Can he help her to heal? Or will he be the one to push her over the edge?

not meant
to be
broken

Cora Reilly

Copyright ©2014 Cora Reilly
All Rights Reserved. This book or any portion thereof may not be
reproduced or used in any manner whatsoever without the express written
permission of the author except for the use of brief quotations in a book review.

This is a work of fiction. All names, characters, businesses,
events and places are either the product of the author's imagination or used fictitiously.

Cover design by Romantic Book Affairs Designs
Book design by Inkstain Design Studio

not meant

to be

broken

chapter one
Amber

Regret pressed down on my chest, an invisible weight threatening to crush me.

This was a new beginning.

I couldn't let my fear rule the rest of my life.

I risked a glance at Dad. His hands clutched the steering wheel as if it was the only thing keeping him rooted, his anchor against the despair. My happiness wasn't the only thing on the line if I failed.

He didn't look my way. He almost never did. His brown eyes were far away, caught somewhere in the past. Lost in a time when things were easier, a time when I was still myself, when I knew how to be happy.

Those moments of untainted bliss were out of my reach. The darkness overshadowed the memories, dragging me down into an abyss I struggled to escape.

I turned back to the window, the cars and houses a blurry streak of color as we drove by. Motion sickness mingled with nerves in my stomach.

Why did I ever think this was a good idea?

After three years of hiding at home, the walls were beginning to close in on me; most days I couldn't even stand the sight of my room. Yet it was a safe place for me, possibly the only one I still had. A place where no one ever bothered me. I could be alone, except for the few hours I spent with Dad after he came home from work.

But I couldn't go on like this or I'd never learn to live again.

Learning to live again.

Dad wanted me to try. He'd been worrying too much about me for the last three years—and for entirely different reasons than most parents worried about their teenage children. I never truly got the chance to be a teenager. The incident prevented that. At only nineteen, the weight bearing down on my soul made me feel like I'd lived for much too long already.

I felt old, worn out, drained.

The happy young girl from before was gone, *replaced* by a shadow of my former self.

Sometimes I didn't even recognize myself. I could only guess how much worse it was for Dad and my brother to witness how I'd changed. How I'd slowly morphed into a corpse, going through the motions of the day because I had to, not because I wanted to.

Dad cleared his throat. "This is good, you know? You need to live a little, socialize."

Forcing a smile, I nodded, not that Dad could see it. His gaze was still focused straight ahead.

Socialize.

I wished it was as easy as it sounded.

Dad steered the car off the highway toward the gas station. "I have to fuel up the car, Amber."

He parked the car at the gas pump and finally turned to me. He didn't meet my eyes, though. "Do you need anything? A snack?"

"I need to go to the restroom." I'd been holding it the whole time, but I doubted I could hold on much longer.

Dad glanced around until his eyes settled on the door leading to the restrooms. "All right?"

The hesitation lingered in his voice, reminding me of the indisputable truth that even this would be a struggle.

Even as my throat constricted, I shoved the door open. Swallowing thickly, I gripped my purse tightly.

Dad hovered to my right. "Do you want me to come with you?"

Flushing, I shook my head. "It's fine. Fuel up the car. I'm right over there."

If I wanted to live on my own, I'd have to be able to go to the bathroom unsupervised. I hurried toward the restrooms. The ladies' room was on the left, and luckily no husbands or boyfriends were waiting for their significant other. I opened the door and peeked inside, finding it vacant. Only when I locked myself in the stall did I dare to breathe again.

I flushed the toilet then heard the door opening and two female voices talking. My heart beat skyrocketed and the door handle was slippery in my sweaty hand.

No danger.

My brain knew that, but my body ignored reason and went into flight mode. Holding my breath, I slipped out of the stall and almost jerked back seeing how close one of the women was as she waited in front of it.

The other woman was at the sink, redoing her makeup.

I rushed out of the restroom without washing my hands, knowing it was awfully unhygienic. The women's expressions made their disgust clear. In their eyes, I must be a freak. Fumbling for my disinfectant wipes in my purse, I almost bumped into someone.

A tall man made a move as if to steady me, and I jumped back with a choked sob.

Panic seized my body. I started running, clutching my purse for dear life, and flung myself into the passenger seat. Sweat trickled down my spine and my breath came in short gasps.

Dad stared at me with wide eyes and reached for me. I flinched.

He dropped his hand. "Amber, what happened?"

"Nothing," I bit out. "I'm fine, Dad."

I wasn't. We both knew it.

"It's okay. Breathe deeply. The therapist said it might happen …" He trailed off. I'd refused to see a therapist for months, but Dad was seeing one. He didn't talk to me about it, but I'd overheard him discuss his sessions with Brian.

Socialize.

Any form of closeness was pure torture for me. How could I socialize if two harmless women in a restroom made me lose it? If a man on the way to the toilet sent me into a panic attack?

I hated it when people looked at me as if I was a freak because of the way I acted. I *tried* so hard to be like them, tried to act normal.

Yet acting normal required being close to people, but allowing closeness reminded me of what happened. And that was the one thing I feared even more than the closeness itself. The memories, being reminded of what had happened and what I'd lost, it was too much for me to bear. They reminded me of what could never be.

I was broken.

Broken with no chance to ever be mended.

Broken.

I would never be like I was before.

It was easier to accept that I'd be broken for the rest of my life. Some things weren't meant to be broken, and therefore couldn't be mended. Ever. I was one of those things. Whatever had been shattered all those years ago, and I was pretty sure it was myself, my entire being, would never be whole again.

It wasn't like breaking a vase and simply putting it back together with some glue. There was no such thing as glue for a broken soul, a shattered person like myself.

I made that realization a few months after the incident, and somehow accepting that made my life so much harder, but easier at the same time. It was harder because I knew there wasn't any hope, but easier because *finally* I accepted there wasn't any hope. Having hope and having to see your hopes destroyed over and over again was so much worse than not having any hope at all. Even complete strangers could see that I wasn't normal. That was why I'd barely left the house for the last three years, despite Dad's efforts to bring me back to life. He gave up eventually and even hired a retired teacher to homeschool me for the last two years of high school. I'd had plenty of friends before the incident, but afterward the thought of facing any of them ever again was too terrifying.

Peterborough was a small town. Rumors about the incident spread like wildfire and speculations were all over the news.

The only people who had meager knowledge about the incident were Dad, my brother Brian, and the hospital staff that treated me in the weeks afterward, but even they didn't know everything. And if I had any say in the matter, it would remain that way until the day I died. I'd take the truth into my grave.

I'd already have succeeded, if Dad hadn't saved me twice. After my second attempted suicide, he started sobbing. I couldn't remember ever having seen my dad cry in earnest. He'd told me he wouldn't survive if he lost me too, not after having already lost Mom to cancer when I was only twelve.

Even Brian, my invincible brother, had had tears in his eyes when he visited me in the hospital after my second try. After that, I decided I would try to bear my life for their sake. I wouldn't hurt them more than absolutely necessary. Dad was suffering enough, forced to watch me every day while Brian had left for college shortly before the incident. *He* was spared most of the drama.

When I suggested to Dad that I wanted to start a new life, I didn't have the slightest clue how to do it exactly. The only thing that had been clear from the beginning was that I had to leave my hometown. Dad came up with a solution that sounded good in theory: I would move in with my brother Brian and his best friend. Now it seemed like a certain way to make their lives miserable.

We were almost there, only a few more minutes until I'd arrive at my new home. A feeling of sickness spread in my stomach. Fighting it, I closed my eyes for an instant to push it down.

"Are you alright, Amber?" Dad's worried tone caused me to open my eyes, but I averted my gaze. I couldn't stomach the look of concern and despair on his face.

"I'm fine, Dad," I assured him, avoiding eye contact as I glanced over my shoulder at the pet carrier where my cat Pumpkin was curled up sleeping. Sticking a finger through the grid, I stroked the soft fur on Pumpkin's back, attempting to calm myself. As usual, my cat rewarded me with a low purr and lifted his head so I could scratch his ear. I caught Dad staring at the cat wistfully, and it almost broke my heart. Dad shouldn't have reason to be jealous of a cat.

One of his hands rested between us, as if he hoped I'd take it. God, I wanted to, but the result would hurt him more than me not trying at all.

Our car pulled onto the street where Brian lived. This was it: my chance to start a new life. Dad parked the car and turned off the engine. I didn't move and neither did Dad, but I looked out of the window. My heart leaped into my throat.

There, in front of a four-story brownstone apartment building, stood my brother, staring uncertainly at the car. With his hands shoved into his pant pockets and a deep frown on his forehead, there was no mistaking that he'd rather be somewhere else.

Our eyes met and the worry in his was like a slap in the face. *Always worried.*

Dad pushed open the door and got out of the car before walking toward Brian. They hugged. There was no hesitation, no awkwardness.

I fought back the tears threatening to fall. Taking a deep breath, I opened the door and left the car. I quickly retrieved the box from the backseat, needing the reassuring purring to calm my nerves. Unable to postpone my meeting with my brother any longer, I headed for Brian and Dad. They were talking to another guy. He was even taller than Brian and even more muscular. His dark hair was cut really short, and he was wearing a BU sweatshirt. He must be Zachary, Brian's best friend.

A new wave of panic rushed over me, but I forced my face into a neutral mask. They were watching me as if they expected me to have a hysteric breakdown any minute. At least, that's what Dad's and Brian's expressions told me.

I wouldn't prove them right. I'd be strong for their sake, and maybe I'd even manage to pretend I was happy. It couldn't be that difficult.

I'd seen other people being happy. I could copy them. Dad kept telling me that I needed to be happy again or *they* would win. Deep down I knew that they *had already won*. They'd wanted to break me, and they broke me. They'd won, and that thought made living so much more unbearable. They won, and there was nothing I could do about it.

They had won.

Sighing quietly to myself, I took the last few steps toward Dad, Brian, and Zachary.

chapter two
Zachary

Brian and I had been waiting on the sidewalk for more than thirty minutes. Brian wanted to be there when his father and sister arrived. I didn't understand why we had to wait outside; we would have seen them pull up from our kitchen window.

Brian rubbed his palms against his thighs, his eyes glued to the street. It was no fucking wonder that he was freezing wearing that ridiculous checkered button-down shirt. My sweatshirt did a better job of keeping the cold at bay. With his carefully combed hair, he looked like he was going for the mother-in-law's delight-look.

Brian cleared his throat. "Remember not to touch her, and don't get too close to her, and—"

"And don't ever be alone in a room with her … I know, Brian. The words are practically burned into my ears," I said calmly. "I'll be on my best behavior." I patted his shoulder, feeling how tense he actually was.

His expression made it clear that my best behavior might not be enough. I'd never seen him so tense or anxious before. He was definitely more uptight than me, especially since we started law school a few weeks ago, but this was extreme. We'd been friends since our first year in college four years ago, and we spent a shitload of time together. He was pretty much the only reason why I hadn't dropped out our first year of college—just to spite my father—or why I actually started law school. He'd always been a worrier, and certainly worried more than I did, but I had never seen him like this.

Brian hadn't told me all that much about his sister; he hardly ever spoke of her at all. It had taken more than a year of sharing an apartment before he finally told me that at sixteen she'd experienced hell. Brian didn't like to speak about what happened, and he never mentioned the word rape once.

After Brian's constant words of warning, I was a bit worried about our new living arrangements, but not nearly as much as Brian. Of course we'd have to stop having parties in our apartment—at least the ones with girls and booze. We could still have them. We'd just have to hold them at Kevin's and Bill's place instead.

The sound of a car pulling onto the street caught my attention. A black Jeep came to a halt about thirty feet from us, and a man in his late forties got out. He walked toward Brian and pulled him into an embrace, but that wasn't what had my attention.

Brian's sister pushed open the door and climbed out of the car, a purse pressed to her chest. After hearing Brian talk about her, I'd expected her to be a shell, a shadow, someone your eyes passed over. I never imagined her being so beautiful. She had long wavy caramel-brown hair and pale skin and was about a head shorter than me. An oversized hoodie covered her body and she wore baggy boot-cut jeans. Her eyes were the most startling thing about her. Huge brown eyes. She looked like a deer, fearful, skittish, ready to run at the slightest sign of danger.

I couldn't quite explain it, but I felt an overwhelming sense of protectiveness then. I wanted to keep her safe. She didn't seek our gazes. Instead, she picked up a carrier from the backseat before finally making her way over to us.

amber

I stopped a few feet from Dad, Brian, and Zachary, not sure what to say or do to make this any less awkward. Dad shifted nervously, running his hand over his bald head, his eyes flitting between Brian and me. I met Brian's gaze and forced a smile. Maybe it would have been a real one if he and Dad weren't watching me and waiting for me to collapse at their feet any moment.

After several heartbeats, Brian finally gave me a small smile, but he didn't try to move closer or even hug me. And his smile wasn't the smile I remembered from when I was little or even from four years ago. Now whenever he was around me, his facial expression was a brink of a frown.

It had been two months since I'd last seen him. He'd cut his visit during the summer short and instead spent three weeks in Mexico with a couple of friends. His friend Zachary had been one of them, and I risked a quick glance at him. He hovered behind my dad and Brian but regarded me over their heads. The cautiousness and worry I usually saw reflected on the faces of people around me was missing from his. He smiled in response to my scrutiny, and I quickly looked away. Embarrassment crawled under my skin at my inability to do something as simple as meet his eyes. The awkwardness intensified, and I tightened my hold on the handle of the cat carrier.

"It's good to see you again, Brian," I said eventually, then cringed at how formal it sounded—as if we were distant acquaintances and not siblings. His expression almost brought tears to my eyes. He looked hurt and disappointed. Maybe he was hoping I'd changed in those last couple of months, that we could finally be close again.

"Yeah, it's good to see you too, Am," he murmured, staring at anything but at my face.

It hurt me to see him, to see his disappointment. It was more painful than I thought it would be. Maybe coming here was a mistake. There was still time. I could turn around, get back into the car, and ask Dad to take me back home with him. I could keep hiding, keep hating every breath I took. I could live my tiny lonely shell of a life until it crushed me.

A feeling of dread settled in my chest, threatening to suffocate me. All eyes were on me, watching, waiting, worrying. I couldn't leave now. I couldn't do that to Brian and Dad.

"So," Dad interrupted my thoughts and the uncomfortable silence, scratching the back of his head nervously. A few weeks ago he finally accepted his bald spot had reached the size of a saucer, so he started shaving his head. Obviously he wasn't used to it yet. "Maybe we should go inside."

"Yes, right. That's a good idea," Brian agreed eagerly. I couldn't blame him for wanting to escape the situation. My eyes returned to Zachary. What must he be thinking about us? About me? He hadn't said anything yet, but his blue eyes were attentive, taking it all in. He was even taller up close, more than a head taller than me. He didn't avoid my gaze like my father and brother did, and I felt uncomfortable under his scrutiny. But that wasn't unusual. I always felt that way when people stared at me. It made me feel as if they were judging me, but Zachary's eyes held curiosity in them, not pity.

Brian cleared his throat nervously, his gaze shifting between me and his best friend. "That's Zachary," he said slowly, then he shot Zachary a badly disguised warning glance. "Zachary, that's my sister Amber."

"Hi, Amber," Zachary said with a grin that lit up his entire face. He had a strong prominent jaw, and his face was all angles and sharpness, but his eyes and grin took away some of the hardness. "You can call me Zach."

"Zach," I confirmed, trying to make my voice come out firm but sounding hushed. He didn't try to shake my hand or get closer. If I wasn't mistaken, he hadn't as much as twitched since I'd reached them. Brian had done his job. He probably warned all of his friends and the entire neighborhood of my impending arrival.

I scanned the surrounding houses, even the windows, but nobody was trying to risk a peek at the freakshow that was me. I wasn't sure how I felt about Zach and possibly other people knowing what was wrong with me. This was supposed to be a new start, but how was that even possible if everyone knew I was broken? A brief flash of anger directed at Brian hit me. Then it faded. Zach certainly would have noticed I wasn't quite right on his own.

"I'll get your belongings," Dad said then hesitated. "Okay?"

Warmth spread in my cheeks. If he was worried about leaving me alone with Brian and Zach for a couple of minutes, how was I supposed to survive sharing an apartment with them?

"It's fine, Dad." He practically rushed toward the Jeep. Zach followed after him at a much slower pace, leaving me alone with Brian. Hesitantly, I looked at my brother, catching him watching me with wistful eyes. I willed the corners of my lips into a smile that would wipe that look off his face.

His eyes lit up. "I'm glad you're here," he said quietly. I wanted to believe him, and I knew that he wouldn't deliberately lie to me, but he couldn't possibly want me in his life. Not like this. I was going to mess everything up for him, and for Zach, who was getting in the line of fire without any fault of his own.

"I'm glad too," I lied. The way Brian looked at me, it was clear that he knew I wasn't telling the truth. Maybe I wasn't as good a liar as I thought, or maybe I'd just done it too often. I looked away, unable to bear Brian's scrutiny, and turned toward Zach and Dad who were heading our way, carrying my two suitcases. If I couldn't even stand Brian's closeness for ten minutes, I might have been overly optimistic taking that much luggage with me. I wouldn't last a day.

Dad's eyes found me as he and Zach passed by. For once they did not hold concern I was accustomed to seeing every day. The two of them were talking about college football. Brian joined in on their conversation eagerly. I didn't mind. It made me happy to see him and Dad so animated and relaxed. It wasn't something I saw often when they were around me.

I followed them at a safe distance, stroking Pumpkin's soft fur through the flap at the top of the box. It always managed to calm me. I slipped past Dad, who held the door open for me, careful not to touch him. The hall of the building was narrow and dark, but at least it looked clean. The floor was dark brown wood with scratches all over it, and the bricked walls were painted in a sterile white.

"Our apartment is on the fourth floor, so we should take the elevator," Brian said, heading for the metal doors at the end of the corridor. A beeping noise announced the arrival of the elevator, and a moment later the doors slid open, revealing a small space with barely enough room for six people—or four people with two suitcases. Zach, Brian, and Dad stepped into the elevator without hesitation.

They made it look so easy: setting one foot in front of the other. But my throat was closing up at the sight of the crammed space. I hadn't used an elevator since my hospital stay three years ago. It would be close to impossible not to touch someone. My fingers began shaking as I weighed my options. Pumpkin let out a noise of protest.

My feet were glued to the floor. Move, Amber. *Move*. I tried to force my body to move forward, to step into the elevator, but my muscles refused to bulge. Up until about two seconds ago, Brian, Dad, and Zach had been too absorbed in their conversation to notice my hesitation, but now their attention shifted to me. One set of eyes after the other met mine, trying to figure out what was wrong.

The happiness on Dad's face evaporated and an expression of sadness took its place. A muscle in Brian's cheek twitched, his lips thinning before he stared at the ground. Anywhere but at his sister, the freak show.

Zach was watching me with a deep frown on his face. Now he probably regretted agreeing to let me live in their apartment. And why wouldn't he? I was a mess. I couldn't believe I'd actually hoped this was the beginning of a new life. Tears welled up in my eyes, but I forced them back. The guilt was a vise around my heart.

I was a horrible person for hurting my father and brother like this, but I couldn't step into that elevator.

I hated myself for my next words. "You can go ahead without me.

There's not enough room for all of us. I'll take the next elevator." I stared at a spot on the wall, imagining the pained expression on Dad's face and the despair on Brian's. I didn't want to actually see it.

Dad reached for the button to send the elevator up. A couple of years ago, he might have protested, tried to console me, and waited for me to come around. Now he knew better. The front door swung open and a few young men entered the hall and headed in my direction.

I quickly stepped into the elevator, careful not to touch Dad, Brian, or Zach, who stood immediately to my right. Zach shifted a few inches to give me more room, but there were still only two inches between my shoulder and his arm. Dad jabbed the button with more force than necessary. The doors closed smoothly behind me, and I pressed my back against them. The sense of being trapped washed over me. I focused with all my might on the pink suitcase in front of me, but Brian's brown leather oxfords were in my peripheral vision. No matter where I looked, there were shoes or legs or hands. Bodies. Heat. Breathing.

Too much.

I closed my eyes for an instant and raised the cat carrier, catching Pumpkin's comforting smell. The elevator began to move, too slowly.

Too slow.

Too slow.

Too slow.

My throat tightened, my heart pounding in my ears. The silence pressed in on me. How much longer? I couldn't do this. Couldn't. Couldn't.

I was startled out of my rising panic attack when Zach cleared his throat. My eyes peeled open, and I peered up at him before settling for the safer sight of my belongings again.

"Your room has a clear view of the small park behind the house.

You'll like it. If you're lucky, you might even get to watch squirrels scurrying after joggers for food," he said, a small smile lighting up his face. The dimples around his mouth gave him a boyish appearance and made me forget his intimidating frame for a moment. "I bet your cat will love the squirrels."

Pumpkin's ears perked up as if he realized Zach was talking about him. I opened my mouth to say something when I noticed Dad and Brian watching me as if they expected me to break down crying because Zach had spoken to me. My lips snapped shut. Instead of voicing my reply, I nodded and gave Zach what I hoped was a grateful look. The elevator halted. Before the door slid open completely, I squeezed through and stumbled into the hallway, sucking in a deep breath, relief surging through me at being free.

There were four wooden doors on this floor, two on either side of the elevator. Brian walked past me, startling me. I managed to suppress the gasp rising up my throat and threatening to spill from my lips. I held myself close to the right side to give Zach and Dad room to pass me on the left. Zach's shoulders brushed the wall across from me as he passed by, carrying one of my suitcases as if it weighed nothing. He headed for Brian, who had stopped in front of the last door. Zach was obviously trying to give me as much space as possible. Brian had definitely schooled him well. Heat rose to my head.

How much had he told him?

Brian unlocked the door, and they entered the apartment. Dad turned his head to me, waiting in the doorway, and gave me an encouraging look before disappearing inside. Hesitantly, I walked into my new home. I found myself in a spacious living room with two narrow but high windows. There was a huge flat-screen TV on one wall, surrounded by hundreds of DVDs and Playstation games. Bang & Olufsen loud speakers were attached to every corner of the room. There were two round beige love seats and a long black sofa facing the TV. A sleek glass table was positioned in front of the sofa. There was even a liquor cabinet with more bottles of whiskey, scotch, tequila, and all other kinds of alcohol. More bottles than I'd ever seen. The expensive furniture and the new wooden floor weren't something I'd expected. How was Brian able to afford such a luxurious home? The walls were brick but painted in the same warm beige as the love seats. Through the open door to my left, I could see the kitchen; a corridor branched off the living room and led to more rooms.

"Do you like it?" Zach asked as he set my suitcase down beside the sofa.

Pumpkin wriggled in the cat carrier. I finally shut the apartment door before I put it down and opened the carrier. He strode around the room as if he owned the place, rubbing his chin against the edge of every piece of furniture in his reach.

I gave Zach and Brian an apologetic look, but they seemed more amused than angry about Pumpkin getting fur all over their sofa.

"It's really nice," I said.

Zach grinned and gave Brian an I-told-you-so-look.

"Do you want to see your room?" my brother asked, smiling hopefully.

"That would be great." I followed him into the long corridor. At the end of it was a window that filled the place with daylight. Five doors lined the walls.

"This door leads to my room and that's Zach's room. In between is our shared bathroom," Brian explained, pointing at the three doors on my left side.

We had to share a bathroom? I hadn't even thought about needing to do that.

Don't worry about it.

"This is your room." Brian pointed at the door across the corridor from his room.

Brian pushed open the door and took a few steps back to give me enough space to enter the room without touching him. A smile spread on my face as I stepped into my new home. A huge window flooded everything with light and a king-sized bed was placed against the wall below it. A massive wardrobe took up most of the left side. There was a desk beside the bed and a sofa on the remaining wall. The walls were beige and the bed-linen was purple. Brian must have bought it for me. He was trying to help me feel at home. I walked toward the window and chanced a look at the park below.

"It's beautiful," I said, giving Brian a grateful smile. It was the least I could do for everything he'd done.

He shifted uncomfortably, still not moving from his spot in the doorway, my suitcases positioned next to his legs. Was he worried he'd scare me if he entered the room? "Can you put the suitcases on my bed?"

Brian hesitated before reaching down and dragging my suitcases toward the bed. He hoisted them up and stepped back. We stood so close to each other that he could have touched me if he'd stretched out his arm to its full length. I met his eyes—eyes so full of worry—and drew in a shaky breath, tentatively touching his upper arm for only a second.

"Thank you," I said before pulling my arm back. From the corner of my eye I saw Zach moving away from the doorway and out of view to give us privacy.

Brian's eyes widened in surprise and his face lit up with joy, more joy than such a simple touch should stir in anybody. I stared out of the window, the familiar heaviness of my guilt resting on my shoulders.

"Amber, Brian? I need to get back to Peterborough," Dad shouted.

I followed Brian back to the living room where Dad was waiting for us. Zach had disappeared. He probably thought we needed a family moment. If only he knew that we hadn't had a true family moment for three years. Now everything was complicated and awkward. *My fault*, a small voice in my head taunted me.

Dad took a step toward me, his arms lifting as if he was going to hug me before they dropped back to his sides. "Take good care of her, Brian," he said roughly.

I swallowed.

"Don't worry, Dad." Brian pulled him into a tight embrace. I moved closer to them and accompanied Dad to the entrance door.

"I'll give you a moment to say goodbye," Brian said. Then he left in the direction of the kitchen. Pumpkin perched on the backrest of the love seat, his keen eye watching me.

"I will be alright, Dad," I told him, and like moments before with Brian, I reached out and touched Dad's arm. Again a smile and so much joy.

It was killing me to know that I could bring them so much joy with such a simple gesture.

Dad hovered in the doorway, unable to tear himself away. I wanted this to work for him more than for me. He gave a jerky nod. "You'll be fine. And if you need anything, call me. Any time."

"I will," I said. Dad took a couple of steps into the hallway, but his hesitation was palpable.

I started closing the door but paused and smiled. "You need to socialize too," I reminded him.

He barked out a laugh and finally the hesitation was replaced by a shaky hope. With one last glance back at me, Dad disappeared in the elevator at the end of the hallway. I closed the door, turned around, and let my new reality sink in for a moment. I was really doing this, starting a new life, living in an apartment with Brian and his friend. Voices drifted over to me from the kitchen.

For a moment, I considered joining them, but it would have been too much too soon. I picked up Pumpkin, made my way back to my room, and closed the door behind me, locking it.

I imagined Brian's reaction to my apprehension and grimaced, but I felt safer that way. I plopped down on my bed as I watched Pumpkin discovering his surroundings. This was my new life.

chapter three
Zachary

After saying goodbye to Brian's dad, I disappeared into the kitchen, not wanting to invade in their private goodbye. I grabbed a Coke from the fridge and sank down on a chair at the table. Bringing the bottle to my lips, I took a long gulp. My mind drifted back to the last half hour, the fear and worry on Amber's face as she stood in the elevator with us. She'd looked like a trapped animal. I'd tried to set her at ease with some conversation. I couldn't stand this awkward silence. It was something I'd had to witness many evenings with my parents. I could have sworn it worked. Amber had started to relax.

Brian wasn't kidding when he'd described her condition. Maybe some normalcy would do her good. Brian and his dad probably hadn't treated her like a normal person since that incident. Maybe it would help her to be treated like a woman and not a helpless, fragile porcelain doll.

The door creaked and I looked up to see Brian sitting down on the chair across from me, his expression strained. He hung his head and rubbed his temples, his mouth set in a thin line. I nudged his forehead with the cold bottle and grinned at him encouragingly. The tension started to feel like a nagging headache at the back of my head. It needed to go.

He frowned at me.

"Don't look so worried, Brian. Everything went well so far."

Brian shook his head. "Did you seen what happened in the elevator? She didn't want to step inside because of us."

I put down the bottle and let out a sigh. "She'll get used to it, Brian. This is all new for her."

Brian sighed. "I hope you're right, Zach."

I punched him lightly against the shoulder, grinning. "I'm always right, dude."

Brian snorted, his expression brightening. "You wish."

Smiling to myself, I lifted the bottle to my lips for another gulp. And I truly hoped that I was right. For Brian's and Amber's sake. It had taken me long enough to make Brian loosen up a bit after first meeting him. He took everything too seriously. Recently he'd stopped being so goddamn uptight.

"Just give it time. Don't try to force it. I know you prefer to control everything, but some things are just out of your fucking control."

Brian got up with a roll of his eyes before he went over to our fridge. He didn't look at me when he said, "Believe me, I know I can't control anything about Amber's life. Her past does that."

What was I supposed to say to that? Brian sounded like he was on the fast track to a self-pity party, and while I understood why he was feeling that way, it wouldn't make him or Amber feel better. "Bullshit. The past's just that. It can't control the present if you don't let it."

"*Right.* That's why you still try to piss your father off all the time for the shit he pulled in the past?" Brian glared.

I sat back with raised hands, even as my own anger wanted to burst forth. "Hey, relax. I wanted to help. And pissing my father off makes me feel better in the present, not worse."

"Sorry." He sank back down across from me. "I know you're right, but I can't do a thing. Amber's stuck in the past. It doesn't matter what I or Dad say or do. It's just the way it is."

"But it doesn't have to stay that way."

amber

Laughter.

Their laughter carries in the alley. Echoes off the walls. Fills me up.

And sobs. My sobs.

And moans. Their moans. And grunts. Their grunts.

They ring in my head.

And the smells.

Sweat. The stench of their sweat. Disgusting.

And blood. So much blood. Acid, sweet in my nose and sticky on my skin. Sickening.

Stale cigarette smoke and beer. Their clothes reek of it. And their bodies. Revolting.

And then another smell. Everywhere. Something I've never smelled before. Indescribable. Disgusting. Revolting. Burned into my mind. This smell. How it sticks to my skin just like the blood but so much worse.

And their faces. Taunting. Leering. Lusting.

Frightening. Menacing. Pitiless.

The last faces I'll ever see. Die. I will die. They tell me so.

And I want to. Plead with them even. Beg them to kill me. To end this.

Death is better. Liberating.

So much pain. Unbearable.

Agony. Hot, burning, tearing, ripping. Pure agony.

And the feel of them. On my skin. Their hands. Rough and cruel.

Their bodies. On top of me. Crushing. Unrelenting.

And the pain. So much pain. Too much.

A scream tears itself from the depth of my body and then I can't stop.

I scream and scream. But all I hear is their laughter, their taunts, their grunts...

Blinding light penetrated my eyelids and tore me from the confines of my nightmare. It wasn't just a simple nightmare, a simple fabrication of my mind. No, those were my memories. Seared into my mind.

Forever.

Would it ever stop? Would they ever leave me alone? Would that day ever stop haunting my dreams? Would there ever be a night without nightmares? A night that didn't make me relive the horrors of that day?

I opened my eyes and blinked a few times to clear my vision until I found the reason for the end of my nightmare. Brian stood in the doorway, his hand on the light switch and his horrified eyes on me. Zach towered behind him, his horror matching that of my brother. I must have woken them with my screaming.

My throat felt sore and my body was slick with sweat. *Not their sweat,* I reminded myself and shuddered as the memorized stench filled my nose. Pumpkin was curled up at the end of my bed. He had gotten used to my nightmares and didn't hide under the bed anymore.

"Amber?" Brian whispered and took a hesitant step toward me. He wanted to console me, maybe even hug me. It was written all over his face.

I stared down at the blankets covering my body. Shame rushed through me. "I'm sorry I woke you."

"Don't worry," Zach said quickly.

"You were talking in your sleep, and then you started screaming," Brian said in a very quiet voice.

I talked in my sleep?

My stomach twisted. God, what had I said? The thought that I might have revealed more about what happened made me sick. I lifted my gaze. "I ... I talked?"

Brian grimaced before his expression turned apologetic. "Not much."

Not much? I could barely breathe. I hated to lose control and that was exactly what happened whenever I fell asleep. I swallowed past the lump in my throat. "What ... what did I say?" I stared at Brian pleadingly. He hesitated and chanced a look at Zachary, who was still standing behind him.

"You ... you didn't say much." Brian turned his back to me. This was too much for him. He wasn't used to dealing with this. With *me*.

"Please, I need to know," I whispered.

Brian's shoulders started shaking. Was he crying? I clutched the blankets, needing something to hold on to. Zach stared at my brother for several moments before his eyes met mine. There was sadness in them, but no pity, and I was grateful for that. "You mumble, so I couldn't make out everything. But you said. 'Stop, please stop. Please don't ...'" He stopped and took a deep breath through his nose, his nostrils flaring. He looked as if it cost him all his willpower to say the next words. "'Please, it hurts.'"

I nodded. "Thanks, Zachary," I choked out. I felt sick. It would only be a matter of minutes before I'd throw up.

"Night, Amber," Brian said in a strained whisper. He closed my door and I was alone.

I sat on my bed until I was certain that Zach and Brian had returned to their rooms and I wouldn't meet them in the hallway. My legs shook as I stood, and it took all my strength to grab a bathrobe and walk out of my room. It was dark in the hallway, but light spilled out from beneath the doors to the other two bedrooms.

The darkness threatened to swallow me. I tiptoed toward the bathroom and closed the door behind me as soon as I'd entered. I switched the light on, stumbled toward the toilette bowl, and threw up. I gripped the seat tightly as dizziness flooded my mind. Sinking to my knees, I leaned my head against the edge of the bathtub. My eyes closed on their own accord while I drew in quick shallow breaths through my nose. I felt so drained, and weak, and old, and lifeless.

chapter four

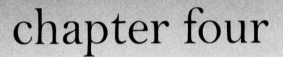

The bowl of cereal in front of me on the table sat untouched. I wasn't hungry. Probably for the first time in my life the mere sight of food made me sick.

Last night. Those screams and the look in Amber's eyes. I pushed the bowl away, not caring that milk spilled over onto the table.

Fuck. I couldn't forget those terrified eyes.

I didn't sleep more than two hours after that. And my sleep was far from sound. Nightmares filled with her screams haunted me. Not that my dreams were even close to being as horrible as hers.

It was nearly ten. Brian hadn't even left his room yet, though he was an early riser. I'd heard movement in his room, but he didn't come out. Maybe he was hiding. Maybe he was afraid to face his sister after last night. If that was the case, I'd kick his ass.

I ran a hand through my hair. This had to be the first time Brian missed a day of law school. My attendance record was far less perfect.

The sound of soft footsteps in the corridor caught my attention; they didn't belong to Brian. I didn't move from my spot on the chair. It was too late to leave anyway. I wouldn't manage to slip out of the kitchen without meeting Amber.

Don't be in a room alone with her.

Brian's words flitted through my mind. The door creaked and I tried to act casual. She didn't have to come into the kitchen if she was uncomfortable. I raised my head and caught her staring at me. She bit her lip and her forehead wrinkled in contemplation. She wore a similar outfit to the one she had on yesterday. Jeans and a hoodie. Didn't those clothes make her sweat? It was fucking warm in the apartment.

After what felt like an eternity, she mumbled "Morning, Zach." A blush spread to her pale cheeks. I could see how conflicted she was. Her body seemed frozen on the spot in the doorway.

I smiled, hoping to set her at ease. "Morning, Amber."

An awkward silence hovered between us, and I contemplated storming past her out of the kitchen, but then a low purr sounded in the room. Amber looked down to her feet, and so did I. Her black cat rubbed its small body against her calves before it waltzed into the kitchen as if it owned the place.

I wasn't exactly a cat person. I'd always wanted a dog when I was younger, but my mother would have had a coronary if she'd found a single dog hair on her Persian rugs.

Without hesitation the cat jumped onto the table and began licking up the spilled milk, watching me the whole time. Its one amber eye was fixed on me, and its body coiled tight as if it was prepared to run in case

I tried to catch it. I'd seen enough cat videos on Youtube to know that cats could be vicious little creatures, so I had absolutely no intention of touching it.

"Pumpkin! Get down!" Amber's indignant exclamation didn't impress the cat. It simply lifted its head for a moment before it continued lapping up the milk. It wasn't a very pretty cat with its missing eye and the crooked tail, but it had character.

Amber took a hesitant step forward then froze, suspiciously watching me as if she expected me to attack her any second. My height and muscles made me look intimidating. My physique was something I worked hard at, but I wasn't violent. I'd never even think about hitting a woman, much less doing what Amber probably feared the most.

Then something changed on her face. Resolve took over. She took another step. When I didn't move, she walked toward the table and grabbed her cat. She put it down and gave it an affectionate pat on the head.

"Sorry," she said with an even deeper blush. The table was between us, and her face made it clear that she was glad about it.

"Don't worry," I assured her with a grin. "But don't let Brian see it. He's a neat freak. Without him the apartment would be slob central."

"I know. His room was always much cleaner than mine when he still lived at home." Her lips curled up into an adorable smile. For some reason, it made me feel better instantly.

"Are you hungry?" I asked. Food was a way to relax people. At least, it always worked wonders for my mood.

She shrugged but her gaze moved to the fruit bowl that was behind me on the counter. I leaned back in my chair and reached for the bowl. Then I put it on the table between us and gave her a wink. She blushed again and averted her eyes with a mumbled "thanks."

She grabbed an apple and bit into it. I *really* wished she would sit down.

"Have you decided yet how you're going to spend your days?" My attempt at conversation startled her slightly, and she held the apple an inch from her lips.

"I'm not sure. Since it's too late to start college, and it wouldn't be a good idea with all the people anyway," she said in an apologetic tone, "I guess I'll just try to get used to everything and then maybe I'll apply for the spring semester."

"I get it. You should take all the time you need. There's really no reason to rush into things. Hell, most days I wish I hadn't started college right after high school and instead traveled the world for a year or two."

"You're in law school like Brian, right?"

"Yeah, it was either that or business school."

Amber's forehead wrinkled. "You make it sound as if you didn't have a choice."

Free will and choosing your own career weren't high on my family's list of priorities. Old money required a certain set of skills—according to my father and grandfather. "My father wants me to take over the family business in a few years, so he thought a law or business degree would be the best preparation for my future tasks."

Shit, I sounded like a wimp, having my father tell me what to do. But it was still the truth, no matter how bad a taste it left in my mouth.

Amber took another bite from her apple, thinking about my words. "But you don't want to?"

I gave a one shoulder shrug. "A law degree will be useful. And maybe if I'm lucky and don't turn into a workaholic like my father, I'll even have time to do the things I love once or twice a month." *Whoa, way to sound like an idiot, Zach.* I liked having money at my disposal, and that was the fucking truth. If I didn't want my old man to turn off my money supply, I'd have to follow his orders. "Sorry. I don't want to bore you with my daddy issues."

Her eyebrows shot up. "You don't need to apologize." She bit her lip. "There is a support group twice a week for women who ... for women like me. I think I'm going to give it a try."

She made it sound as if she'd never been to therapy before. That hardly seemed possible, given the extent of her anxiety. "Have you never been in a support group before?"

"No. There wasn't one in my hometown. And I didn't really—"

My cell phone vibrated in the back pocket of my jeans, and I stood up from the table to yank it out. I shouldn't have moved so quickly.

Amber's eyes widened and she stumbled backward, her back bumping against the counter. I froze, my hand halfway to my pocket and my eyes fixed on the girl in front of me. Fuck. The horrified expression on her face told me she thought I was about to attack her.

"My phone," I said, and my voice actually cracked. I cleared my throat, pulled out my cell slowly, and turned it off. I wasn't in the mood to talk to whoever was calling. "I didn't mean to frighten you."

A deep blush spread across Amber's cheeks. With her skin as pale as it was made it even more obvious. Her gaze dropped to the floor and she stared at the apple that had fallen there. Taking a deep breath, she bent down and picked it up before she chucked it into the trashcan.

"I'm so sorry," she whispered. Her huge brown eyes held embarrassment and guilt when *I* was the one who'd scared the fucking bejeezus out of her.

"There's nothing to be sorry about."

She nodded. Again, it was Pumpkin who saved the situation. He began purring loudly and rolled around on the tiled floor in front of Amber's socked feet.

"Where did you get him?" I asked, glad for an out of the awkwardness. Pumpkin didn't look like a cat that a pet shop would sell.

Surprise followed by graveness crossed her face. "A year after—" She stopped herself and for a second I worried she'd freak out on me again. Thankfully, her expression smoothed in a way that required years of training. Amber must have learned how to hide her true emotions.

"Dad and I went to a pet shelter because he thought I needed company. There were dozens of cats, and they were all trying to gain my attention, purring and nestling against my legs. All except for one. Pumpkin was sitting in the far corner of the room, watching me with his one eye, not moving at all. He didn't even bother to try and get attention. I realized then that it was because he knew nobody would want him the way he was, with his missing eye and crooked tail. He'd given up. Nobody would want a broken creature like him …"

She hesitated, her expression sad and hopeless. "That's why I decided to give him a home, to show him that there was somebody willing to take a broken creature. That there was someone who would love him."

Was Amber still referring to Pumpkin or was she talking about herself? The idea that she thought of herself as broken sent a jolt of fury through me. I was furious at the men who had hurt her. I wished those men were standing right in front of me so I could hurt them like they hurt Amber.

For once I truly wanted to utilize my martial arts training. But somehow I was pretty sure that no matter what I did to those bastards, it wouldn't be nearly as bad as what they'd done to Amber.

"What happened to him?" I asked. The question I really wanted to ask was, "*What happened to you?*" but I doubt she would have answered. If I asked, I bet Brian would iron my goddamn balls with his expensive iron.

Amber didn't even look at me when she replied, "The people in the pet shelter didn't know for sure, but they assume he had been tortured by some boys because he's so afraid of men."

Another thing that she seemed to have in common with her pet. Fuck, I wanted to kill those sick fucks who'd attacked her.

Eventually, she averted her eyes from Pumpkin, who was still stretched out on the floor as if he was staking his claim on the room. Amber met my eyes for a second before her gaze settled on my nose.

A phone rang somewhere in the apartment, and she jumped. "That's mine." She hurried out of the kitchen. I had a feeling she was glad for the opportunity to leave the room. I couldn't blame her. Things had been awkward.

The cat watched me with its one eye, as if it was trying to figure me out. Amber said Pumpkin was scared of men, but so far the cat hadn't run away. I took that as a good sign. Slowly, careful not to startle the cat, I knelt down to make myself smaller. I reached out.

"Don't scratch me, dude."

Pumpkin sniffed my hand, and then he started to rub his head against my palm. He was probably marking his territory, but honestly it didn't feel half bad.

"Good boy," I said.

Amber's feet appeared in my vision as she stepped into the kitchen. She stopped dead in her tracks. Her gaze settled on my palm as I continued to pat Pumpkin's head. She walked a bit closer, but remained out of my reach.

It was unnecessary to point out that I could have grabbed her with a simple lunge.

"He's never let anyone touch him except for me."

I shrugged, feeling a bit smug about it. My first cat encounter went better than expected. "Maybe I'm different. Not all men are alike."

She considered me for a moment, and then she nodded once, accepting my words. She sank down on one of the chairs, watching me. I knew it wasn't much, but it was a start.

Maybe Amber and I could figure out a way to live together without any more awkward encounters.

amber

I sat on the sofa in my room, trying to read a book but my mind kept wandering to the events of the morning. Pumpkin had let Zach touch him. Why did he suddenly start trusting men, especially a man of Zach's size? He was built like a linebacker. Dad would be proud of me for that comparison. Sports weren't really my thing, so making that reference would have impressed him since he was such a football fan.

It had taken Pumpkin several months to let Dad touch him. Maybe my cat was leery of my dad because Dad didn't know how to act around him. Kind of like he didn't know how to act around me.

The sound of the bell startled me, and I jumped up. Pumpkin hissed, leaped off the sofa, and hid under my bed. I tiptoed toward my door and stiffened when I heard several male voices in the apartment. With shaking hands I locked my door and leaned against it to eavesdrop.

There were three male voices that I'd never heard before, and then I could decipher Zach and Brian speaking. Unease swirled in my stomach. I tried to keep my breathing even as I listened to their conversation.

"There's a new club," a man with a deep voice said. "Are you in?"

"Sure, Bill," came Zach's immediate reply.

"Come on, Brian," another male voice urged. I heard the shuffling of feet getting closer to my room, so I checked my lock again.

"I'm not in the mood," Brian said in a tight voice. I bet he was worried about leaving me alone.

"You sound like an old housewife," said the man.

"Stop it, Jason," Zach growled and I cringed. He'd never sounded so … threatening, not when I was around. It was silent for a moment. Then they began talking again but too low for my ears to hear. I guessed they were discussing *me*.

It was something I had grown used to over the year. That didn't change the acute embarrassment I felt every time, though.

I rested my forehead against the door, listening to how the male voices died down as they left the apartment. Pumpkin pressed against my leg, purring loudly. He blinked up at me with his amber eye and meowed.

"It's okay."

Guitar music floated over to me. It was the saddest melody I'd ever heard. Sad but beautiful. Brian was playing the guitar. It had been years since I'd heard him play. I unlocked the door and opened it without a sound, not wanting to draw attention to myself.

Pumpkin dashed past my leg and through the door, heading straight for the living room. I followed him on my tiptoes and peered around the corner. Pumpkin strode over to the sofa where Brian was sitting and playing his guitar. I clamped a hand over my mouth when my cat jumped onto the sofa inches from Brian. He let out a startled gasp and jerked back, almost dropping his guitar. A small smile tugged at the corners of my mouth. After a moment, he straightened and continued his play, never taking his eyes off Pumpkin. Brian wasn't a cat person. Sometimes I wondered if he felt more uncomfortable around me or my cat.

I closed my eyes for an instant as I listened to the sad melody. One song ended and another began, even more haunting than the one before it. When I opened my eyes, I crept closer to the sofa, worried about interrupting my brother. Brian turned his head and apprehension flashed across his face. His fingers stilled on the strings and the music died down in a low sigh.

"Please, don't stop," I whispered, moving a bit closer and plopping down on the love seat on Brian's right. "I missed your playing."

Why was it so difficult to interact with Brian? I could still remember the days when we bantered back and forth and pranked each other like siblings should.

Surprise flickered in his eyes and then a smile brightened his expression. He bent over his guitar and began to play a happier melody. I closed my eyes and leaned my head against the backrest of the love seat. When I was little, Brian often played for me, and it had always calmed me when I was upset. But after the incident, nothing could calm me, and Brian hadn't played in front of me ever since. I'd thought he'd given up on it completely. Now I was glad to learn he hadn't.

I had taken enough from Dad and him.

chapter five

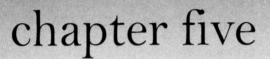

T he music was blaring at full volume when we entered the crowded club, the bass a living breathing thing in my body. Jason and Bill set off instantly on their hunt for a meaningless fling with one of the girls swaying their hips in rhythm to the hip-hop beats. Jason and Bill wore the same floral shirt; it was some sort of inside joke that was supposed to impress the chicks. I doubted that the Beach Boys look made girls want to drop their panties.

I stalked over to the bar with Kevin at my heels and ordered a vodka martini, my favorite drink. Kevin got his usual nonalcoholic beer and gave me a pained smile when a drunk girl leaned against the bar next to him, batting her eyelashes.

Kevin was a chick magnet—that would never change. The lucky bastard. Not that I had reason to complain. Always the gentleman, he didn't have the guts to send her away. Instead, he just ignored her advances, which was proving more and more difficult by the minute. She ran a hand through his long blond hair. A year ago he would have readily taken her up on her obvious offer, but ever since he met Reagan everything had changed. The guys and I often taunted him about being whipped, but I had to admit that his relationship with Reagan was something to admire. Sometimes the two of them reminded me of lovesick puppies.

Kevin's forced smile turned into a frown when the girl began to feel him up, running her hand up and down his chest. I heaved a monumental sigh and took it upon myself to save his life. I bent down toward the girl, and her eyes snapped up to meet mine, still continuing that unnerving batting of her eyelashes. It made me dizzy to watch the rapid movement.

I gave her my coldest smile. "Get lost, babe, we're not interested."

She looked offended and opened her mouth for a come back. I spared her the effort and growled, "Get lost." She left with a huff, giving me one last deathly glare.

"That wasn't very nice, Zach," Kevin said, trying to hide his grin behind the bottle of O'Doul's in his hand.

I shrugged and leaned back against the bar. "You should be grateful. I saved you. I'm sure Reagan wouldn't like that girl having her hands all over you."

"Reagan trusts me," he said with fervor, his eyes lighting up at the mere mention of his girlfriend's name.

I rolled my eyes. Sometimes their lovey-dovey displays made me sick. My gaze caught sight of long blonde hair and a body I knew all too well. Just the distraction I needed.

Kevin nudged my side. "Brittany's homing in on you. I'm gone. Maybe I'll find Jason or Bill somewhere on the dance floor."

With that he disappeared into the crowd, as if the Devil was after him. And for him, Brittany was the Devil incarnate. The two hated each other with fervor. Kevin found her arrogant, self-centered, narcissistic, vain, and rude. Brittany was all of those things, but she was also fucking hot and a good lay.

I glanced in her direction, and she smirked at me. I stifled a groan and kept my face indifferent. The girl was confident enough. I didn't need to add to that by acknowledging her undeniably irresistible body.

She sauntered over to me, a sultry smile playing on her red-painted lips. Men often took Brittany for stupid; she was anything but, and that made her even more dangerous. She went to business school and was the daughter of one of my father's best customers and friends.

Her eyes traveled over my body as I leaned against the bar, vodka martini in hand. Not in the mood for pleasantries, I didn't smile at her. Brittany and I'd been fuck buddies for almost a year, and though recently she seemed to want more, I couldn't imagine wanting anything more than hot sex from her. Just like I did, I knew she had other partners and one-night stands. I wanted our relationship to remain one that was no strings attached.

"Hi, Zach," she said in a husky voice, perching on a barstool beside me and crossing her long legs. "Do you like my new dress?"

Of course Brittany was as obnoxious and self-centered as usual. I let my eyes wander over her dress, if you could even call it that. I'd classify it as underwear. It hardly left anything to the imagination. Not that there was anything I hadn't seen yet.

The flimsy red piece of fabric ended high on her thighs, barely covering her butt, and the plunging neckline would have made a hooker blush. Brittany loved to openly display her best assets, at least during her free time. When you saw her on campus in her modest skirts and cashmere sweaters, you wouldn't recognize her as the same person. She knew which side of herself to present at any time.

If it weren't for her hot body, I wouldn't have put up with her for so long.

"The dress is nice," I commented dryly before raising my drink to my lips and taking another sip.

Brittany's face darkened. "Nice?" She was about to throw one of her temper tantrums.

I sighed quietly. "God damn sexy, fucking hot …"

She smiled, satisfied, and grabbed my arm, sliding her high-heeled foot between my legs and rubbing it along my inner thigh. "How about a dance?" She hopped off the stool and pulled me toward the dance floor.

I resisted her tugging and she pouted. "You won't regret it." Then she licked her lips in a way that almost made me moan. I knew this was a game for her. She had acting skills worthy of an Oscar. You would never believe she was the same woman who attended luncheons at my father's company in custom-tailored business suits.

Knowing that it would only make her more insistent, I didn't resist any longer. I moved my body in rhythm to the hammering beat and ran my hands over Brittany's hips while she ground her body against me, her butt causing delicious friction against my groin.

She knew what she was doing, and I was never strong enough to resist. Despite my previous annoyance, I grew hard and let out a low growl. Brittany reached behind herself and cupped my cock through my pants, squeezing lightly while we kept rocking to the music. Her touch was a promise of what was to come. I nuzzled my face against her neck and sucked her skin into my mouth. She let out a low moan and ground herself even more insistently against me.

"Fuck," I growled into her ear.

"Just what I've been thinking." She grinned wickedly at me and led me across the dance floor toward the back door of the club. For once it wasn't raining, not that I would have cared if it had. The small back alley was deserted. Just what we needed.

She pushed me hard against the wall, and I rested against it, glad that it was there to keep me steady. All my blood had gathered in a certain part of my body, so I needed something to lean on for support. She smiled seductively and sank down on her knees in front of me. I had to give it to her. She didn't mind getting dirty. Brittany licked her lips again and reached for my jeans. I stared up at the night sky.

Unbidden thoughts of Amber penetrated my mind. Where the hell did they come from? This was not the moment to think about her. Her beautiful, shy smile made Brittany's sexy smile appear so horribly cheap. I felt almost guilty for wanting to fuck Brittany.

Damn it. But I really, really wanted to fuck Britt.

Brittany pulled my zipper down and released my cock from its prison. I was about to protest, but then Brittany's hot mouth closed around the tip of my cock and every sane thought left my mind. I groaned and leaned my head against the hard brick wall. Grabbing the back of Brittany's head, I kept her in place, thrusting my cock into her mouth. She didn't mind and seemed comfortable enough. Hell, that woman knew what she was doing! Her tongue swirled around my tip. Then she sucked me into her mouth as deep as it would go.

I started thrusting again, and she hummed against my cock, the vibrations sending jolts of pleasure through me. She gripped my butt as I fucked her mouth. The sounds she made as she sucked drove me fucking insane with arousal. Fuck, she was good. With a groan, I came into her mouth.

"Fuck." I exhaled. She rose to her feet and wiped her mouth with the back of her hand before she smiled at me triumphantly. "I told you, you wouldn't regret it. I keep my promises."

She leaned into my body and kissed me hard. I could taste myself on her lips. Snarling into her mouth, I gripped her ass and squeezed it hard. With my hands on her ass, I lifted her off the ground, and she wrapped her legs around my waist, grinding herself against my groin. I turned us around and pressed her up against the wall, jerking my hips against her. Being with Brittany made me forget my problems. Everything was simple and uncomplicated with her. This was just hot, raw sex and nothing else.

No promises, no regrets.

Just a meaningless fling.

I set her down and disposed of the condom before pulling up my jeans. Brittany leaned against the wall, looking fucking pleased with herself.

She kissed my cheek. "Let's continue at your place."

I frowned. I'd taken her home a few times before, but Brian also couldn't stand the sight of her, so those sleepovers were few and far between. And now with Amber being our new roommate, it was completely out of the question.

"That won't work," I said.

Her blue eyes narrowed and her lips thinned. I knew what that meant: temper tantrum.

"Why?" she demanded.

I straightened to my full height and slid my hands into my pockets.

"Because Brian's sister has moved in with us."

"So what? Is she such a prude that she can't listen to us having a bit of fun?"

I didn't like how she talked about Amber. "Stop it," I said tightly but my reaction only made it worse.

"What is it? Are you screwing her too? Is she a good fuck? Better than me?"

I took a step toward her, scowling. Her eyes widened in shock. "Don't talk about her like that."

"Fuck you!" she spat. "You can find someone else to suck your dick!" She stomped toward the door, disappearing in the building.

I ran a hand through my hair and closed my eyes. As pleasurable as sex was with Brittany, I wasn't sure if that was enough to put up with her personality. The door opened again, and I expected Brittany to return, but it was only Kevin.

He grinned at me. "Brittany just stalked past me. She looked royally pissed." That fact obviously brought him great pleasure.

When I didn't say anything, he continued, "What happened? Didn't you live up to her expectations?"

I rolled my eyes at him. "My performance was outstanding as usual."

Kevin snorted. "You look ready to leave."

"I'm so ready to leave."

"So what got her panties in a twist, then?" he inquired as we headed back into the club.

"She wanted to go to my place for seconds and wasn't happy when I told her no. With Amber staying at the apartment, bringing Brittany home wouldn't be a good idea. It would only upset Amber if she had to listen to us."

Kevin scanned my face as we left the club, heading in the direction of the car. It was unnerving to have him watching me like that. "What?" I snapped.

"You like her," Kevin commented.

"Whom?"

"Brian's sister of course," he said before he plopped into the driver's seat. I didn't know how he could stand the taste of nonalcoholic beer, but as long as it allowed for him to be my chauffeur, he could drink that piss water whenever he wanted.

"Don't even think about it," I warned him.

His expression turned serious. "Why not?"

"The girl went through hell. She sure as hell isn't ready for a relationship," I said a bit sharper than intended. *And neither am I*, I added in my mind.

"You mean she isn't ready for sex? Don't tell me you are that much of an asshole that you can't imagine being with her because you would have to live without sex for a while?"

I scowled at him. "Shut up, Kev," I taunted him with the name Reagan used for him. "It's not like you know anything about it."

Kevin gave me a pointed look. "I was exactly like you, Zach. I was always looking for the next fling, and I couldn't imagine being without sex for long. But then I met Reagan."

A snarky comment rested on the tip of my tongue, but he kept talking. "Reagan was recovering from a bad breakup when we met, and she made it pretty clear that she wasn't ready to jump in bed with me right away. But I was willing to wait because I cared about her."

"How long have you waited?" I blurted out.

He looked uncomfortable talking about the subject. Before meeting

Reagan, he always bragged about his sexual endeavors. "A couple of months."

"A couple of months!"

How could he have gone without sex for so long? I knew a few weeks after they started dating, Reagan had spent her nights at Kevin's apartment. How did he manage to keep his hands off of her while she was lying next to him in bed?

My disbelief must have been on my face because Kevin shook his head. "You are an idiot, Zach." He started the engine.

"Aren't we going to wait for Jason and Bill?" I asked.

"They found some girls they're spending the night with." Kevin's expression turned into a scowl.

I chuckled. "I'm sure they'll have fun."

"You know, since I met Reagan I've realized that my life before her was empty. Some day you will see that being in a relationship is more satisfying than screwing around."

"For fuck's sake! Stop with that holier-than-thou attitude. You sound like a saint. Believe me, my lifestyle is very satisfying," I said with a grin.

"You're an asshole, Zach," Kevin muttered, his fingers tightening around the steering wheel. Why did he even care?

I shrugged. "So I've been told before," I said casually. "Why don't you ever get on Bill's or Jason's case with your new found morals?"

"Because they are lost causes."

"And I'm not?" I barked out a laugh.

Kevin didn't reply.

The rest of the ride passed in silence, and I was damn grateful for that. I wouldn't have been able to endure any more lectures from him. Sex was all I needed.

chapter six
Amber

It was silent in the apartment. I was alone and for the first time in days, the protective wall I always had around me when Zach and Brian were around was down, and I felt almost relaxed. I walked out of my room and into the bathroom. I locked the door, even though I knew Brian and Zach wouldn't be home for a while. Law school kept them busy most mornings, yet a tiny part of me felt safer with the lock in place.

I rushed through my shower routine as usual. Showers brought up too many horrible memories—memories I wanted to forget. The first few weeks after I'd woken in the hospital, I would shower for hours every day. I'd scrub my skin with scalding hot water until I drew blood. I'd tried to wash away their smell, but it was burned into my memory, and even after all those years I could still smell them on my skin. No matter how much vanilla scented shower gel I used, their stench remained.

The psychiatrists told me that it was all in my head. They didn't know how it was to smell those bastards on me. To see their leering faces whenever I closed my eyes. To hear their vile words haunting my dreams. To feel their hands on me. Maybe it was only my imagination because all of that was in the past, but for me it was part of my reality. I was trapped with the memories of that day for the rest of my life.

I shut the water off and stepped out of the shower before more horrible thoughts could take hold of me. Wrapped one towel around my body, I twisted another one into a turban atop my head to keep my hair in place before I unlocked the door.

Pumpkin was meowing loudly. I followed the noise into the living room and found him sitting on the love seat, looking tense. I took a few steps toward him when I noticed movement in the corner of my eye.

"Nice towel," said a male voice.

I whirled around, tightly clutching the tiny towel against my body. My muscles seized with fear. On the sofa sat two men, both of them tall and imposing. Terrifying. One of them had dark skin, and he looked impossibly strong. The other was leaner but no less intimidating.

My breath stuck in my throat, and my vision narrowed, turning black at the corners.

It will happen again.

Happen again.

Happen again.

Happen again.

I couldn't breathe, couldn't run, couldn't do anything.

The smaller man with blond hair stood and walked toward me, a leering grin on his face. It reminded me so much of the grins of that night.

Their grins. Taunting and leering.

I backed away from him, shaking my head desperately. The blond man took another step closer to me and the man with the dark skin got up, looking angry and dangerous.

"*No!*" I wanted to scream, but nothing came out of my mouth.

"Hey, we're not going to hurt you," said the blond man.

I'd heard those words before, and shortly after they were uttered my life had been destroyed. *We won't hurt you. You'll enjoy it. You like it rough, bitch, don't you? Scream for us.*

"Bill, you're frightening her, you idiot!" shouted the other man.

My bare back hit the wall. I was trapped.

Trapped.

Trapped.

The words rang in my ears, mingling with my screams from long ago in my head. I sank down to the floor and hugged my legs to my chest, rocking my body back and forth. Whimpers slipped past my lips and the taste of my tears lingered on my tongue.

"Fuck! That's all your damn fault, Bill, you fucking idiot!"

"Shut up, Jason! What are we going to do?"

"She looks like she's in shock."

"We need to call Brian."

"Are you fucking insane, Jason? Brian will kill us. Call Zach. He'll know what to do."

They were shouting, and they were so close. Too close. Too close.

Fear paralyzed me. Memories, haunting and terrifying, kept flashing through my mind. I rocked harder.

Make them go away, please. God, please, don't let them hurt me again.

"Try to shake her out of it, Jason. Maybe you'll get through to her."

A warm hand on my arm. Touching. Gripping. A scream ripped from my throat, raw and desperate. I pulled my knees tighter against myself, shielding me from what was to come, even though I knew it was futile. It didn't stop them from hurting me last time, and it wouldn't stop those men this time either. I retreated into myself, seeking shelter in the darkness of my mind where I was safe.

zachary

This lecture was by far the most boring thing I'd ever had to endure. Mergers and Acquisitions, or what I liked to call it: how to make rich bastards like my father even richer. I rested my forehead on my arm, drowning out the monotone voice of the professor and trying to get the sleep that I didn't manage to get last night.

My phone vibrated in my pocket, startling me, and my head shot up in surprise. I must have dozed off. I pulled it out without the professor noticing and checked the caller ID: Jason.

What the fuck did he want now of all times? The dumbass knew I was busy. I ignored him and returned my gaze to the professor with his checkered jacket and corduroy pants. The vibrating stopped and I was about to return my phone into my pocket when it beeped once, announcing the arrival of a message. I groaned and the person next to me shot me a withering look, which I returned with the same fervor.

Fucking idiot.

I stared down at my cell and read the message Jason had sent.

Bill and I need your help. Emergency!! A problem with Brian's sister.

My eyes widened. What had those idiots done this time? I grabbed my things and hurried out of the room, ignoring the disapproving scowl of the professor.

As soon as I was outside, I called Jason. "What the fuck has happened?"

"Zach, thank god. Brian's sister, she's having some kind of panic attack."

"Where is she?"

"In your apartment ..." He sounded sorry. And damn would he be sorry when Brian found out.

"What the hell are you doing there?" I asked, already getting into my Hummer.

"Well ..."

"I don't fucking care. I'll be there in a few minutes." Brian and I should have never given those two morons a spare key. I hung up on Jason and called Brian. He was going be furious once he found out what had happened. I knew Bill and Jason would never do anything to Amber, but after what she went through, having two unknown men in the apartment was probably a damn shock.

"Zach?" Brian whispered, probably trying not to disturb his lecture.

"I'm on my way home. Jason called. Your sister is having a panic attack in the apartment," I said in a rush. There was a second of silence before Brian exploded.

"What have they done? I swear by God I'll kill them if they did anything to Amber!"

"Bill and Jason wouldn't do anything." I tried to calm him down but he was beyond reasoning with him.

"I'll kill them!" The line went dead.

I sped home in record time. Brian's car wasn't there yet. I didn't waste any time and ran up the stairs two at a time. The door to the apartment was ajar, and I pushed it open. I froze at the scene before me.

Jason and Bill were sitting on the sofa, both looking pretty close to distraught. No fucking wonder. Amber cowered on the ground, her back against the wall, and she was rocking back and forth. Her face was buried against her naked legs. Her wet dark hair spilled out of the towel wrapped around her head. She wasn't wearing anything but a bath towel. I stormed toward the two idiots on the sofa and grabbed Bill by the collar of his shirt, yanking him to his feet.

"What the fuck happened here?"

"We didn't know she would freak out like that!" he muttered. I wanted to break every bone in his body.

"What. The. Fuck. Did. You. Do?" I spat out each word, barely able to contain my anger. Bill always tended to fuck things up.

"Bill was curious about Brian's sister because Brian is so damn secretive when it comes to her, so we decided to pay her a visit. We just wanted to talk, and then she came out of the bathroom in her towel, and when she saw us, she freaked out," Jason explained hastily.

I released Bill from my grip and turned toward Amber, taking a hesitant step closer to her. I didn't know what to do. Steps sounded in the hall and a moment later the door flew open and Brian stormed in, his eyes wild and furious. In his button-down shirt and oxfords his facial expression looked out of place on his face. He glanced at his cowering sister, and then he stomped past me and toward Bill. He punched him hard in the face. Jason backed away at once, raising his hands in surrender.

"What the fuck?" Bill seethed, holding his nose, which was bleeding pretty badly. Blood dripped down his lips and chin and onto his ugly-ass shirt.

Brian glowered at him. "I told you to stay away from her! Why couldn't you listen for once?"

Bill shrugged, still holding his nose. "I thought you exaggerated when you said she was scared of men. I didn't know that it was so…" he chanced a look at Amber, apparently trying to come up with a word to describe the situation "…serious," he finished lamely.

"I'm sorry, Brian. If I'd known …" Jason trailed off, shrugging.

Brian ignored him and approached Amber then knelt a few feet away from her.

"Amber?" he said softly. "Amber, it's me, Brian."

She didn't react. Cautiously, I moved closer to them, and Brian sent me a desperate look, but I didn't know how to help him. He crawled even closer to his sister and frowned deeply. "Jason, give me the blanket," he ordered.

I followed his gaze. The towel had slipped slightly because of the way Amber pressed her legs against her body. Her thighs were completely exposed. I would have been able to see more if I'd moved my gaze further up. I averted my eyes, not wanting to violate her in that way.

She didn't even notice that she was half naked. I crouched down beside Brian as he tried to cover her with the blanket. She jerked back, letting out a heartbreaking whimper. Brian closed his eyes for a moment, fighting tears. I squeezed his shoulder, and he looked at me gratefully. He moved closer to Amber and put the blanket over her legs. She'd become as still as a statue.

"Amber," he whispered again. Her shoulders began to shake.

Brian drew in a shuddering breath, looking close to breaking.

"Amber," I tried to gain her attention but got nothing.

A knock startled all of us, and we turned toward the open door. Kevin stood there, his eyes wide as he looked at Amber.

"I got home a few minutes ago, and I heard a scream," he said eventually. He shared the apartment down the hall with Jason and Bill. If he heard the scream, the entire floor had heard it too.

Brian pinched the bridge of his nose. "Amber ... I don't know what to do. It's probably best if we call a doctor."

Kevin looked from Amber to Brian. "Reagan came home with me. Maybe she can help."

Maybe a woman wouldn't frighten Amber so much.

Brian considered his suggestion for a moment before he nodded. "Yes, can you get her?"

"I'll be back in a sec." With a last glance in Amber's direction, Kevin disappeared from our view.

I stood up and began pacing. The tension in my body made me feel like I was about to burst. Amber's nightmare from the previous night had been horrible to witness, but this ... fuck, this was on another level.

Kevin returned with Reagan at his side. Her red hair was up in a high ponytail, and her shorts and workout shirt were drenched in sweat. She must have jogged over here from her apartment.

Brian practically jumped to his feet and clutched Reagan's hands. "Reagan, thank God you're here. Maybe you can get through to her."

Shock washed over Reagan's face when she spotted Amber. She tensed and for a heart-stopping moment I thought she was about to say she couldn't do this, couldn't handle Amber.

Then Reagan snapped out of her daze and straightened her shoulders. Kevin once mentioned that she had a horse, and the way Reagan now approached Amber reminded me of someone trying not to spook a wild horse.

Slowly, Reagan walked over to Amber and lowered herself to the floor a good distance away from Amber, pausing for a moment before crawling closer to Amber.

Amber didn't stop rocking. She probably hadn't even noticed the other girl yet. Reagan extended a hand and touched Amber's shoulder. Amber jerked back, but Reagan didn't let go. "Shhh. It's alright. Everything is alright," she cooed.

Amber relaxed visibly.

With her freckles and lanky limbs, Reagan didn't look very intimidating.

"Go away," she mouthed at us, her eyes imploring. Brian hesitated but I gripped his arm.

"Come on, Brian. Let's go into the kitchen. Reagan needs some time alone with Amber."

"I guess you are right."

Kevin, Bill, and Jason started to follow us, but I turned around to the two idiots who'd caused the mess. "You…" I pointed at them "…get lost. You've done enough damage for one day."

Jason looked miserable, but Bill just shrugged and left the apartment. Asshole. I shook my head at his behavior and walked into the kitchen. Brian, Kevin, and I sat down around the table and stared at each other for a moment.

Kevin kept throwing glances my way. Maybe he'd finally realized that Amber wasn't ready for any kind of relationship. Especially not with me. I wasn't the right guy for a girl like her. He'd been trying to set me up with several friends of Reagan, but even his matchmaking obsession had its limits.

"Reagan will help her," he said eventually. I wasn't sure if it was meant to console me or Brian. Brian didn't even raise his head from where it rested on the table. No sounds were coming from the living room. I wished I knew what was happening. What if Reagan couldn't talk Amber out of her panic attack? Seeing her like that, so broken and frightened, it was the worst thing I'd ever witnessed. I hated feeling so fucking helpless.

amber

Someone touched my shoulder. I tried to get away from the person, away from the pain that would follow.

"Shhh … it's all right. Everything is all right," a woman said. Her voice sounded kind, not threatening at all. I relaxed but I didn't dare lift my head. I didn't want to see what was going on around me. Someone sat beside me and our shoulders brushed lightly. I shivered but didn't pull back. Something about the person made me calm.

"Amber?" the woman asked softly.

I turned my head to the side and lifted it from my knees. Kind brown eyes returned my gaze. Next to me sat a girl about my age, with long legs crossed at the ankles in front of her, red hair pulled into a ponytail. She must have been working out when she found me. She was wearing turquoise Nike running shoes and matching shorts.

She smiled. "'I'm Reagan. A friend of your brother." God, I hoped Brian hadn't called her out of the gym to deal with me.

I wiped the wetness from my cheeks and sat up a bit straighter. I wasn't sure how much time had passed since I'd lost control of myself. I remembered hearing Brian's and Zach's voices while I was drowning in my panic.

"I'm Kevin's girlfriend. He lives in the apartment at the end of the hall. He's friends with Zach and Brian. I don't think you've met him yet," she chattered in a light tone, completely ignoring the fact that we were sitting on the floor because I had a breakdown. *God*, I was still only dressed in a towel and the blanket that rested over my legs. What a pathetic sight. She didn't say anything about my state, though, and I was infinitely grateful for that.

"I'm Amber, Brian's sister," I said lamely, though she probably knew that already. She smiled and rose to her feet, holding her hand out for me to take.

"Let's go to your room. We can go there to talk some more."

I took her hand and stood on shaky legs. She was a few inches taller than me and built like a hurdle runner, all long limbs and thin body. She quickly released me and grimaced.

"Sorry. I'm sweaty. I really need to shower. Do I stink very badly?"

"Not very badly," I said.

She laughed. "Well, that's a relief!"

A tiny smile tugged at my lips. I led her toward my room, where Pumpkin was pacing in front of the door. He nudged my calf as I entered. Then he peered up at Reagan before striding over to the sofa and curling up on it. Reagan was watching him with obvious unease. I supposed everyone was scared of something, even a harmless cat. I took a few clothes out of the drawer.

"Why don't you take a shower in our bathroom while I get dressed?" I held up my jeans and shirt. "The bathroom is next door."

"Thanks, but I can shower at Kevin's. That's where I left the bag with my clean clothes anyway."

"Oh, okay." I paused. She leaned against my door, her eyes taking in the bare walls and empty desk. "How long have you been living here?"

"For a few days," I said. I really wanted to get out of my towel and into my comfortable clothes, but I couldn't undress with Reagan in the room. "I haven't gotten a chance to put up pictures yet."

"What kind of pictures? I love Miró and modern art in general."

I flushed. "I don't know. I'll have to buy a few prints and frames."

Reagan's eyes darted to the clothes I still held in my hand. "I can turn around … or do you need me to go outside?"

I quickly shook my head. "No, turning around is fine." I wasn't sure if it was, but I would try. She turned her back to me and reached for her ponytail, pulling out the hair tie.

Not taking my eyes off of her, I dropped the towel and dressed in record time. "It's okay."

Reagan faced me. "How about we go looking for pictures together? I know an amazing art store that sells beautiful bargain prints."

I didn't give my anxieties time to take over. "Sure. That sounds good."

"Great!" She walked over to my desk and grabbed my phone. "I'll put my number into your contacts." Her fingers typed at lightning speed, and a beep sounded. She pulled out her phone from the holder around her upper arm. "And now I have your number too. Send me a message if you feel up to going shopping."

I nodded. "If I don't, will you remind me again?" Sometimes I needed a little push. This social life thing … this whole living thing was new for me.

"You bet I will! I can't wait." She glanced at the watch around her wrist. "Shit. I need to hurry. I have Russian literature in ninety minutes. I can't go there looking like a train wreck." She scanned my face. "Are you going to be okay? I have a perfect attendance record. It wouldn't be a problem if I skipped once. I could stay with you and we could grab something to eat."

"No, I'm okay. Really." I didn't want Reagan to miss class because of me. It was bad enough that I'd caused her and everyone else to worry so much because of my breakdown. "Russian literature? So you're in college."

With her hand on the door handle, she said, "Yeah, I'm majoring in Russian and French."

"Wow. Maybe you can tell me more about it when we go shopping?"

"Deal. But I should warn you. Once I start talking about it, I probably won't stop." She waved as she slipped out and closed the door. Somehow a day that could have become the biggest nightmare in months had turned out okay thanks to Reagan. She seemed relaxed and in control of her life. Maybe we could become friends.

zachary

Reagan appeared in the kitchen and walked over to Kevin. She slung her arms around his neck and kissed the top of his head, smiling. "I need to grab a shower. I don't want to be late for my classes."

Brian's head shot up from his arm. "How's Amber?" I'd never seen him like this. He'd always been a pensive guy, but right now he was bordering on depressed. Not that I could blame him. It had been hell for me to watch Amber like that, so how much worse was it for Brian?

Reagan gave Brian a reassuring smile as she straightened. "She's fine," she said. "She agreed to go shopping with me." She turned to face Kevin. "Remember that art store I talked about?"

Kevin smiled. "Of course. You showed me their website. I'm sure

Amber will love it."

"I know. We'll buy a few prints for her room."

Brian's eyebrows climbed up his forehead. "She said yes?"

Reagan nodded. "I really need to go now."

"I'll join you," Kevin said quickly, practically leaping off the chair. The way he undressed Reagan with his eyes, I doubted he had only showering in mind. They left the kitchen, holding hands.

Brian followed them with his gaze, his shoulders tense. I punched his arm lightly. "Reagan said Amber is okay. Stop worrying."

"How can I stop worrying, Zach? You saw her."

I leaned back with my chair until it rested against the counter and the front legs were in the air. He was right, but freaking out about it like Brian did wouldn't help anyone, least of all Amber. "Do you have classes in the afternoon?"

"Yeah, but I won't go. I don't want to leave Amber alone after what happened today. And I can't focus on stuff like that right now."

"Me too." Not that I usually needed a reason to skip classes. "Do you want to order pizza? I'm starving."

"Are you sure you don't want to go? You've been bailing on classes a lot lately."

"You can't get rid of me so easily. So how about that pizza?" We'd eaten pizza or other fast food almost every day since we'd moved in together, and it certainly wasn't healthy, but neither of us could cook.

"Then pizza it is again," Brian agreed halfheartedly, reaching for the phone to call our favorite pizza restaurant.

"I could cook something for us." The quiet words startled Brian and me. I almost tipped sideways in my chair and had to hold onto the counter to keep my balance. Amber lingered in the doorway, looking uncomfortable and embarrassed as she gnawed on her lower lip.

"That sounds like a great idea," I said with a smile. Some of the tension leaked out of her body. I couldn't believe she was the same girl who'd been cowering on the floor less than thirty minutes ago. "Well ... unless your cooking skills are anything like Brian's. I'm not in the mood for food poisoning."

Brian didn't laugh and didn't react in any way to my jab. I kicked him under the table to shake him out of his stupor. She let out a small breathy laugh. "I think my cooking skills are quite alright. Dad never complained." The smile vanished from her face, and she chanced a look at Brian.

"Amber is a fantastic cook," he said finally. "You're in for a treat." He couldn't even look her in the eye. Instead, he was staring at the table. Could he act any more obvious? "You don't need to cook. Maybe you should rest? You're probably exhausted."

Her lips tightened. "I'm not. I'd really like to cook, but if you don't want me to, then that's okay."

Brian shook his head hastily. "No, I love your cooking. I just thought that you needed to rest after ... never mind."

Amber blushed and averted her gaze. Oh for fuck's sake! Watching them interact was almost painful. Brian was the biggest moron ever.

"I'll check the fridge and cupboard to see what I have to work with," she said eventually and stepped into the room. Brian sat rigidly on his chair, probably worried he'd scare her if he moved the wrong way, and I didn't dare to move much either. But it was getting uncomfortable with my chair standing on two legs, so I let it fall back on its front legs with a low thud. Amber jumped slightly, and Brian shot me a glare.

Amber ignored us mostly and even moved past us to get to the fridge, but Brian kept watching her as if he expected her to have another panic attack. I was torn between breaking the silence and keeping my mouth shut. Amber turned to us after a few minutes of rummaging and gestured at a few items on the kitchen counter. "I think I could cook Penne Arrabiata from this. Is that alright? We really need to go grocery shopping if I'm supposed to cook more often."

"Knock yourself out," I said. "I'm always down for pasta."

"Sounds good," Brian said.

She began to work, and I rose from my chair to grab the sports magazine that was lying on the counter behind Brian. His hand shot out. "What are you doing?" His eyes darted to Amber, who noticed as usual.

Her face filled with embarrassment. "You don't have to sit there like statues, you know? You can move. I don't mind."

Brian glared at me as if it was all my fault and handed me the magazine. He needed to stop being so fucking careful. I began to read, watching Amber from the corner of my eye every now and then. She seemed content and happy while she cooked, her face more relaxed than I'd ever seen it before.

"Ready," she said and the smell of pasta flooded my senses. It smelled delicious. She carried the pot over to the table and put it down. "Will you set the table?"

Brian and I both rose at once and froze when we realized that we were now standing over her. She looked fragile and delicate and the urge to protect her flared inside of me. She didn't flinch. She ignored us and sat down on a chair. Brian and I took that as our cue to grab plates and put them on the table. We dug in as soon as we sat down.

"So good." I offered praise between bites of pasta.

She hummed in response, sucking a piece of spaghetti into her mouth. Tomato sauce coated her lips, and I felt the ridiculous urge to lean over and kiss her.

"I missed your cooking," Brian said.

"I want to apologize for…" swallowed hard, her gaze flitting toward the living room for an instant "…for being such a bother."

I swallowed the pasta in my mouth. Brian reached out for her but thought better of it and returned his hand to his side, giving her a forced smile. "You aren't a bother, Amber."

"It's good to have a girl in the apartment who can cook for us, do the laundry, and clean everything," I joked, winking at her.

She let out a laugh that sounded like tinkling bells. It was beautiful. "I'm not going to do your dirty laundry."

Did she know how beautiful she was? I wanted to slap myself. I shouldn't be thinking about her in such a way. She was Brian's sister, after all, and that was only the tip of the iceberg of things standing between us.

"There's a support group meeting today. I think I might want to go," she said, chancing a glance at Brian.

He put his fork down at once and made a move to get up. "I can drive you there."

"That would be great. It's at seven, so you have enough time to finish your pasta." She leaned back in her chair and rolled her eyes at me when Brian wasn't looking.

I stifled a laugh. Fuck, that girl was worming her way into my heart, and I didn't have the first clue how to stop it.

chapter seven

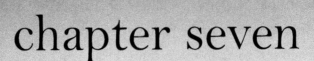

Nerves fluttered in my stomach. Why did I have to mention the support group? Now I had to go or Brian would worry. Would I have to talk about what had happened? I wanted to forget, not drag everything back to the surface. But Dad and Brian set their hopes on the group helping. I grabbed my purse and slung it over my shoulder. I would do this for them.

Brian was already waiting in the living room when I entered. I gave him a smile that probably looked very forced, but it was the best I could do. He held the door open for me, and I walked past him into the hallway, careful to keep my distance. Straightening my back and sucking in a deep breath, I headed into the elevator. Brian joined me after a moment, cautious and worried—as always. He kept as much space between us as possible and pressed the button. The elevator began moving, and the awkward silence between us was threatening to suffocate me. I wanted my relationship with Brian to return to normal, to how it had been before that day that had ruined everything. But how could it ever get back to normal if I couldn't even hug him or take his hand? The elevator stopped and we strode toward Brian's car. I buckled myself up. Brian kept his gaze fixed on the windshield and sat rigidly as we drove off.

"The support group will help you," he said into the silence.

I decided to play along. "I'm sure it will." I tightened the hold on my purse to hide the trembling of my hands.

We parked in front of the part of Massachusetts General hospital, where the support group meeting was being held. "Do you want me to bring you to the door?" Brian asked as I unbuckled.

"No." I wasn't a toddler. I needed to do this on my own, even if I felt safer with someone I knew.

Brian froze with his hand on the seat buckle. "Are you sure?" Upon seeing my expression, he nodded. "Okay. I can wait until the meeting is over if you want."

I raised my head to look at him. "No, Brian, it's alright. I don't know how long it's going to take, and I'm sure you have better things to do than sit in the car. I'll call you once I'm done."

He looked hesitant but after a moment he said, "Okay, but wait inside for me. I'll call you when I pull up."

I got out of the car and threw the door shut. With one last worried glance, Brian drove away. I drew in a shaky breath as I headed toward the glass entrance and stepped into the brightly lit lobby. This outpatient center was part of the psychiatric department of MGH, but my worry that everyone would look at me like I was weird was completely unfounded. Except for an elderly woman behind the welcome desk, there was only a tall girl with dark brown hair in the lobby. I was supposed to register, but the thought of sitting down in circle with people who'd gone through the same thing that I had suddenly seemed impossible. The mere idea made my stomach roil. *Calm down.*

The tall girl was looking at a bulletin board on the wall. I walked toward her slowly, not yet ready to register with the receptionist, and the girl turned to me when I stopped beside her. She was older than I'd first thought, maybe twenty, but she was so skinny that she'd looked younger from afar.

A smile broke out on her thin face, and she stepped aside, so I could look at the bulletin board as well. "Hi, I'm Olivia," she said. She didn't try to shake my hand or to make any attempt at physical contact, and I liked her for it.

"I'm Amber," I told her.

"Are you here for the eating disorder support group?" she asked, her expression hopeful.

I hesitated. I knew that I had neglected my body over the last three years and hadn't been in the sun for the same amount of time, but did I look like I was trying to starve myself? From afar Olivia hadn't looked that thin, but now that I was standing next to her, I saw that she was wearing a thick winter coat to hide her body. Her skinny hands peeked out from it, like the hands of a skeleton, her fingers spindly twigs. Her cheekbones were protruding, and I could see her blue veins through the skin at her throat and hands. The shadows under her eyes were even worse than mine.

"Actually, I'm here for …" I hesitated, not able to voice it. I pointed my index finger at the name of the group.

Olivia's eyes followed my finger and then they widened slightly. Her shoulders slumped. "Oh," she mumbled. "I was hoping you were in my support group. You seem nice and I really don't want to go. I should probably stop rambling." She let out an embarrassed laugh.

I gave her a smile. "I don't really want to go to this group either but …" I trailed off. A thought popped into my head, and though I knew it wasn't fair toward Brian or Dad, I couldn't shake it off. "Why don't we just sit somewhere and talk, only the two of us?"

"That sounds perfect. Our own personal support group," she whispered. "I'd really like that. There's a park around the corner, but it'll be getting dark soon."

The woman behind the desk was watching us. She probably wondered why we hadn't checked in yet. "Is there a coffee shop close by?"

"Yes, a Starbucks is a five minute walk away. I can lead the way."

We walked in silence and finally settled in two seats in a corner of the shop. It was the most private spot we could find. I kept glancing at the other customers, worried someone would approach us. So far I'd managed not to bump into anyone. The number of people at Starbucks was far more than I was used to, but I tried to ignore my anxiety. I'd ordered a pumpkin latte, but Olivia only wanted a peppermint tea. "So who made you go to the support group?" I asked.

She sipped at her tea. "My mother. She's worried about me. I had to move back in with her after I spent a few weeks in hospital. I missed a lot of classes."

She talked about her problems without being embarrassed. I wished I could do that.

"What about you?"

"Nobody really made me go, but my father and brother really want me to get better."

"Better how?"

I took a spoonful of foam, letting it melt on my tongue and enjoying the burst of pumpkin spice in my mouth. "I'm not good with people."

"You're good with me," Olivia said, tugging her legs under herself, making herself even smaller. She was still wearing her coat. "I didn't notice anything strange about you."

I pondered that. She was right. I had followed her into the coffee shop without a single freak-out. Well, I did check how many men were sitting in the coffee shop, but that had been more of a passing thing. Being around Olivia was easy. "Sometimes I panic," I said. I hoped she wouldn't push the matter. I really didn't want to elaborate any further.

She nodded as if she got it, then said, "Maybe we should establish ground rules. Topics that are off-limits." She fiddled with the tea bag but didn't avoid my gaze. She hadn't once averted her eyes from me. Maybe I could learn a thing or two from her. Despite her obvious indifference—I could at least hide my brokenness most of the time—she didn't try to hide.

"I'll start. Off-limits: diet, food, college, weight, boyfriends, healthy living, my father." Her brows drew together. "I'm pretty sure I forgot something."

I cradled my cup. "I hate the question 'what happened?'. I don't like to talk about the past."

"That's all?"

"It is." So what now? "I moved to Boston less than a week ago."

"It's too late to start college," she said then rolled her eyes. "Okay. So college is only off-limits if it's about me."

I smiled. "I didn't come to start college. At least, not right away. I moved in with my brother and his best friend."

"That takes guts. My siblings and I fight all the time. I actually miss my roommate, even though she was a bitch."

"How many siblings do you have?"

"One sister, who's two years younger, and a younger brother, who's thirteen." Olivia spent the next hour recounting her life with her family. I loved listening to her, and she obviously didn't mind talking. A few minutes after the end of the scheduled support group meeting, we arrived back at the center. A hint of guilt filled me at the thought of having bailed on the support group. I couldn't tell Brian. He wouldn't understand. I checked my cell phone for a message from him. I'd written him ten minutes ago, but he hadn't replied yet.

zachary

I tried to block out the conversation, but it was impossible. I plopped down on the couch and watched Brian pace the room, cell phone pressed against his ear. This conversation had been going on forever. How had Brian not lost his shit yet? If it had been Brittany who was bothering me like that, I would have hung up ten minutes ago.

"Lauren, I don't have time right now," Brian said for the hundredth time, and his voice had an edgy tone to it. I smirked. I couldn't hear what she was saying in return, but the rising of her voice told me that she was pissed—as usual.

"Lauren …" Brian, always the gentleman, tried to placate her. In vain of course. There was more screaming on the other end of the phone that I could hear.

"I need to pick up my sister."

I shook my head and rolled my eyes.

"I don't think it's a good idea if Zach picks her up," Brian said, though he sounded as if he was going to give in.

"I can pick her up if you want."

Lauren would keep bothering him until he went over to see her. The woman was insistent and bothersome, but Brian seemed to like her for some incomprehensible, twisted reason. I had no right to judge him anyway. I wasn't one to talk. I still had my own twisted arrangement with Brittany, the queen of all bitches.

"I'll get her. Send her a message." I shot him a smirk and grabbed my car keys before I left the apartment.

I hadn't thought about Amber's reaction when I agreed to pick her up. When I pulled up in the parking lot, shock spread across her face. She was talking with a girl that looked as if she was trying to starve herself. I got out of my car and walked toward them but stopped a few feet away.

Her dark brows drew together. "Hey, Zach, what are you doing here?"

"I'm here to pick you up. Brian needed to deal with something." *With his bitchy on-and-off-again girlfriend*, I added in my head. I wasn't even sure if Amber knew about Lauren. Somehow I doubted Brian had told her.

She tried for a smile. "Oh, okay. That's nice of you." Tension leaked from her voice. Was she scared of being in a car alone with me?

"That's Olivia," she said with a nod toward the skinny girl.

Olivia smiled but didn't try to shake my hand. Amber must have met her in the support group. She glanced over to a red Lexus that was parked next to my car. "That's my mother," she said with a grimace. "I've got to go. See you soon, Amber?"

"Same place same time next week?" A look I couldn't decipher passed between them. Then Olivia slipped into her mother's car, and they drove off. Now it was only Amber and me. An awkward silence ensued.

"Ready to head home?" I asked, giving her my most encouraging smile to set her at ease. It seemed to work because she followed me toward my Hummer. Her eyes widened when she caught sight of it, and I couldn't help but grin. "That's huge," she said in surprise. It was. My father gave it to me as a gift for starting law school, a bribe—and the only form of love he knew. But I couldn't tell Amber that.

"I'm not trying to compensate for anything here!" I said with a wink and immediately wished someone would smash my fucking big mouth in.

Amber looked away.

"I'm sorry. I didn't mean to. I—" I shut up before I could fuck up even worse.

"It's ok," she said with a shrug. "Please don't apologize." She climbed into the passenger seat with some difficulties, and I walked around the car and sat down behind the steering wheel. She fumbled with the buckle of the seat belt. I hesitated. Should I try to help her? I would have to touch her, and that would make her very uncomfortable at the very least.

"Do you want me to help?" I asked eventually.

Amber froze and raised her head, uncertainty reflected in her eyes. I already regretted having asked her, but I couldn't take it back. Her eyes locked with mine and her hands dropped from the seat belt. "Yes, thank you."

I tried to hide my surprise as I reached for the belt, careful not to touch her body. She tensed but didn't say anything. I fastened the seat belt as fast as possible and pulled away from her to give her room. "Done," I told her, trying to act casual. I started the engine and took off from the parking lot. She relaxed.

I turned the radio on. "What music do you like to listen to?"

"Taylor Swift."

"Really?"

She laughed at the look on my face. "Actually, I was just trying to see your reaction. You don't look like the kind of guy who listens to Taylor Swift."

"I'll see what I can do for you." I started searching the radio for something she might like and eventually settled on a station that was playing Adele. "Okay?"

She bobbed her head. "Better than okay. I love Adele." She leaned back and gazed out of the side window. "You know, you're the only man apart from Brian and Dad that I've been alone with in years without wanting to bolt."

I risked a quick glance in her direction. Her gaze was soft and melancholic. "I don't like being in cars. I usually feel trapped, but I'm ok now." She started humming along with "Rolling in the Deep."

I didn't know what to say, and she didn't seem to expect a reaction. I drummed the beat of the song on the steering wheel, and she rewarded me with her smile. I wanted to see that look on her face again. I'd do anything for it.

chapter eight
Amber

I felt horrible for bailing on therapy yesterday. Brian had been disappointed when I finally worked up the courage to tell him. He couldn't understand that talking to Olivia had actually helped and had brought me a tiny step closer to normalcy. I kept my eyes fixed on my plate and took another bite from the stew that I'd prepared for us.

The bell rang, startling me. Zach rose from his chair and walked out of the kitchen to get the door. I didn't even flinch anymore when he or Brian moved around me. Being in their company 24-7 was obviously helping in some strange way. Reagan's voice sounded from the living room, then steps rang out and she and Zach appeared in the kitchen. Kevin hovered in the doorway, his gaze flitting over to me then back to Reagan. I lowered my head, feeling my cheeks burn in embarrassment.

"Hi, Amber. Hi, Brian," she said as she plopped down on the free chair next to me. Her red hair hung in waves down her back.

"Your hair is gorgeous," I said without thinking.

She grinned. "Kevin keeps telling me too, but I hate the color." She held up the DVD *The Devil Wears Prada*. "I thought we could have a movie night. It's been too long since we had one." Her eyes shone with excitement. "So what do you say?"

Brian lowered his fork, his expression uncertain. I knew why. He avoided my gaze as he said, "I don't know."

"That sounds great," I said before Brian could say anything else. Reagan flashed me a grin, clapping her hands. "Then let's get on with it!"

"We won't watch a chick-flick," Zach said with a smirk, pointing his fork at the DVD Reagan was still holding up. Reagan rolled her eyes, and I had to stifle a laugh.

"Whatever," she muttered, though she had difficulties keeping a straight face. "What would you suggest? *Rambo*, the complete edition?"

"No, that one's reserved for Valentine's Day."

I choked on my water, which made Zach's smile widen.

"I'm sure we can compromise on something," Reagan said.

"We're still eating," Brian reminded her, pointing with his fork to his plate.

Reagan pouted. "Well, then eat faster!"

I shook my head with a smile. I was already done eating and put my plate into the sink. Kevin and Reagan walked into the living room, and I followed a few feet behind them. They sat down on one of the love seats, and I chose the one across from them, pulling my legs up and rested my chin on my knees. Brian and Zach entered the room, and I could tell that my brother was worried again. I wished he would stop looking at me like I was a porcelain doll that would shatter at any moment. I knew that my mental state was very questionable, but his worry kept reminding me of that fact and it made acting normal even more difficult. He plopped down on the sofa and chanced another look at me while Zach browsed their DVD cabinet.

He straightened. "Crank!" He lifted a DVD with a man in a business suit and a gun in his hand. I'd never heard of that movie. Reagan seemed to know it, though, and she wasn't too enthusiastic about watching it. I nodded my agreement anyway. It was better than watching a love story. I relaxed into the love seat and turned my gaze to the TV as the opening credits started to run.

Some time in the middle of the movie, my eyes landed on Reagan and Kevin. They were snuggled against one another on the love seat, looking like two people in love. Kevin kept running his hands up and down Reagan's back, occasionally planting a kiss on her temple, or throat, or cheek until she turned her head and captured his lips with her mouth. Usually, displays of affection brought back memories, but what I witnessed between Reagan and Kevin was far more than physical closeness. It was a display of love, of trust, of tenderness.

My heart clenched. That was something I would never have. My eyes brimmed with tears, and it was getting harder to breathe. I swallowed and pushed all the longing, all the despair, all the wistfulness down where it belonged—buried in the depth of my mind with the dying embers of my hope. *You better get used to the hell that's your life, Amber, and stop longing for something you'll never have,* a cruel voice in my head said. For some reason that voice sounded a lot like one of the men that had ruined my life.

My throat tightened painfully, and bile rose in my throat, but I fought against it. Another breakdown would freak out Brian. I didn't want him to worry more.

"I'll get some popcorn," I announced and was relieved to hear that my voice wasn't shaking. I felt everyone's eyes on me when I rose from the love seat and walked out of the room. I closed the kitchen door behind me and drew in a deep breath as I closed my eyes. After I'd calmed down, I searched the cupboards for microwave popcorn. With shaky hands, I put it into the microwave and leaned against the counter.

Reagan stepped into the room and closed the door. I tensed. She looked uncomfortable and hesitant while she hovered next to me. I was not use to seeing that expression on her face.

"Amber, I'm sorry. I didn't think about it. That was completely inconsiderate of me," she said.

I turned away from the microwave to look at her. "What do you mean?"

"Kevin and I, we shouldn't have ... not in front of you," she whispered, pressing a hand against her forehead, covering her red eyebrows.

Please don't apologize for that. It's all I ever wanted. I shook my head, horrified. "No, Reagan. No. Please, don't act different around me."

"But it bothered you," Reagan said, her brows drawing together. "I don't want to bring up any bad memories for you."

I swallowed, ignoring the tears prickling in my eyes. The mentioning of my past brought up images that I didn't want to see. Not ever again. I gripped the counter tightly in an attempt to keep it together. *Be strong, Amber.*

"Amber?" Reagan's voice was gentle and full of concern.

I drew in a deep breath before I faced her with new resolution. "When I saw you and Kevin, it didn't bring up any memories because I've never experienced anything even close to that. I've never been in love. I've never been that close to someone. I've never wrapped my arms around someone and thought this is home. I've never looked into someone's eyes and felt butterflies in my stomach. I've never made love to someone, and I won't. Ever. I feel like I've come to an impasse, like my future is a blind alley. I will never know how it feels to lie in someone's arms, to be in love, to kiss someone. Never."

My voice broke and I had to turn my back to Reagan or she would have seen the tears streaming down my cheeks. I felt pathetic and guilty for burdening Reagan with my problems. I'd buried my fears, worries, and longings for so long. But with my new life they'd resurfaced, and I wasn't able to push them away.

I wanted to live a normal life. I wanted to experience love and trust. I wanted happiness. I wanted all of that so desperately and knowing that I could never have any of it killed me.

Reagan touched my shoulder, turning me toward her. "Amber, whatever happened doesn't define who you are forever. You are in control of your life, and you can be happy and in love if you only give life a chance." Without warning, she wrapped her arms around me.

I froze at first, but then I melted into her touch. I hugged her back and buried my face in the crook her neck, and then I wasn't able to stop the sobs. Reagan's arms around me tightened, and for the first time in years I found comfort in someone's touch. It was so overwhelming that all my walls seemed to tumble, and I cried like I hadn't ever cried in front of someone.

"I want to give life a chance, but I'm broken." After a moment I pulled back, feeling embarrassed and guilty. "I'm sorry, Reagan."

She shook her head, her expression determined. "No. Don't apologize for your tears," she said. "And you're wrong, Amber."

I was startled by her words.

"You aren't broken. You will experience love. I know you will. You've been strong enough to move in with Brian and Zach, and you will be strong enough to find your happiness."

The microwave beeped, and I was glad for the distraction. I opened the door, took the popcorn out, and turned to head back into the living room.

"Wait," Reagan said. She raised a tissue to my face and dried the remains of my tears. I did the same for her, and after checking our reflection in the window, we returned to the living room. After our conversation, I actually felt better. Reagan met my eyes across the room before she sat down on Kevin's lap. I put the popcorn into a bowl on the table and sat down on the love seat with my legs pulled against my chest. I rested my chin on my knees and focused on the TV. I felt eyes on me and tilted my head to the side to find Zach staring at me. He smiled and I couldn't help but smile back.

zachary

I buried my face into my pillow. I felt like shit as if my body had been overrun by a truck repeatedly. For once this wasn't the effects of a night spent partying with the guys. My stomach constricted. With a hoarse groan, I rolled over onto my back and stared at the white ceiling. The motion sent a new wave of sickness through my body. "Fuck." My stomach's contents wanted to see daylight, and I'd be damned if I was going to let that happen in my room. I swung my legs over the edge of my bed, and my hand shot to my head when the dizziness set in.

"Fuck," I groaned as I stumbled to my feet and out of my room. My vision turned blurry for a moment, but I managed to find the bathroom.

Once there, I emptied my stomach into the toilet bowl. The last time I'd hurled like that was in my freshman year at college after doing two keg stands in a row. A hangover, that I could deal with—especially if it entailed a fucking great night of fun. But this shit? I couldn't even remember the last time I had the flu.

I dragged my sorry ass back to my room and flopped down on the bed, not bothering to cover myself with the blanket. I was drenched in sweat. My boxers and T-shirt stuck to my skin, but I couldn't even bring myself to change clothes right now. A knock at the door caused me to lift my head a few inches, though I let it plop down on the pillow almost instantly because it took too much effort.

"Zach?"

I replied with an unintelligible grunt. The door opened and Brian entered, dressed and groomed, not one hair out of place as usual. He let his gaze wander over my sprawled-out form.

"You look like shit."

I grimaced. "Hadn't noticed."

"I take it that you won't be attending classes today?" he said with a smirk.

I flipped him the bird then snatched up a book from the floor and chucked it at him.

"Have fun," he called as he dashed out of the room, slamming the door shut before the book could hit him in the head. Instead, it banged against the door and fell to the ground. I closed my eyes and tried to ignore the turning of my stomach.

Some time later, another knock disturbed my silent suffering, but it was softer than the one before.

Amber? I sat up slightly and straightened my clothes. "Come in."

The door opened and Amber poked her head in, hair still damp and curling at the tips. I gave her a smile, and she stepped into the room, her foot bumping against the book that I'd thrown at Brian. Amber stared down at it with a little frown. "Is this supposed to be lying here?"

I shook my head. "Nah, I aimed it at Brian, but he was too fast."

One corner of her mouth pulled up into an almost smile as she picked it up and placed it on a dresser. I didn't want to ask, worried about unsettling her, but I was starting to wonder what she was doing in my room. Her eyes wandered around, taking in my trophies and the posters of Patagonia on the walls, then eventually her gaze returned to my face. "I made chicken soup for you, and I wondered if you'd like to eat some now."

I sat up fully. "You cooked for me?"

Amber nodded, biting her lip, and her cheeks turned a soft pink. *Holy shit*, she was fucking beautiful.

"Brian told me that you aren't feeling well and that you're staying at home. He said I should order pizza, but with an upset stomach that would be stupid, so I made soup. It will soothe your stomach."

The only person who'd ever made soup for me was Theresa, the nanny my parents hired so my father could jet around the world and work while my mother drowned her loneliness in alcohol. Misunderstanding my silence and my frown, her face flushed an even deeper shade of red. "I mean ... you don't have to eat my soup. If you'd rather have pizza, I can order—"

"No!" I half screamed. She jumped. "Sorry." I paused. "I want your soup. I don't think my stomach could handle pizza right now."

Her eyes lit up. "I'll get it for you." She hurried out of the room and returned with a tray.

"Where did you find a tray?" I asked as she set it down on my nightstand. I sent a silent thanks to the powers above that the packet with condoms was stored in my top drawer and not in plain sight.

"It was at the back of the kitchen cupboard."

"I didn't even know we had one. Must be a leftover from the previous owner."

"It has its uses," Amber said, leaning against my desk. I chanced a look at the tray. A plate with steaming chicken soup was positioned in the middle. But that wasn't all. There was a mug with a pale liquid. I took a whiff. Chamomile tea. I scrunched up my nose.

"It will help your stomach," Amber said sternly as she noticed my expression.

"I hate the taste."

She smiled slightly. "You will get used to it."

I grabbed the tray and positioned it on my lap, careful not to spill anything. Amber turned around on her way to the door. "Will you keep me company?" I blurted out. Slowly, she turned around, surprise flashing across her face.

"You don't have to. I'm sure you've got better things to do than keep a dying man company." I let out a melodramatic sigh.

She let out a laugh, her expression and body relaxing visibly. "Actually, I've got nothing better to do right now, but you don't look as if you're dying." There was an amused twinkle in her brown eyes that I'd never seen before. For once the haunted look had left her beautiful face.

She sat down on my office chair. I was surprised that she'd chosen to sit so close to me. Weak and sick with the flu, I probably looked pretty pathetic, not at all dangerous or threatening. But I'd never been happier about looking pathetic. At least Amber felt comfortable in my company.

When I was done eating the soup, the tea was cold. Maybe Amber would show mercy and not force me drink it, but I had no such luck.

"You should really drink it. Don't you want to get better?"

I gulped the disgusting liquid down, making a face. Amber smiled and I decided that the horrible taste was worth seeing her smile. Her eyes returned to the trophies I'd won in karate and in martial arts. "Those are yours?"

I nodded, not sure if it might intimidate her.

"Dad always wanted me to learn self-defense."

"I could teach you some day," I suggested, though I wasn't sure how to do it, since it would probably require physical contact.

To my surprise, Amber seemed to consider my suggestion, and I could have grinned stupidly because I was so happy.

She found the frame with a photo of my parents and me at my graduation on my desk behind a pile of ignored books. "Your parents?"

I leaned back against the headboard and nodded. "Yes."

"They look nice, but your mother looks so young," she said.

"They do look nice. And my mother was twenty-two when she had me. My father is fifteen years older than her. She was an intern at his company when they met."

She studied my face. "You don't get along?"

"We hardly see each other. They are too busy." Well, my father was. My mother spent most of her time with her therapist or at our country club, at least when she wasn't in rehab.

"What about when you were younger?"

"They were busy then too."

"Oh," she said. She brought her legs up to her chest and curled her socked toes around the edge of the seat. "So what's up with all the Patagonia posters? Did you travel there?"

"No," I said, looking at my favorite poster of the Los Glaciares National Park. "But one day I will. I want to travel South America from top to bottom."

"That would take a while."

"Six months to a year if you want to do it properly," I said absentmindedly. "Guess I'll have to wait until I'm retired for that to happen."

"Or you could take a year off before you start to work and follow your dream." Amber shook her head. "That sounded cheesy."

"No," I said softly. "I should, but I can't. Some things just aren't meant to be."

"I know," she said, her brown eyes boring into my own.

The next three days while I was confined to my bed, Amber brought me food—and chamomile tea despite my pleas and protests—and kept me company. I'd never enjoyed being ill so much before.

I wasn't sure if her newfound comfort around me would last after I recovered, but I hoped she would realize that she could feel safe with me. Brian didn't know about the time that Amber had been spending in my room, and somehow I knew it was better that way. He was weird when it came to Amber. Couldn't he see that she longed for normalcy?

chapter nine
Amber

I walked out of my room with Pumpkin at my heels. He was hungry and wouldn't stop complaining loudly. I hurried through the living room and into the kitchen, stopping in my tracks when I saw Zach sitting at the table. He looked much better than the days before. I was still shocked about my courage to spend so much time with him over the last few days, but he'd looked so helpless and I just couldn't let him down. I liked to take care of people, especially since most of the time over these last few years it had been the other way around. Before the incident I'd considered working as a doctor, but now I associated too many bad memories with hospitals. People always tried to take care of me, and helping Zach had made me feel useful. I enjoyed spending time with him.

"Good morning, Amber." Zach's words tore me from my thoughts.

I gave him a smile. He grinned in return, his spoon filled with cereal hovering a few inches in front of his face. For a moment, I marveled at how blue his eyes were.

"Are you feeling better?" I asked as I walked into the kitchen and picked up cat food from the cupboard.

"Yes, and all thanks to your cooking skills. If I'd followed Brian's advice and eaten pizza, I would have been in hospital by now." He let out a low chuckle. It was more of a rumble from deep in his chest. I loved the sound.

I laughed and shook my head. "Maybe that was Brian's intention."

Zach's booming laugh filled the kitchen and a grin tugged at my lips. It felt good to make him laugh. It almost made me feel happy. He looked even more handsome when he laughed than when he was just his normal self. I felt my cheeks heat in embarrassment and hastily bent over Pumpkin's feeding bowl to hide my red face from Zach. Had I just thought of him as handsome? Usually, there were only two categories of men for me: very intimidating and slightly less intimidating. Apparently, a third category had been added to that. Handsome. I found Zach handsome. This realization shocked me so much that I must have remained bent over Pumpkin's bowl for a couple of minutes without giving him any food. He meowed loudly, giving me a reproachful look with his amber eye. Had Zachary noticed anything? My cheeks warmed even more, and I hurriedly filled the bowl, straightening to my full height before I faced Zach. Fortunately, he was immersed in a sports magazine and hadn't noticed my strange behavior.

"Will you stay home today?" I asked before I could stop myself.

Zach raised his head and smiled. "Yes, I'm not feeling fit enough for classes." He winked at me, and again I felt myself blush. I busied myself with the apple that I was eating to avoid embarrassing myself even more. I leaned against the counter. Zach rose from his chair. I waited for the usual tensing of my muscles but nothing happened. Maybe the last couple of days with Zach had changed something. I felt almost elated when I pondered the possibility.

Zach knelt down beside Pumpkin and began petting his neck, causing my cat to purr in approval. I smiled softly. He raised his head. "Are you up for some video games? Maybe I'll even let you win."

"Maybe I'm good and you don't need to let me win," I countered with raised eyebrows.

"Are you any good?"

I let out a sigh and shook my head. "No, probably not."

"Fantastic!" Zach stood up straight and strode into the living room. I followed him and sank down on the love seat, facing the TV screen. Zach plopped down on the sofa and handed one of the controllers to me. The video game turned out to be car racing, and I sucked at it. Most of the time I was busy not crashing against the walls or other cars. Zach was trying not to laugh at me, but I could tell that he had trouble hiding his grin.

"Having fun?" I asked sarcastically.

Zach gave me an apologetic look, though his grin was ruining the effect. "Sorry. I'll make up for it. Today, I'm going to cook for us."

I probably didn't look too enthusiastic about his idea, because Zach made a mock hurt face. It turned out that my worries weren't unfounded. The macaroni and cheese Zach prepared for us was hardly edible. I ate it anyway, not wanting to hurt his feelings.

"Tell me this isn't the most disgusting thing you've ever eaten," Zach said, sticking his fork back into his pile of macaroni.

"It's not that bad." He raised one dark eyebrow, not believing me for a second. Something fluttered in my belly. "Okay, it's pretty horrible. But it's not the worst thing I've ever eaten. Just promise me you will never cook again." A strand of hair fell out of my ponytail, and I twirled it around my finger. Zach followed the movement with his eyes. "You have beautiful hair," he said.

My hand froze as heat slowly crawled up my neck. "Thanks." I lowered my hand, suddenly self-conscious. I didn't look away, caught in his intense gaze. The silence stretched between us. For a moment, I wondered how it would be to lean across the table and touch my lips to his.

zachary

Amber's gaze sent a shiver down my back. I wanted to pull her to me and kiss her pink lips. Brian stalked into the room. The wakeup call I needed. Fuck, what was I thinking? I couldn't kiss Amber. She wouldn't want me to. It would scare her. Brian looked irritated and tired. Not a good sign. I knew he'd spent the day with Lauren, and they probably had another fight.

His gaze darted between Amber and me, and a flicker of anger flashed in his eyes. I almost groaned. He was in one of his moods. I hoped he would get over it before he said something stupid.

"What are you doing?" He focused on me for a second before his gaze moved on to Amber. She rose from her chair and shrugged. "We had dinner and then we decided to play some Playstation."

"Play some Playstation," Brian said doubtfully. "Why is it that you don't seem to mind spending time alone with Zach? You hardly know him at all."

What the hell was he doing? "Brian—" I began in a warning tone.

"Stay out of it. This is between my sister and me," he interrupted as he walked to where she stood. When he'd almost reached her, she stiffened and took a step back, probably scared of the anger radiating off of him. Apparently, her reaction to him was the last straw for Brian.

"God, Amber I'm your brother! Do you think I would hurt you?" he demanded, his expression hurt.

She stared at him with wide eyes. "No," she said quickly. Again, Brian moved toward her, closer and closer, until she took a step back. Why did he have to push her like this?

His face contorted with pain and despair, and it was nearly too much to watch. "Why did you move back then? I would never hurt you," Brian said in a broken tone.

Amber looked thoroughly shaken. "I'm sorry! I … didn't mean to …" Her voice died away, and she stumbled toward the front door, tore it open, and disappeared.

"Damn, Brian, what was that for?" I asked furiously.

His eyes grew wide, and he shook his head slowly. "I just got carried away. Lauren and I, we had a fight, and then when I saw Amber with you, smiling. I lost it."

I snorted as I pulled a jacket on.

"What are you doing?"

I glowered at him, grabbing the keys to the apartment. "Your sister just ran out and it's dark outside and raining."

Guilt flashed across his face. "If something happens to her—"

"It won't. I'm sure she's close by," I told him and jogged out of the apartment and down the stairs. I didn't have the patience to wait for the elevator to arrive. I wasn't sure if Brian was following, but I didn't want look over my shoulder. I stepped out of the building and instantly the rain lashed against my face. It was icy cold.

A sigh of relief left my lips when I caught sight of Amber. She stood on the sidewalk, her hair and clothes soaked and clinging to her body, making me aware of everything she was usually hiding. She wasn't moving, but as I got closer, I noticed that her shoulders were shaking. She stiffened when she heard my steps.

"Amber?" I said cautiously, stopping a few feet away from where she stood. "Brian didn't mean what he said."

"He's right though. I shouldn't treat Brian and Dad like this." She turned around to me, her face full of self-hatred.

I couldn't bear seeing her like that. "It's not your fault."

"Whose fault is it, then?" she asked sharply, her eyes hollow and desperate.

I stared at her, the rain pouring down on us. "Those men," I replied calmly.

She blanched and lowered her gaze to the ground, wrapping her arms tightly around her chest. "Sometimes I think that I deserved what happened, that it happened for a reason, that it was my fault."

I was so shocked by her words that at first I didn't know what to do. "No. That's nonsense. Fucking nonsense and you know it," I said firmly. "Don't blame yourself for what happened. You could just as well blame me or Brian or your dad."

"But it wasn't your fault!" she objected, her wide eyes filled with tears.

"It wasn't your fault either," I told her, and we looked at each other for a moment, the pattering of rain the only sound around us. She closed her eyes, and tears trickled down her pale cheeks, mingling with the raindrops on her skin. I took the risk and walked over to her, so close that

I could have touched her if I tried. In slow motion, her eyelids slid open and she stared at me. She didn't react how I expected her to, though—scared and intimidated. She simply looked at me with unfathomable sadness in her brown eyes. Before I had time to think about my actions, I raised my hand and brought it closer to her face. Her eyes followed the movement, but she didn't flinch or make any attempt to stop me. Maybe I was making a big mistake that I'd regret later, but I couldn't stop myself. I felt the need to touch her. My fingertips brushed against her cold cheek, and the touch felt like electricity. Her eyes were soft and inquiring, and she didn't look away. Slowly, very carefully I wiped the tears off her cheeks. It was futile since the tears were replaced by raindrops almost instantly, but it didn't matter. All that mattered in this moment was that Amber allowed me to touch her. She raised a trembling hand, her eyes uncertain and resolved all at once, and Amber covered my hand with hers. It looked so small and delicate in comparison to mine. With soft pressure she pushed my palm against her cheek, and she tilted her head, leaning into my touch. The feel of her cheek cupped in my palm, her eyes shining with trust, I felt something I'd never felt before. It scared me a bit, but at the same time I wanted to embrace it and relish in it.

From the corner of my eye, I noticed movement, and I turned my head slightly in that direction. Brian had stopped in front of the building, and he was watching us with a mixture of jealousy and disbelief.

Amber dropped her hand from mine, like she'd been burned, and ever so slowly I lowered my palm from her cheek.

"Thank you, Zach," she whispered, her eyes flitting over to Brian. I watched as she walked toward him, and after a moment of hesitation I followed. Amber stopped right in front of him and lifted her head until she was looking at him. "Brian …" She began in a small voice, but Brian shook his head, stopping her from continuing. Amber closed her mouth, anxiety filling her face.

"I came to apologize," he said hesitantly, his gaze still flitting between Amber and me.

"It's my fault," Amber whispered, but again Brian shook his head, his expression determined. "No, Amber. It wasn't. I know it's hard for you to allow closeness." For a fleeting moment, he looked directly at me. "And I shouldn't vent my anger on you."

Amber bit her lip, and Brian stiffened when she reached out for him. She curled her fingers around his hand and held on to it for a few moments. "I will try to get better, Brian. I want this more than anything," she told him before releasing him.

Brian swallowed visibly and gave her a small smile. "I know you will get better," he said, but then his eyes swung to me and his expression hardened. "Why don't you go back inside? You'll catch a cold."

Amber stared back and forth between Brian and me, hesitating.

"Go on. Brian's right." I gave her a smile and nodded my head in the direction of the entrance door. Slowly, she turned around and disappeared inside the building. As soon as she was out of sight, Brian advanced on me, his eyes burning with fury. "What the fuck are you doing with my sister?"

We stood nose to nose. My muscles tightened in anticipation. "Brian, I'm not doing anything with your sister. I like Amber."

"You like her? You like her!" he shouted, his expression a mask of anger. He jammed his palms against my chest. I stumbled a step back, fighting down the urge to defend myself. Brian was my friend. "Amber isn't Brittany or any of the whores you usually hang around with," he continued.

"Brian—" I tried to calm him down and put a hand on his shoulder, but he shook it off, looking barely like himself in that moment. He balled his hands to fists. I really hoped he wasn't planning on punching me.

"No! You will listen to what I have to say. I won't let you play your sick games with Amber. She's broken and hurt, and I won't allow you to take advantage of her," he growled.

My own anger spiked. "Don't you dare accusing me of such things! I'm not playing any games. I like her and I'm just trying to help her. What the fuck is your problem?"

Brian let out a dark laugh. "You like her and want to help her? You don't even know her!"

I opened my mouth to protest, but he cut me off.

"So you think you know her, know what she went through? You don't know anything. Do you understand how broken she is?" I shook my head slowly and swallowed a large lump in my throat. Brian didn't even notice my reaction. "Three guys gang-raped her. They beat her and raped her, and then they left her for dead in the bushes. When a jogger found Amber, she was more dead than alive, and when Dad and I first saw her she was in a coma. And when she finally woke, she wasn't my sister anymore. She was someone else, someone broken and desperate and terrified. *You* don't know anything, Zach. You didn't see her in the hospital three years ago. You didn't have to witness how she tried to starve herself, how she took all those pills to kill herself, how she slit her wrists. You don't know a fucking thing!" Brian shouted, his voice breaking.

I was so shocked by what he'd said I could barely stand on my legs.

Brian stared up at the sky. "Amber might not be happy but at least she isn't on the edge of another suicide attempt. Leave her alone."

I didn't know what to say. Brian lowered his head and looked at me almost pleadingly. "Listen, Zach. I know you're a good guy, but you're not good for Amber. Your other girls move on after you're done with them, but Amber would fall apart. I won't allow it."

"I would never hurt her, Brian," I promised without hesitation.

"You can't help it. You've never been in a serious relationship. Just leave Amber alone. I saw the way she was looking at you. I should have known. Girls are drawn to you like magnets."

How was Amber looking at me?

He took a deep breath and his shoulders slumped, looking as if every bit of his strength was gone. "Don't make her hope for something that can't ever be." His expression turned fierce again, and he fixed his narrowed eyes on me. "Because if you hurt her, I swear I will be your worst nightmare and you'll wish you were never born. Stay away from Amber." Brian turned around and went back inside. I knew this wasn't an empty threat. Brian looked dead serious.

But I also knew I couldn't stay away from Amber. I'd made Amber smile. She'd allowed me to touch her. I was a good friend. The problem was I was fairly sure I didn't only want to be friends with her. And Brian was right. I wasn't boyfriend material.

chapter ten

Amber

The next morning, I still couldn't believe that I'd actually let Zach touch my cheek. That I actually wanted him to touch me. I wasn't scared. The look in his eyes had been so gentle that I just knew he wouldn't hurt me. Zach always made me feel like a normal girl. He made me believe that there was the chance of a normal life for me. And when I looked at him, I just … I didn't even know what it was that I was feeling. It was something I'd never felt before, and it confused and scared me. I spent so many years feeling numb. I thought I was empty and lost, but now I wasn't so sure anymore.

I needed to talk to someone about my feelings. I slowly rose from my bed and walked out of my room. Pumpkin followed me and jumped onto the sofa in the living room, curling up into a tight ball and watching me with his amber eye. I was alone in the apartment. Zach and Brian had classes, and they wouldn't be home for a few more hours. I picked up my mobile and sent Reagan a text.

Need to talk. Can we meet for coffee?

Her reply was almost instant: **Sure! I'm over at Kevin's.**

She spent more time there than in her own apartment. Jason and Bill didn't seem to mind, which was no surprise to me; I couldn't imagine anyone not liking Reagan's company.

Hesitantly, I lifted my hand and knocked on their apartment door. It made me nervous to think that Jason or Bill might open the door, but they had been avoiding me since my breakdown, which I was more than thankful for.

Reagan opened the door. "Come in."

She led me into the kitchen. Random furniture pieces made up the kitchen set. Not everyone could afford a designer kitchen like Zach. "Sorry for bothering you. Kevin and you probably wanted to spend some time together."

"Nonsense. I always have time for girl talk," she said with a smile. We took seats at the kitchen table, and Reagan scanned my face. "So what's up?"

I bit my lip anxiously, thinking of a way to explain what was bothering me. "I wanted to talk about Zach." I took a deep breath and told her how I'd let Zach touch my cheek the day before, which sounded almost ridiculous when voiced out loud, but it was a huge step for me. Pausing, I tried to find words for the feelings surging through me.

Reagan could barely contain her curiosity, but she remained silent, waiting for me to continue.

"I feel normal around him. It's strange because I've known him for only a short time. But I just feel comfortable when he's around." Reagan looked like she was going to burst from excitement at any moment. "But with Brian—" I let out a small sigh. "With Brian everything is so tense and awkward. I'm always careful how to act around him because I know he's monitoring me. I wish our relationship would return to how it was before the incident."

Reagan gave me an understanding smile. She took my hand and squeezed. Physical closeness with her seemed so casual, so normal. "I'm sure it will get better between Brian and you."

I shook my head. "I barely see him anymore, even though we live in an apartment together. He's always somewhere else. I don't even know what he's doing when he's gone all night, and sometimes I think he's avoiding me. Maybe he can't bear to be in an apartment with me at night because of my nightmares. Sometimes I talk or scream when I sleep." I trailed off, feeling a lump rising in my throat.

Reagan tightened her grip on my hand when she spoke. "No, Amber. Brian is an idiot for not telling you. This entire secrecy thing didn't accomplish anything."

I frowned at her, not sure what she is talking about.

She let out a sigh. "Brian is gone so often because he's spending time with his girlfriend."

My eyes widened. "Brian's got a girlfriend?"

Reagan nodded. "Yes, Lauren. They've been having an on-and-off-again relationship for a few months, and she's a bit of a tight-ass. She wants to control every aspect of his life. She calls him all the time and wants to spend every second with him."

I was shocked and hurt. "Why didn't he tell me?"

"Apparently, he thinks that it would bother you," Reagan said with a shrug.

"He should have told me," I murmured. Why couldn't he act normal around me? Why did he have to make me feel like a freak?

I stared out of the large window. "Sometimes I feel like I don't know him at all. It's like we've become strangers."

"Don't you think it's a good sign that you let Zach touch you? It's only a matter of time before you can hug your brother. Don't be too hard on yourself. Change takes time."

"You're probably right."

"So you like Zach?"

I didn't really know the answer to her question. Of course I liked Zach. But how much did I like him? The reason I wanted to talk to her was so she could tell me. "I really don't know, Reagan. When I'm with him, I feel like I'm a normal girl, like I belong here. Sometimes when I'm around him I feel like I could manage to be happy. Everything seems so easy. Sometimes I am able to forget. He makes me forget."

Reagan squeezed my hand. "Have you told him?"

My eyes widened and I shook my head hastily. "No, of course not. How could I tell him? I mean. I don't really know what it is that I feel for him, and he probably won't return my feelings—whatever they are."

Reagan frowned and opened her mouth to object, but I continued.

"Zach can have any girl he wants. Why would he take someone like me, someone who's broken?"

Reagan interrupted me instantly. "You aren't broken, Amber."

"But I feel like it, Reagan. I feel like those men have soiled me, like their filthy hands have tarnished me in some irrevocable way. I feel dirty and tainted, and how could Zach want something like that? How could he ever want someone like me?" I gestured at myself.

Reagan sat perfectly still, only her head was shaking back and forth slowly. "You aren't dirty, Amber."

The sob that I'd been holding back slipped out. "But I feel so dirty, Reagan, so dirty, and it just won't go away no matter what I do." I buried my face in my palms. I heard Reagan move, and then she wrapped her arms around me and pulled me against her body. "Oh Amber, don't ... don't you dare think of yourself like that! You aren't dirty or broken or tainted or any of those other nasty words. You're kind and caring and beautiful. You just have to allow yourself to see how wonderful you are."

I let her closeness and words comfort me, though I couldn't believe what she was saying. I wanted to believe her, but it seemed impossible. Feeling dirty had become a part of my life. "I'm sorry for crying all over you again," I apologized as I pulled back and wiped the tears from my face.

Reagan shook her head vehemently. "Everyone needs a good cry now and then." She paused, resolution filling her eyes. "And now we need to find a solution for you and Zach."

"Reagan ..." I said.

She tilted her head. "You said that you wanted to be close to someone, that you wanted something like Kevin and I have. Maybe Zach can give you that. Maybe it's meant to be. I've got a good feeling about the two of you."

I bit my lip, gazing at her anxiously. "Reagan, how could I ever let myself be so close to someone? I don't even let people hug me or touch me. Guys want to be able to touch their girlfriends."

It felt surreal to even speak about the possibility of me ever becoming Zach's girlfriend, or becoming anyone's girlfriend for that matter. Love and falling in love had always seemed out of my reach, but during my talk with Reagan I'd realized that was exactly what was happening to me. I was on the fast track of falling in love with Zach.

"Amber, first of all, that's not exactly the truth."

I frowned.

"You hug people. Me for example."

"Reagan, you're not a man."

"There isn't that much of a difference."

"There is for me," I whispered.

"If you can hug me, you can hug others too," she said in a firm tone. I didn't object because somehow her words seemed logical, and they gave me hope.

"And," she continued with a small, knowing smile, "you let men touch you. Zach, for example. Or have you forgotten how he touched your cheek yesterday?"

How could I forget? The memory was seared into my mind. The look on my face must have pleased Reagan immensely because she smiled brightly.

"But I can't expect Zach to be satisfied with touching my cheek for all of eternity. He's going to want more, and I don't know if I can give him that." The smile slipped from my face as the hard truth of my words set in.

Reagan shook her head. "Before you came here you thought you'd never let someone hug you or a man touch you, and look at what you've already accomplished in such a short time! It will take time, Amber, but you will be able to allow more closeness. You just need to take one little step after the other."

Maybe she was right. Maybe I could do it. "I don't even know if Zach likes me. He could just be nice to me because Brian is his best friend."

"He likes you, Amber. I'm sure of it, and Kevin agrees," Reagan said.

"You talked with Kevin about me and Zach?" I asked, a little embarrassed.

"No, Kevin mentioned that he noticed how Zach looked at you and how he talked about you. It's really obvious that he likes you very much."

"But why hasn't Zach said anything to me?"

Reagan let out a small laugh. "He's probably worried about your reaction and that you don't feel the same way."

I worried my lower lip, lost in my thoughts. The situation was probably as difficult for Zach as it was for me. If he had feelings for me—and that was a big if in my mind—he had to be worried that I'd freak out if he told me. I certainly wouldn't tell him about my feelings until I was sure he actually returned them.

Reagan smacked the tabletop. "I have a wonderful idea. Let's go out together. You, Zach, Kevin, and me."

"Don't you think Zach will think it's a double date?"

"So what? Don't you want to know if he's interested in you?"

I didn't say anything. What if the answer was no and he wasn't interested in me?

Reagan must have guessed my thoughts. "He does like you, Amber. Trust me."

zachary

Brian and I headed toward the parking lot of BU.

"Someone's waiting for you," Brian said snidely.

I followed his gaze and groaned. Brittany was leaning against her red Mercedes and was waiting for me with a seductive smile on her face. We hadn't spoken since our encounter in the club. I assumed that she was still angry at me because I didn't taken her home with me after our fuck, but apparently she'd forgiven me.

"Could you wait for me?" I asked Brian when he turned to walk toward his car. He raised his eyebrows. "Are you sure? Brittany seems to plan on taking you somewhere."

"I'm sure, Brian."

He nodded. I went to talk to Brittany. She stood tall and smirked. The skinny jeans, tight top, and leather jacket was nothing in comparison to what she wore at parties, but as usual she drew quite a bit of attention toward her. All the guys lingering in the parking lot looked like they were sporting a hard-on simply from looking at her body. I stopped in front of her. She threw her arms around my neck before pressing a kiss on my lips. I grabbed her arms and pried them off, taking a step back. She narrowed her eyes at me.

"What are you doing?" she demanded, her red-painted lips pulled into a tight line.

"Whatever there is between us is over, Brittany," I told her. As long as I wasn't sure about my feelings for Amber, I couldn't keep seeing Brittany. I needed to sort out the mess that was my emotions. I could practically see my father rolling his eyes at me. He didn't approve of emotions.

"What's that supposed to mean?"

"It means that we won't be seeing each other anymore," I said calmly.

Brittany looked as if she wanted nothing more than to slap my face. Maybe I deserved it, but we were never going to be exclusive. It wasn't as if this was a breakup.

She lifted her chin, glowering at me. "We'll see about that, Zach," she said icily. The she got into her car and drove off. She was probably off to tell her father, who would then call my father, who would then call me.

"She looked angry," Brian commented as I walked up to him.

"I told her that it's over between us. She didn't take it too well," I said flatly.

"I'm glad you got rid off her. She's such a bitch."

I chuckled. "Says the man who's dating Lauren."

"Lauren isn't like Brittany," he objected.

I rolled my eyes. Lauren was a bitch. Everyone knew that. My exact point was proven once more when Brian dropped me in front of our apartment building and quickly sped away because Lauren needed to see him. They were supposed to study together. The girl was a control freak.

I was surprised when I entered the apartment to find Reagan and Amber sitting on the sofa.

"Hi, girls," I greeted them and walked past them toward my room to drop my bag off before I returned to the living room. I could tell that they'd been discussing me, but I wasn't sure if it was because I'd messed up in some way or if it was general girl talk.

"So, Zach, do you have any plans for the afternoon?" Reagan asked with a wide grin. I raised my eyebrows and chanced a look at Amber, but she was avoiding my eyes. I frowned at Reagan. "No, why?"

"Great. We want to go ice-skating. Kevin, Amber, and I … we thought you might like to join us?" It was worded as a question, but

Reagan looked like she would cause me bodily harm if I refused. Not that I would have since I wanted to spend more time with Amber, but I wasn't sure if she was comfortable with the idea of ice-skating on an ice rink filled with people. And what was more: this sounded suspiciously like a ploy from Reagan. Was she playing match-maker? I really hoped she hadn't talked Amber into this.

Reagan stood. "So what do you say?"

"I'm in," I said. From the corner of my eye, I noticed Amber smiling slightly and exchanging a look with Reagan. What the hell was going on?

Thirty minutes later, we arrived at the ice-rink, and luckily it wasn't as crowded as I'd expected, but it wasn't exactly deserted either. There were definitely more people than I thought Amber could handle. We borrowed skates and sat down on a bench near the ice. Amber's eyes kept flitting toward the ice and the people on it while she put on the skates. I sat next to her, keeping a few inches between us. She seemed comfortable with my closeness, and I couldn't stop thinking of how she'd let me touch her cheek last night. She turned her head and caught me staring at her. She blushed.

"Have you ever ice-skated?" I asked to distract her from her obvious embarrassment.

"Yes, but that was when I was twelve. I'm not sure how good I'm at it now," she admitted.

I smiled at her. "Don't worry. I'm sure you'll do fine." I rose to my feet and realized with a start that Reagan and Kevin were already on the ice, having left Amber and me alone. Amber put her gloves on and stood, swaying slightly on the skates. I would have steadied her, but I wasn't sure if she'd appreciate my touch. Instead, I went ahead and waited for her on the ice. She grabbed the boards tightly when she stepped onto the ice. I could tell that it would take time for her to get used to the feeling of being on skates. I played ice hockey for a few years when I was a kid and felt confident on the ice, but I wasn't sure how to help Amber.

She turned around to me, smiling apologetically. "You can go ahead. You don't need to wait for me."

I grinned at her. "You're the only reason why I'm here." The words left my mouth before I could stop them, and I awaited Amber's reaction with trepidation. I wasn't sure what I expected but certainly not what Amber did. She smiled at me and her cheeks tinged a soft pink. I smiled at her in return, feeling happier than I'd felt in forever.

Amber bit her lip and let go of the boards. Slowly, she extended her gloved hand and held it out to me. "Maybe you can help me?"

I was stunned and I hoped it didn't show. I curled my fingers around her hand, careful to keep my grip light. "Okay?" I asked.

She nodded simply. I carefully led her across the ice, steadying her with my grip on her hand. Her hold on me tightened a few times when she swayed. She never let go of me. I kept my eyes on our surroundings, trying to avoid getting too close to other people. There was an arm's length between Amber's body and mine, and I longed to get even closer to her, but I didn't want to push my luck. Suddenly, her left skate slid to the side and she lost her balance. It was a split-second decision: either let her fall to the ground and maybe she'd hurt herself or I steady her with my other arm. It was more instinct than anything else as I wrapped my arm around her waist to keep her upright. Her body tensed beneath my touch, and I let go of her waist as soon as she'd regained her balance. To my surprise she kept a hold on my left hand, not giving any indication that my arm around her waist had bothered her.

"Thank you," she said.

She was trying to be strong, and I admired her for it. I caught Reagan and Kevin watching us with smiles on their faces, but I tried to ignore them. I wanted to be angry with them for meddling in my life, but when I felt Amber's hand in mine as we slid across the ice, I almost felt the need to thank them.

amber

I'd wanted this for so long, so very long, this taste of normalcy. Being a part of normal life. The feeling was intoxicating. Was this happiness? It had to be very close. This was the closest I'd come to feeling happy in years. The smile didn't leave my face, and for once it wasn't forced. It felt so easy to smile around Zach.

You're the only reason why I'm here. Zach's words were on repeat in my head, and they filled me with strange warmth. He liked me. Maybe Reagan was right and he didn't just see his best friend's sister when he looked at me. It made me hopeful. Though, I knew it was dangerous for me to allow myself to hope, I couldn't help it. I chanced a look up at Zach's face. At his strong jaw, his blue eyes, his high cheekbones. For a second, his eyes darted over to me. He squeezed my hand gently as we continued gliding over the ice. Maybe it was because of the gloves between us, but I didn't mind his touch at all. Instead of frightening me, it gave me a strange sense of being safe. How was that even possible?

Zach was huge and strong. He was everything I'd been scared of in the last three years, and yet I wasn't afraid of him.

"Hey!" Reagan's voice carried over to us, and I found her standing with Kevin near the exit of the ice and she was waving. "Let's grab dinner!"

Zach and I exchanged a disappointed look and skated over to where they stood. I could have spent hours skating beside Zach, his hand around mine, his body so close that I could feel his warmth. Reagan flashed me a grin when Zach wasn't looking, and I had to stifle laughter. Zach and I stepped off the ice; we were still holding hands. I stared down at our gloved hands in amazement. It felt so good. Zach followed my gaze then met my eyes. I wished I knew what was going on in his head. He didn't let go of my hand until we sat down on a bench to remove the skates from our feet. His warmth lingered on my skin, and I wondered how it would be to touch him without the gloves. I missed Zach's touch. His hand around mine was a feeling I wanted to experience over and over again.

Reagan scooted over to me. "Looks like it's going great between you and Zach. You are so sweet together. You'd make such a cute couple."

I cast a quick glance at Zach to make sure he hadn't overheard what Reagan said, but he was talking with Kevin about one of his professors.

We had dinner at the rink, fries and burgers, but I hardly tasted what I was eating because I was too distracted by the way Zach kept looking at me.

We arrived back at the apartment building and stepped into the elevator together. I pressed my back against the wall. The space was too small for me to feel comfortable—that definitely hadn't changed. Reagan took my hand in hers, and I squeezed her fingers, silently thanking her for the support. I didn't dare to look at Kevin or Zach to see if they noticed anything. It wasn't as bad as last time, but as soon as the doors slid open, I stepped out and drew in a deep breath. Kevin and Reagan waved at us and headed for their apartment. Suddenly, I felt nervous about being alone with Zach. It felt like something had changed between us, but I wasn't sure if Zach felt the same way.

We walked in silence to our apartment, and the second we entered, Brian advanced on us. "Where have you been?" he snarled. "I've been out of my mind with worry!"

I shrunk back. It wasn't voluntarily, but my body acted on its own accord. He halted, his expression one of despair. Slowly, his shoulders slumped and he took a step back, the pain in his eyes almost too much to bear.

"Relax, Brian. We were just ice-skating with Reagan and Kevin," Zach tried to explain, but Brian wasn't listening. He glared at Zach. "Don't you remember what I told you?"

Zach tensed. "Didn't you listen to what I just said? We were out with Kevin and Reagan."

Brian shook his head. Then he disappeared in his room without another word.

"What did he tell you?" I asked.

Zach looked uncomfortable. "Nothing." His face gave nothing away, but I knew something had happened between Brian and him, and that something had to do with me.

"Brian will calm down soon," Zach said.

I gave him a weak smile and shook my head. "I need to talk to him."

"Are you sure?" Zach asked. We were standing so close, closer than I'd have thought possible before today. "I could try to talk to him."

"I'm his sister. I'm the reason why he's like this. I need to do this."

Zach hesitated, looking like he wanted to say more, but then he nodded and headed for the kitchen. I went ahead and knocked at Brian's door.

"Go away, Zach," Brian shouted. "I don't want to deal with you right now."

"It's me, Brian." It was silent in the room, and I feared that maybe he didn't want to see me either. Why was he being so difficult?

"Come in," Brian said so quietly I almost didn't hear him. I eased open the door and stepped into the room. Brian was sitting on his bed, his elbows propped up on his legs. He raised his head. Our eyes met and I could tell that he was on the verge of tears. The struggle was obvious on his face.

I hesitated, unsure of what to do. I pushed my anxiety aside and closed the door behind me. His eyes followed me as I moved toward his bed, and slowly his face filled with confusion. I sank down onto the mattress an arm's length away from him. Brian sat up straight. He was silent, waiting for me to make the first step. I took a deep breath and reached for his hand resting on his legs. Tentatively, I covered it with mine.

Brian froze and stared down at our hands like he'd never seen a hand before.

"Brian?" I said softly, and he lifted his gaze to look at me. He didn't try to grab my hand or move at all.

"Amber?" His voice shook with emotions, and the small flicker of hope in his eyes encouraged me further. I could do this. I could be a good sister to Brian. I was in control of my fears. I could conquer them.

"I'm sorry if I upset you," I told him.

He shook his head slowly. "I was just so worried when I came home and you weren't there. I sent you several texts but you never replied."

"My cell phone was in my bag. I didn't check it while we were at the rink."

"So you spent the day with Zach?"

"We were just ice-skating together. It was Reagan's idea."

"You're spending a lot of time with Zach."

"Are you jealous?"

"Maybe," he admitted begrudgingly. "But that's not why I don't want you to hang out with Zach."

"Then why?"

"He's not good for you."

"Not good for me? I like spending time with him. I like how he makes me feel. How can that not be good?"

Brian paled. "Please don't tell me you're falling for him."

I wanted to deny it, but I couldn't lie to Brian again. "I don't know," I said quietly.

"Fuck," he muttered then hastily added, "sorry." His eyes wandered over my face. "I mean it, Amber. Zach is one of the last guys you should fall for. He's not good for you."

I got up, frustrated and confused. "You're his friend. How can you say something like that? Why are you even friends with him if you think so badly of him?"

"Zach is a good friend. He is my best friend. That's why I know about his history with girls. He never settles. For him girls are just good for one thing." He paused to see if I understood. I nodded, getting what he meant. I wasn't stupid.

"But why? Zach seems like a good guy. He doesn't strike me as someone who would use girls."

Brian shrugged. "It's because of his parents, I guess. Their marriage is a train wreck from what he tells me. His father cheats with girls that are Zach's age, and his mother drinks because of it. Zach thinks he's like his father." Brian stood to pace the room, and I tensed. He pointed at me. "That's why he isn't good for you."

I flushed. "I'm trying to get better, Brian. It's all I want. I want to be happy. I want to date. I want to love someone like Mom loved Dad." I swallowed.

"You do?" Brian asked softly. Why was it such a surprise to him? I nodded. "I thought you only came here to get Dad off your back, not because you actually wanted to get better."

"It started like that, but I realized that I actually want this. I want a life."

Brian looked like I'd given him a huge present. "That's great, Amber. I'm glad you want to live. For a while, I was really worried you were going to try to end things again."

I lowered my face, embarrassed for what I put them through. "I don't want to kill myself anymore." I peered up at him as tears welled in my eyes. "I want to move on. But you have to let me."

"I'm not stopping you from moving on. But not with Zach."

"Why?"

Brian looked at me worriedly. "I just don't want you to get hurt."

"Do you think Zach would hurt me?"

Brian shook his head without hesitation. "No, not on purpose, and he knows that I'd kill him if he did."

"Brian," I scolded. "Don't say such things."

Brian's eyes were soft as he spoke. "But it's the truth, Amber. I couldn't live with myself if someone hurt you again. I still can't forgive myself that I wasn't there to protect you when it happened." Self-hatred flashed in his eyes, and I was taken aback by his words. I never realized that Brian blamed himself for what had happened. If he just told me this before, then I could have convinced him that it wasn't his fault. I never blamed him or Dad. If I blamed anyone it was myself.

"Brian, nothing that happened was your fault. You couldn't have done anything even if you'd been there. There were three of them." My voice got stuck in my throat as the images of that day flashed in my mind, and I closed my eyes tightly in an attempt to banish them.

"Amber." His pained voice drifted into my ears, and I opened my eyes and looked at him with a weak smile. "I'm okay," I said.

"When you are with Zach, you seem so much more relaxed than with me. Why?"

I bit my lip with uncertainty. "With you, I have the feeling that you're always watching me, waiting for me to freak out or have breakdown, and it makes me feel scrutinized."

"I never meant to put pressure on you, Amber. I'm just always so worried about you."

"I know, but maybe you can pretend I'm a normal girl and not a broken porcelain doll," I said softly, smiling hopefully.

"I'll do my best," he promised.

"That's all I'm asking for."

"About Zach—"

I held up my hand. "I know, you don't want me to spend time with him. But I can't help how I feel." At the look on his face, I said, "I don't even know if I'll act on my feelings. I don't even know what exactly they are. I don't know if I even want to figure them out. I'm not exactly girlfriend material either."

"Don't say that."

"We both know it's true," I said. "I know you worry and you want to protect me, but I need to find my own path. Please don't threaten Zach. It's not his fault that I like him. He probably doesn't even feel the same way, so you have nothing to worry about."

Brian snorted. "I wish that was true." He shook his head. "I need to get out of here for a while. I'll be back in a couple of hours." I stepped back as he passed and a few moments later the front door was slammed shut. What did he mean? Had Zach said something to Brian? I really wished I knew if Zach was interested in me or not.

I walked into the kitchen. Zach stood in front of the open fridge, drinking out of a milk carton. He quickly lowered it when he saw me, smiling apologetically. He looked like a child caught with its hand in the cookie jar. "Sorry. I was planning on finishing it."

I smiled. "Good, I don't want your cooties."

He laughed then downed the rest of the milk.

"That's kind of gross, you know?" I asked, still in the doorway. My eyes traveled over his body, from head to toe. The way his abs strained against his thin white shirt, the way his biceps flexed, his broad shoulders, and the outline of a tattoo on his back coming through the fabric. I couldn't make out what it was. Then I realized what I was doing. Was I really checking out Zach?

His eyes met mine. "I know, that's why I only do it when I'm alone." Had he caught me staring? Heat flooded my cheeks. He chucked the carton in the trash can then turned back to me.

"Good to know." A swarm of butterflies fluttered in my stomach. I tried to remind myself of what Brian had said about Zach, that he wasn't good for me, that he wasn't boyfriend material, but my heart and body didn't want to listen to reason. I'd never felt like this.

"So, did you talk to Brian?" Zach asked as he leaned back against the counter, arms crossed over his chest.

I nodded. "Yes, we straightened things out."

"I'm glad you did."

"Me too." My cheeks still felt hot, but I couldn't look away. Some crazy, daring, normal part of me considered bridging the distance between us, touching my lips to his, pressing my palms against his strong chest and leaning against him, feeling safe in his arms.

Could I even feel safe in someone's arms? Could I feel safe in Zach's arms?

chapter eleven
Zachary

Amber averted her gaze. If it were any other girl I would have said that she was attracted to me, but with Amber I wasn't sure. She had been staring at me, but was she actually checking me out? I wasn't vain but I knew the effect my body had on many women. It's why I never had trouble finding someone to spend the night with, but Amber wasn't like that. I didn't want to misinterpret her actions. Too much was at stake. She'd gone through so much. If I did something wrong, not only would Brian hunt me down and probably castrate me, but I would hate myself as well. I knew how toxic people could be for each other. My father hadn't managed to be faithful to my mother for longer than a few months at a time. It fucking broke her heart. He always told me I was exactly like him, and I feared he was right. Could I risk getting close to Amber?

Our time spent on the ice had been great, and I just wanted to take her hand again, but I wasn't sure if she wanted me to. Fuck, I wanted to kiss her, wanted to run my hands over her body, wanted to ... And that was the problem.

Amber took a few steps into the kitchen and leaned against the counter, an arm's length away. One of her hands rested on the counter top, and she was drawing small circles with her forefinger. It would be so easy to reach out and touch her. I'd never been nervous around women, but with Amber everything was different. I was turning into a fucking pussy.

Being this close to her, I could see the soft dusting of freckles on her nose and that her eyes weren't exactly brown. They were brown close to the center but turned a dark green toward the corners of her irises. They were fucking amazing. She tilted her head toward me, and her long hair fell to the side, revealing her slender neck. I wanted to trail my tongue over it, wanted to taste her, even though it was wrong.

"Brian told me to stay away from you," she said. She might as well have thrown a bucket of water into my face.

"He did?" She nodded. "What else did he say?"

She shrugged. He probably told her about Brittany and the other girls and God knows what else. It was probably for the best. "I should go to my room," I muttered.

She put her hand on mine, stopping me. I stared down at her small pale hand on my tanned skin. Slowly, I lifted my gaze. "You don't want me to leave?"

She shook her head.

My skin tingled were she touched me. It would be so easy to turn my hand around and close my palm around her hand, pull her against me, and press my lips against hers.

"But I thought Brian told you to stay away from me?"

"He did. But I can make my own decisions."

"And what did you decide?"

She smiled. "I like spending time with you. I don't want to stay away from you."

"Good. I don't want you to stay away from me."

She pulled her hand back. Disappointment washed over me. What did this mean? That we would only be friends? We'd been so close we could have kissed.

"How about a midnight snack?"

"Sure," I said quickly, trying to drag my thoughts away from kissing her. "I could go for a grilled cheese sandwich."

She straightened her back, her eyes on my face. When she licked her lower lip, every muscle in my body tensed in anticipation. Then she turned, opened the fridge, and the moment was over.

I dreamed of Amber that night. Of how her skin had felt against mine, of how pink her lips had been, of how it would feel to run my hand over her body. I hated myself for always going there, for always imagining how it would be to see her naked and touch her. I actually had a fucking boner. "Fuck," I muttered. Brian was right. I should stay the fuck away from Amber.

I rose from my bed and stretched my arms over my head. I needed to take care of business in the shower.

There was a knock at my door and before I could react, it swung open and Reagan entered. I casually dropped my hands so they concealed my hard-on. What the hell was Reagan doing in my room? She closed the door and turned around to me. I raised my eyebrows inquiringly. I wasn't wearing anything but briefs, but Reagan didn't seem to be bothered by it. Actually, she ignored my body completely.

Reagan walked past me and sat down on my bed, patting the place beside her. I frowned and didn't move from my spot in the middle of my room. She was dressed in running shorts and a tank top, but at least she wasn't sweaty.

She narrowed her eyes. "Sit."

"Are you getting all dominatrix with me?" I asked as I plopped down beside her.

"No. Not that I don't think that you don't need a woman who tells you what to do now and then."

"Where's Kevin?"

"He's still asleep. It's the weekend after all."

"You do realize that sitting on my bed might look strange?" I said. I didn't want to imagine how Kevin would react if he found his girlfriend in my bed. I doubted that he'd give me the chance to explain the situation to him. Maybe I was a man-whore, but my friends' girlfriends were definitely off limits.

She rolled her eyes. "Don't be stupid. I'm not attracted to you. Nobody would think that I'd have an affair with you."

"You're breaking my heart," I said in a fake, hurt tone.

Reagan crossed her legs, a determined look on her face. "We don't have time for this nonsense right now. I came to talk to you before Amber wakes up. I don't want her to know that I'm here."

Now she had my undivided attention. "Is anything wrong?"

Reagan shook her head. "Nothing is wrong, except for the fact that you haven't told Amber about your feelings."

I opened my mouth to protest, but she cut me off. "Don't deny your feelings. They're obvious." Her eyes softened slightly. "Listen, Zach, you need to do the first step and tell Amber. She's too scared that you might reject her. I can see how good you are for each other. You just need to admit how you feel about her."

Brian would object to that. "Are you sure that Amber has feelings for me?"

"Are you blind?"

"I don't want to push Amber into anything she's not ready for," I said cautiously. And what was worse: I wasn't even sure if I was ready for a committed relationship.

"Admitting one's feelings and seeing each other doesn't mean that you need to get physical. Amber isn't Brittany."

Annoyance rocked through me. Why did everyone have to bring up Brittany? "I know that, Reagan. Why do you think I'm being so careful?"

"What's really holding you back, Zach? Are you worried you can't go without sex for a while?"

"I'm a guy," I said, annoyed. "Of course I'm thinking about sex. I've never had a serious relationship ... unless you count the few no-strings-attached girlfriends I've had over the years. I'm not even sure if I could stay faithful to a girlfriend I could actually screw, but with Amber I'd be forced to live like a monk for God knows how long."

Reagan's lips tightened with disgust. "If that's your reasoning, then you're a pig." She stood abruptly. "Kevin told me you think you are like your cheating, home-wrecking father, but our parents don't define who we are or who we become. There's something called choice. Maybe you should stop following in your father's footsteps like a mindless sheep and figure out what you really want." My phone started buzzing on the nightstand, the screen flashing with Brittany's name. "If screwing around is all you want, then you should answer that call. But then you better stay away from Amber. I won't watch you break her heart. I expected more from you." With one last glower, she whirled around and stormed out of my room, slamming the door shut.

"Bitch," I muttered. I expected more from you? Really? My father always said that to me. I could never do anything right in his eyes and apparently the same applied to Reagan, Kevin, and Brian. Fuck them. This was my life. I picked up the phone. "Hey, Britt, do you want to come over? I need you."

I thrust into Brittany one last time, the subsiding waves of my orgasm surging through me. Brittany lifted her head from the pillow where she'd buried her face to stifle her moans. She was stretched out on the bed, her butt propped up. She loved that position, and I didn't mind watching her hot ass during sex. I pulled out of her and disposed of the condom. Then I stood and stared down at her sweat-slicked skin. She rolled onto her back, arms raised over her head, a satisfied smirk on her face. Guilt gripped my chest. While I'd fucked Britt, images of Amber kept popping into my head. She'd wormed her way into my brain, and now I couldn't get her out. Britt ran her toes up my thighs until she reached my balls. She began massaging them with her foot and a jolt of lust made my softening cock jerk awake again. What was I doing? Sex with Britt was hot, mind-blowing, uncomplicated, and yet deep down I wanted more. I wanted Amber.

I pulled away and Britt's foot dropped from my balls. She sat up, frowning. "What? Don't tell me you can't go another round."

I could definitely go another round, and my already hardening cock wanted to, but I had to stop this madness. Reagan was right. I expected I would become like my father. I wasn't even trying to be a better man. I ran a hand through my hair. I was an asshole. How could I explain my reasoning to Britt without a major scene? Soft steps padded past my door. Amber. I cringed. Had she heard anything? Fuck. I'd told Britt we needed to be quiet because of Brian, but she had let a few moans slip out.

Her eyes narrowed. "Is that her?"

"What?"

"Someone walked past your door just now and you got a strange look on your face. That was Brian's sister, right?"

I forced a shrug. "So what?"

"So what?" Britt repeated, rising from the bed. "Did you want to make her jealous?"

I laughed. "No, of course not."

"Then why did you invite me over after what you said in the club?"

That was a good question. Maybe I was trying to push Amber away, but I didn't want to do that anymore. I wanted to give this thing with Amber a chance.

"Oh my God, you have a crush on that girl." She grabbed the blanket and wrapped it around her body and walked toward my door. "I'll clean up and then I'm gone." I was surprised that Britt didn't try to fight. I wished she wouldn't take a shower here, but I could hardly tell her to get dressed reeking of sex. She stepped out of my room, but she didn't head for the bathroom. She was on her way toward the living room. Oh shit.

chapter twelve
Amber

I curled up my legs beside me on the sofa and picked up the newest Mercy Thompson book. Pumpkin was stretched out beside me, his tail twitching occasionally in his sleep. Steps echoed down the hall, and a blond woman hurried into the living room. She was naked except for the blanket wrapped around her body. I lowered the book, eyes wide.

Her gaze zeroed in on me. "So you're Amber?"

Was she Brian's girlfriend Lauren? Why was she standing in the middle of the apartment half-naked?

"Uh, yes?" I said with uncertainty in my voice. "Are you Lauren?"

The girl moved closer. She was tall and her skin was sweaty. "No, I'm Brittany." She scanned me from head to toe, and I couldn't help but feel small under her scrutiny. What did she want?

"Britt!" Zach stumbled into the living room, fumbling with the zipper of his jeans, his upper body naked. He froze when he spotted me sitting on the sofa. My stomach tightened. The book slipped from my fingers and tumbled onto the sofa. Pumpkin leaped away with a startled hiss then dashed off. Nobody said anything. My eyes were glued to Zach's face. His hair was disheveled and slightly sweaty, as was his upper body. I could feel Brittany's eyes boring into me like knives. Now I understood why she wasn't wearing clothes. She and Zach just had sex in his room. Hurt welled up inside me. I couldn't help but feel betrayed, which was ridiculous since Zach and I weren't together, but after the ice rink I thought something had changed between us. I shouldn't have believed Reagan. Of course, Zach didn't have feelings for me. How could he when he had someone like Brittany? I could never compete with her body, her experience, her confidence. I snatched up my book and jumped up from the sofa. Not looking at Zach or Britt, I walked around the love seat and headed for my room.

"I'm sorry." I didn't even know what I was apologizing for. I had every right to be in the living room. "I'll give you some privacy."

Maybe Brittany wanted to continue their adventures in the living room. I wouldn't be staying to watch. Sickness rose within me like a flash flood. I was the stupidest person alive for thinking there could ever be something between Zach and me.

Words from long ago, words my attackers had whispered into my ears when they were done with me crept into my mind. *Nobody's ever going to want you now, you dirty little slut. You should be glad that we kill you.* And at that point I'd actually been glad for the mercy of death. I didn't want to die anymore, but the fear that those men could have been right made me want to hide in a dark corner and never come out. *Nobody's ever going to want you now.*

"Amber, wait," Zach said, reaching for me as I passed him. I jerked back and collided with the wall. Pain shot through my arm from the impact.

"What's the matter with her?" Brittany asked.

Heat flooded my cheeks. I couldn't bear the thought of Zach touching me after he'd had sex with another woman. For several seconds, neither Zach nor I moved. He dropped his arm, hands clenching to fists. My eyes followed his tendons straining, up to his biceps, his wide shoulders, sculpted pecs and abs, down to the fine trail of dark hair disappearing under the waistband of his jeans. Brittany had touched every inch of the skin my eyes trailed over. That thought sent another wave of embarrassment, mixed with hurt, through me.

"Can you give us a moment?" Zach asked. With a start, I realized he wasn't talking to me.

Brittany huffed. "Really?"

"No," I said quickly. "I should go." I almost tripped over my feet in my haste to get into my room.

Zach hurried after me. "Amber, please give me a chance to explain."

What was there to explain? It wasn't any of my business if he had a girlfriend.

"Explain? The only person you owe an explanation to is me!" Brittany hissed. She was also coming after us. "Why don't you start with why you give me a booty call when you're obviously caught up in some kind of messed-up puppy love with *that girl*?" She narrowed her eyes at me. "Or is that some kind of sick kinky thing between the two of you? Do you like to listen to Zach fucking other women?"

I stared. "Excuse me?" I asked, my voice rising. For a moment, I was startled by my own bravery. She had no right to talk to me like that. I had done nothing wrong here.

"Oh, don't give me that innocent look."

"Brittany, shut up," Zach snarled.

Brian's door opened and he poked his disheveled head out. His eyes took in the scene, his face twisting into a mask of fury. "What the hell is going on here?" He stepped out in his pajamas. At least one person wasn't half-naked.

"I don't know," I said. "I was on my way to my room." I gestured at my door. Brian didn't even look at me. He glared at Zach with so much anger, it actually worried me.

Brittany threw her hands up. "You know what? I'm done here." She whirled around and disappeared in Zach's room. She slammed the door shut.

"We need to talk," Brian ordered, seizing Zach's arm, who shook it off like a bothersome fly. "I need to talk to Amber first."

"The fuck you will!" Brian slammed his palms against Zach's chest. Apparently, Zach hadn't expected the assault and crashed with his back against the wall. In a blink, he was on Brian and shoved him hard. He hurled Brian against his door with so much force that it broke out of the hinges and the door crashed to the ground. Brian caught his balance against the doorframe. He looked ready to pounce on Zach again. I couldn't let that happen. They'd been friends for years. Every muscle in Zach's body was taught in anticipation of a fight. If the trophies in his room were any indication, he'd wipe the floor with my brother.

I stepped between them as they were about to start their fight, and they both recoiled in surprise. My arms were stretched out between them, palms resting against both their chests. For a moment I was so stunned by my courage, I gaped at my hands. I was wedged between two guys who were furious and towered over me in a narrow corridor, and I was actually touching them without dissolving into a puddle of misery. Adrenaline was pounding in my veins. I cleared my throat and slowly lowered my arms. My fingertips tingled where I'd touched Zach's chest.

"Stop it," I said firmly, then added, "please."

Zach slumped against the wall. "Sorry for your door." He nodded toward the ground. Brian turned and picked it up from the floor. "That's the least of my worries."

"Brian," I said in warning.

Brian tried to get the door back on its hinges but failed. "Let me help," Zach said, moving toward my brother.

"I don't want your fucking help."

Zach ignored him and together they managed to put up the door, but it didn't move properly. "It's broken," Brian said in frustration, then he turned his attention to me. As if the word broken had reminded him that I was still there. "Are you okay?"

Admist all the fighting, I'd briefly forgotten why everything had started. Of course, Brittany chose that moment to step out of Zach's room, dressed in black skinny jeans and a leather jacket. She looked amazing. I averted my gaze, feeling empty and tired. She left without another word, for which I was grateful, but her mere presence had revved up the tension between Zach and Brian by several notches. "I'm fine. Why wouldn't I be?" I tried to sound casual.

"You promised not to bring any of your sluts here."

"Brian!" I hated that word. "This is Zach's apartment as much as it is yours. He can have over whomever he wants. And just because a girl goes home with a guy doesn't mean she's a slut."

"The girls Zach usually chooses are."

"The girls aren't any more at fault than Zach. You could just as well call him a slut."

"He is a male slut," Brian said. "That's why I wanted you to stay away from him."

Zach leaned against the wall, his jaw tight. "I'm here, you know? And I like sex, so sue me. What's your problem anyway? Don't tell me you visit Lauren several times a week because you like her jabbering. You go there for sex."

"My problem is that you're messing with my sister. I don't care if you screw around. I don't care if you don't realize how pathetic that is. But I care about Amber. So stop pretending that you give a shit about her, when clearly you don't. I won't let Amber be another notch on your belt."

I was done with this conversation. Without another word, I entered my room and closed the door, then leaned against it, eyes closed. I supposed it was good that I knew where I stood with Zach now before I got really emotionally invested. More emotionally invested? Who was I kidding? I was already helplessly in love with him.

I was on my way out of the apartment for a Sunday morning walk to clear my head, when Zach jogged after me, dressed in sweatpants and a tight black T-shirt. He was barefoot. "Amber, please wait." I'd avoided him since our awkward confrontation yesterday. But Brian had left the apartment late last night and hadn't come back. He was probably with Lauren. "I really need to talk to you."

I hesitated. "Why? You don't owe me an explanation."

"But I want to," he said, his eyes pleading.

"Okay, but I wanted to go on a walk."

"I'll just put some shoes on. I'll be back in a sec."

We sat down on a bench in the park beside the apartment building. Neither Zach nor I had said anything in the five minutes it had taken to get here. Maybe Zach hoped I'd start the conversation, but I didn't know what to say. I brought up my knees, pressing them against my chest. A chilly breeze picked up, ruffling my hair and sending a shiver down my back. My naked feet were cold in my Converse. Zach didn't seem to mind the freezing temperatures. His hoodie was probably warmer than my thin jacket.

"So," I began, wanting to get past the awkward silence. I rested my chin on my knees and tilted my head to look at Zach. We sat on opposite ends of the bench, almost a foot between us. Part of me wanted to scoot over and snuggle up against Zach's strong chest. Maybe it was for the best that I'd fallen for a guy I couldn't have. That way, at least, I could experience a crush without actually having to risk a relationship.

"I'm sorry for yesterday."

"Why?" I frowned. "It's not like you aren't allowed to bring your girlfriend to your own apartment."

"Britt isn't my girlfriend." He sighed. "Never mind. That's not the point."

"Then what's the point?"

"I shouldn't have brought Britt to the apartment. I shouldn't have met her at all."

"Why?" I whispered, caught up in his intense gaze.

He stared down at his lap, his brows drawn together. "Fuck," he muttered, then grimaced. "I'm not good at this. I really like you Amber."

Hope flooded my body, but I couldn't make a big deal out of nothing. I gave a small shrug. "I like you too," I said. "You're my brother's best friend."

His eyes flickered over my face. "That's not what I meant. I don't like you like a friend."

"You don't?" I wanted to reach out and trail my fingertips over the dark stubble on his jaw. I wanted to lean close and draw in his scent, which was a mix of peppermint and something spicy.

He angled his body so he was facing me. Now there were only a few inches between his knee and my foot. And still I wanted to scoot closer. I should have felt uncomfortable, maybe even scared. Zach was had a formidable appearance with his tall frame and muscles, but when I was around him, the possibilities seemed endless, as if happiness was actually in my reach, as if I could grab onto it if I only stretched out my hand. Zach made me hope for something I thought was out of my grasp, he made me long for something I dreaded for so long.

"Amber, I'm attracted to you. I want to be with you." My breath caught in my throat. He must have mistook my reaction for fear because he turned away, his shoulders sagging. "I know you probably don't feel the same way, and maybe I shouldn't have brought it up at all. I'm sorry if I scared you."

I laughed and Zach frowned at me. "You didn't scare me. At least not in the way you probably think."

"I'm confused," he said with an adorable expression. There was a dimple in his left cheek I wanted to kiss. In my head, I always wanted, wanted, wanted. I wished I could actually go through with it.

"I'm not scared of you," I said, and I realized it was true. Even though I knew Zach was much stronger than me and was physically capable of doing what those men had done, I knew he wouldn't. "I'm scared of how you make me feel."

"Isn't that the same thing?"

"No. I'm scared because you make me hope for something I thought I wasn't capable of. I'm scared of hope."

Zach looked lost. "I'm not good with subtlety. I know women always want men to figure out what they mean without spelling it out, but I really need you to spell it out for me. I don't want to mess this up."

I smiled. "I don't want to be just friends. I want more."

"More?"

"I think I'm falling for you." The moment the words left my mouth worry twisted my stomach. Why did I have to say I was falling in love for him? That was probably a huge red flag for most guys, but from what I knew about Zach it would be a death sentence for any budding relationship. But I was done being cautious. The last few years caution and fear had been my prison. I wanted to break out of them. I needed to.

Relief filled Zach's face. "Good."

"Good?" I whispered.

"Yeah, because I think I'm falling for you too."

My heart exploded with joy. I bit my lip, unsure of what to do now. Zach's eyes flitted toward my lips, but he made no move to kiss me. I knelt on the bench and eased closer to Zach. He froze, his eyes never leaving my face. My knees bumped his thigh, his heat radiating through our clothes. I rested my hand on his shoulder, felt the muscles flex under my touch. Slowly, I leaned closer and touched my lips to his in a feather-light kiss. Nerves fluttered in my stomach. I couldn't believe I was actually doing this. I braced myself for an onslaught of bad memories, but none came. There was only the softness of Zach's lips, his warmth, his scent. I pressed my other palm against his chest, feeling the steady beating of his heart. His hand, which had rested on the armrest, touched my waist very lightly. I jumped and Zach pulled back immediately. "Too much?"

I snatched up his hand and put it back to the same spot on my waist. "No, it's okay. I was just surprised."

I wasn't sure anymore what was too much. Zach made me believe that maybe I could break down every single wall that I'd built around myself after the incident. Walls that had seemed impenetrable, walls that had dominated my life for years, that had isolated me to the point of utter loneliness and despair, I suddenly seemed able to conquer.

I didn't try to deepen the kiss, neither did Zach, though he probably wanted to. Eventually, I sat back on my haunches. "So," he said, a smile slowly building on his face.

"So."

"Does that mean we …" He trailed off.

I thought of yesterday, of Brittany in only a towel, of what she and Zach must have been doing before she walked into the living room. "No."

His expression fell. "Because of yesterday."

"That too," I admitted. "But it's not a definite no. I just think we need to discuss a few things before we take this any further." Heat rushed into my cheeks. I couldn't believe I managed to say the words. I felt in control of my fate for maybe the first time in three years.

Zach nodded, relaxing under my touch, and I realized my hands were still on his chest and shoulder. I dropped them and folded them in my lap. "So you're giving me a second chance?"

"You never got a first chance to begin with," I said teasingly. Was this how normal girls my age felt?

He grinned and warmth filled my stomach. I wanted to kiss him again, but that would contradict what I just suggested. "How about we go on a date?" he asked. "Tonight?"

I nodded. I couldn't believe that going on a date was actually part of my reality now.

zachary

"Tonight," she agreed. There was a hint of uncertainty on her face. "But I still think we need to talk about things before we go out."

"Okay, let's do it then." Another gust of wind blasted over us and Amber shivered. Normally, I'd have wrapped my arms around her to keep her warm, but I didn't want to overwhelm her. "Do you want to go inside?"

"No." She shook her head. "Brian might be home by now, and he'll complicate things."

I grimaced. I'd forgotten about Brian. He'd be royally pissed if he found out I was going on a date with Amber, and even more pissed when he found out I wanted to take things further with her. "He'll try to stop us from going out."

Amber sighed. "I know. But this is my life. I can't live in a cocoon forever."

"Brian won't like it."

"Oh, he definitely won't like it, but he'll deal." Amber gave a delicate shrug. "So let's talk."

I felt oddly nervous. "Brian probably told you that I don't have a great track record with relationships."

"He did. So what about Brittany? What's going on between you two?"

"Nothing." Amber looked doubtful. "We've been seeing each other for about one year, but it's been only physical. And it wasn't exclusive. We both saw other people."

She stared down at her hands. "So it was about sex?"

"Yeah." I was actually embarrassed. When Amber said it like that, it made me sound like an asshole, which I probably was. "I never found someone that I wanted to be serious about."

"You know I can't give you what those women did. I want a relationship. I want something that's meaningful."

"I want the same," I said.

Reagan had been right. If I didn't want to be like my father, I had to choose a different path. Not the one I'd been treading so far. I'd never liked a girl like I did Amber. But I couldn't lie to Amber. "I don't know how good I'll be at this relationship thing. It's new for me."

Amber smiled. "I can't promise anything either. It's new for me as well. I've never had a boyfriend." She swallowed. "Before the incident, I liked a guy but I never got the chance to be with him."

Anger surged through me when I thought of what had happened to her, but I pushed it aside. "I really want to try."

"Me too. That's all we can do. Try." She searched my face. "You know physical closeness is hard for me. I can't promise that I'll ever be ready to sleep with you." She swallowed. "I don't even know if I'll ever be ready to do more than kissing." Embarrassment twisted her expression.

I didn't like the thought of never doing more than kissing Amber, but I couldn't tell her that. "I know. We just have to take our relationship one step at a time."

"That sounds good. But are you sure you are willing to wait for me to be ready. What about your…" I could tell she was searching for the right wording "…needs or urges?"

I burst out laughing. Amber flushed. "Sorry, but that sounds like I'm some kind of animal who can't control his urges."

Something shifted in Amber's face, and my gut tightened in horror. The men who'd raped Amber had been like animals. No worse. Monsters. "Amber. I'm—"

She held up a hand and I shut up. Her chin wobbled as if she was about to lose it. "You're right. You aren't an animal. But you have needs."

"Don't worry about my needs. I can take care of them." She frowned. "You know? His right hand is a man's best friend?" I winked.

Amber choked on a laugh. "Oh, okay. Right. I didn't think of that. But will that be enough?"

I carefully closed my hand around hers. "Don't worry. I can handle it." I was on the verge of laughter again, but I fought it. "You have to promise that you'll always tell me when something is too much for you. I don't want to pressure you."

She nodded. "I promise. So what are we going to do for our first date tonight?"

"How about watching a movie?"

"I haven't been in a movie theater in years." *Since the rape ... that's* what she didn't say.

"We can do something else."

She squeezed my hand. "No, I'd love to watch a movie."

I couldn't believe Amber agreed to go out with me after everything Brian had told her, after what she'd witnessed yesterday. I wanted this to work out. I wouldn't mess up.

chapter thirteen

Amber

I'd been staring at the display of clothes in my wardrobe for almost thirty minutes, and I still wasn't sure what to wear to the date. I wanted to look nice for Zach. Unfortunately, the majority of clothes I owned were meant to hide my body and make me as inconspicuous as possible. A door slammed shut in the apartment and someone stomped past my room. Brian. The way his steps sounded, his time with Lauren hadn't gone too well. He still hadn't even told me about his girlfriend. I really hoped he wouldn't make a scene when he found out Zach and I were going out tonight.

I still couldn't believe that Zach and I were going to try a relationship. Zach wasn't perfect, but neither was I. Maybe this was bound to end horribly, but I had to give it an attempt. A normal life. Nerves twisted my stomach. I focused on the task at hand and picked out black—not-quite skinny but tighter than my usual style—jeans and a purple tank top I had never worn before. I bought it online because I loved the color, but then I never felt comfortable wearing it because it hugged my body in all the places I wanted to hide. I brushed out my hair, put on a light touch of makeup, and slipped on ballet flats. Then I checked my reflection in the floor-length mirror attached to the door. It was actually the first time I'd used it.

Taking a deep breath, I left my room and headed toward the living room. Zach was already there. He wore dark jeans and a nice white shirt. He rolled up the sleeves, revealing strong forearms and tanned skin. He turned his head and caught me staring. His eyes roamed over me. I wished I knew what he was thinking. "You look beautiful," he said.

Trying to hide my nervousness, I strode toward him. He held out his hand, palm upward. Without hesitation, I put my hand in his. How could something as simple as holding hands feel so right? I wasn't sure what it was about Zach that made this possible. I was just glad that he gave me the chance to explore a normal life. Music was blasting from Brian's room. At least he wouldn't try to stop us.

We arrived in the parking lot of the movie theater. We'd been holding hands all through the ride, and I missed his touch when we let go of each other to get out of the car. The parking lot was crowded with people, mostly our age from what I could see. So many people. I hesitated beside the car. Zach held out his hand, and I took it, glad for his presence. I clutched his hand as we approached the movie theater. The inside was brightly illuminated, and it was even more crowded than the parking lot. As we entered, noises washed over me. Laughter and conversation. I couldn't remember the last time I'd been surrounded by so many people.

"Do you want popcorn or something else?"

My eyes darted toward the counter. "Popcorn sounds great." We joined the long line of people waiting for their turn. A group of high school boys got in line behind us, all tall and loud. One of them bumped into me and panic surged through me. I pressed against Zach, seeking his protection.

He shoved the guy back. "Watch it," he snarled. The boy's eyes widened. Then he exchanged a look with his friends that made it obvious he thought Zach was overreacting, but they all backed a few steps away, giving me more room. Zach was impressive, really.

He gazed down at me and whispered, "Are you okay? We can leave if you want."

"No," I said. "I'm fine."

He wrapped an arm around my shoulder protectively. "Too much?"

I smiled. "No."

In Zach's arms, the people and the noise weren't half as scary. His scent and warmth enveloped me in a cocoon of safety. We got our popcorn and then we headed for our seats. The seats beside ours were both occupied, and both with men. Swallowing my rising panic, I sank down and scooted as close to Zach as possible. He slung his arm around me. As he scanned my face his expression turned worried. I forced a smile and eased my head down on his shoulder. The lights dimmed and the commercials started. Zach rested the popcorn on his lap, and our hands kept brushing against one another. Every time it happened, a small shiver ran through me. Even though I was snuggled up against him, and his arm was around my shoulder, those occasional touches felt intimate and thrilling. They stirred something in my belly making me wonder how his touch would feel in other places, but I had a long way to go before that was an option.

After the movie, Zach and I returned to our car and drove home. "I didn't even think how crowded the movie theater would be," he said after a while. "Sorry."

"No. I really enjoyed it."

"You did?" He tossed me a doubtful look.

"I enjoyed having your arm around me," I admitted.

Zach grinned. "Good, because I like putting my arm around you."

A message flashed on my mobile when we got out of the car behind our building. It was from Brian and said: **Where are you???**

"Brian?" Zach guessed as we walked up to the front door of our apartment building.

"He wants to know where I am."

"He'll know soon enough," Zach said. We stepped into the elevator, and I smiled despite the worry I felt. "Maybe we should pretend we met in the hallway."

Zach laughed. "You want to lie to Brian about us?"

"It's just one date."

Zach frowned. "I don't want this to be our last date."

"Neither do I."

"So if we decide to give this dating thing a chance, we need to tell your brother."

I sighed and slumped against the elevator wall. "You're right. So are we dating now?" The question made me oddly nervous.

Zach twisted closer. Was he going to kiss me? I bit my lip. He towered a head over me. We were in a narrow space, and this time I wasn't the one in control. Could I handle that? Zach stopped and only took my hand. Had he seen the doubt on my face? "We're dating," he said. Suddenly a huge weight had been lifted off my chest. I stood on my tiptoes, curled my hand around Zach's neck, and pulled his face toward me, brushing my lips against his. The contact sent a thrill through my body. I wondered how it would be to deepen the kiss, but the elevator wasn't the place for that. I was already surprised that I had kissed him at all. The elevator doors slid open, and we stepped out. When we entered the apartment, Brian was sitting on the sofa. His eyes darted to our linked hands then over to Zach and then to me. He jerked up from his seat. This was going to end badly.

zachary

Brian looked like he wanted to kill me. I squeezed Amber's hand. "Maybe you should go into your room."

Brian came around the sofa and headed straight for me. I never took my eyes off him. I hadn't done anything wrong, no matter how much he wanted me to feel that way. "Brian," Amber said in a warning tone. "This is what I want. Don't give Zach trouble."

"You don't even know what *this* is. You've got no clue what you're getting yourself into," Brian muttered. He treated her as if she was some stupid kid.

Amber narrowed her eyes. "How can you say that? I want a normal life. I want a boyfriend. I want experience, closeness, and love." She snapped her mouth shut, looking embarrassed.

Love, huh? I forced my face to remain passive. I couldn't let Amber see how the mere mention of love had shocked me, but Brian must have seen something in my expression. I knew she didn't mean that she loved me, but I still couldn't help but be worried. The word love referred to a sort of commitment, one I never even considered. Love had ruined my mother.

"I only want to talk to Zach," Brian said.

"Talk?" Amber looked doubtful. I probably did too. Brian wanted to kick my fucking ass. "I don't think that's a good—" The ringing of her phone interrupted her. She stared down at the screen then replied, "It's Reagan. She's at Kevin's and wants to talk." Just then a knock sounded at our door.

Amber let go of my hand and opened the door. "Where you waiting in front of the door this whole time? How did you get here so fast?"

Reagan smiled, but her eyes darted between Brian and me. It was probably obvious that we were about to start arguing. She took Amber's arm and pulled her away. "Let the boys deal with their testosterone." Both girls disappeared into the kitchen.

Brian waited for the door to close before he spoke, "What's going on here?" I could tell how much it cost him to talk calmly.

"Amber and I went on a date."

"A date?" Brian clenched his jaw.

"We want to give it a try."

"What a try?"

"A relationship ..."

Brian snorted. "You've got to be kidding." He kept his voice low.

"Amber isn't ready for a relationship. You can't just use her as your guinea pig to see if you're capable of not sleeping around."

"She's not my guinea pig. Your sister and I discussed this. We both want to try it."

Brian shook his head. "Damn it! Why couldn't you have listened to me?" Suddenly he didn't look angry anymore. He sank down on the armrest of the sofa.

I put a hand on his shoulder, but he shook it off. "Listen, man, I'd never do anything that would hurt your sister. I really care about her," I said, trying to be the voice of reason.

"Maybe not on purpose, Zach, but you are a womanizer. I doubt you can keep your dick in your pants for more than a couple of weeks."

I clenched my fists. "Amber and I will make this work. Will you help stop me from messing up or will you stand by and keep glowering at me like I'm the second coming of Satan?"

Brian stood. He was a few inches shorter than me, but somehow he managed to get us nose to nose. "For some reason Amber wants to give you a chance. I haven't seen her this happy since those bastards raped her. I won't try to interfere because Amber would be angry if I did, but if you mess this up, if you hurt her, if you break her heart … our friendship is over. I'll move out and never talk to you again, so you'd better not fuck up. Understood?"

I felt a twinge of worry. A lot was on the line. I stood to lose not only Amber but also Brian if I messed up. And so far my life had been a series of mess-ups. "Understood," I said simply.

amber

Reagan and I stepped into the kitchen. She sat down at the table, but I stayed close to the door to listen to Brian and Zach's conversation. If they started shouting, I would have to get between them to break it up.

"So you and Zach went on a date?"

I'd sent Reagan a text earlier to tell her about it. I nodded.

"Tell me everything." She pulled out the chair beside her. "And please sit down. Your brother isn't going to kill Zach."

"I'm not so sure."

"Zach's got about fifty pounds of muscle on your brother. There's no way in hell Brian could beat Zach in a fight."

"Is that supposed to calm me?"

Reagan patted the chair, and I plopped into it. "So how was it?"

"It was nice."

"Nice? Did you kiss?"

"Yeah, but…" my cheeks flamed "…not really, you know?"

"So no tongue?"

I wished I could be as open about these things as Reagan. "I wanted to, but I was worried it would be too much. Or that Zach would want more if we really kissed."

"Zach knows about your past. He wouldn't think you'd be ready to get down and dirty because you French-kissed him," she said. "And you can tell him 'no' when something is too much for you. Zach's got his faults, but he would never ever force you to do something you don't want."

I'd said 'no' in the past. I had screamed it till my throat was raw. I begged, cried, pleaded, whimpered, but that 'no' had meant nothing to them. Zach wasn't like that. I knew that. Reagan touched my hand. "You have to voice what you want and don't want. Believe me, Zach won't mind if you're open with him about your desires."

It sounded so easy but even the word desire made me flush with embarrassment. "I don't even know what I want."

"You'll find out together. If there's one good thing about Zach's extensive experience, it is that he's probably good at pleasing women."

"Oh God." I buried my face in my palms. "I don't even know if I can feel something like that. Maybe what happened has made me numb."

Reagan searched my face. "You worry that you can't feel pleasure." I gave a small nod. "Have you never tried to touch yourself?"

My skin felt so hot, it was a miracle that I hadn't combusted yet. "No."

"Why?"

I gave her a look. "Because after what happened, I couldn't even think about anything like that without reliving it."

"And now?"

"I feel attracted to Zach." I paused. "I want to kiss him."

She grinned. "So when you see Zach's muscled body, you do feel something?"

I definitely felt something whenever I saw Zach. "Yeah, I guess. It's complicated. I don't know what to do."

"You have to be in control, Amber. Be the one to make the first step. Take matters in your own hands. Show Zach what you want. He's probably as unsure and confused as you are. He needs your guidance."

"Right. You said it yourself … He's experienced and I'm not."

"That's got nothing to do with it. He's never been with a girl like you. His usual women drop their panties with one smile from him. They most definitely weren't virgins."

Tears sprang into my eyes. "I'm not a virgin," I whispered harshly.

"Yes, you *are*," Reagan half-growled. "What those three assholes did to you was against your will. You never *slept* with a guy. You were violated. That doesn't count." She blinked rapidly.

I drew in a deep breath through my nose, forcing back the tears. I wasn't going to cry. I'd shed too many tears over what happened. "It doesn't feel like it."

"When—*if* you ever decide to sleep with Zach or someone else, you'll see what I mean."

"I don't know if I can ever sleep with Zach."

"One step at a time. Just remember to take control."

"Okay," I said. Take control ... was that even something I could do? Maybe Reagan was right. Maybe I needed to finally get my control back. And what better way to do it than with Zach? He wouldn't hurt me.

The door swung open, and Zach entered. His eyes darted between Reagan and me, and a familiar warmth settled in my stomach. "Everything okay?"

I smiled. "Yes." I tried to look past him. "Where's Brian?"

"In his room."

"Is he okay with us?"

"As okay as he can be." Zach took a carton of orange juice from the fridge and took one big gulp.

"Pig," Reagan said. "You could use a glass."

Zach winked at me. "Amber doesn't mind."

Reagan stood. "I should get back to Kevin. He's probably already sulking." She gave me a meaningful look as she passed by us and disappeared. Zach put the orange juice back into the fridge. It was already almost eleven, but I couldn't stop thinking about what Reagan had said.

I wanted to kiss, Zach. *Take control.*

I bit my lip.

"You have a strange look on your face," Zach said with a grin. Then his face became serious. "Are we okay? Did Reagan say anything about me? Anything bad?"

I laughed. "No." I gathered my courage. "I want to kiss you."

Zach's eyebrows shot up. "You can kiss me whenever you want. You kissed me today."

"I mean," I said, my voice turning into a whisper, "I want a real kiss." Could this get any more embarrassing?

Zach straightened, surprised. "Sure."

"Can you sit down?" The words rushed out of me.

Confusion flickered over his face, but he sank down on the chair Reagan had sat in without protest. I stood and slowly walked over to him. With him sitting, I had a couple of inches on him. He tilted his head up, not making any move to reach out for me. His hands rested on his thighs. He was trying to look as harmless as a man of his size and stature possibly could. Was Reagan right? Was he as nervous about this as I was? Who knew what Brian had threatened him with? I stepped between his legs and put my hands down on his shoulders. *Take control.*

I'd kissed two boys before the incident, but this felt new. I wasn't that girl anymore. She'd been broken, crushed, obliterated. For a long time I'd mourned her, had cried over the fact that she was lost to me forever and with her, my happiness, my life, my future vanished. Maybe what had been broken couldn't be mended. Maybe I could never be the girl from the past, but I could become someone new.

Zach's eyes searched my face. I'd thought I could never trust a man again. *Take control,* I reminded myself again. It was a mere kiss, a kiss I'd been dreaming about for days now. But what if the worst happened and I had a panic attack? Would Zach decide I wasn't worth the trouble?

"Tell me what you're thinking," Zach murmured. Something stirred in me at the worry in his tone. I wanted this. I wanted to feel Zach's lips on mine.

I brought my face closer to his until our breath mingled. Zach's blue eyes bored into me, soft and encouraging. Maybe my brother was right. Maybe Zach was a mistake, but he was a mistake I wanted to make. It would be *my choice*. I pressed my mouth against his, my eyes closing. Gathering my courage, I touched my tongue to his lips, hoping he'd understand it as permission and take lead. Zach lifted one arm and gently cupped my cheek. Then he opened his mouth and his tongue slipped past my lips. He was hot and tasted so good, and every brush of his tongue against mine sent a small shiver of pleasure through my body. I could even feel it in my toes. *My choice*. His tongue became more demanding, and heat pooled in my belly. I wasn't even sure what I was feeling, but it was so good, so freeing. I never wanted this to stop, this feeling of being in control of my body, my wants and needs. Zach's other hand came up to touch my back. My legs felt weak as our mouths glided over each other's. I raked my fingers through Zach's hair. I hardly thought it was possible, but the sensations cursing through my body got even more intense. I pulled back to catch my breath, my eyes fluttering open and meeting Zach's gaze. The corners of his lips turned up, and I couldn't help but smile back.

"You okay?" he asked softly, lowering his hand from my cheek.

"Better than okay." My skin was still burning, but this time it wasn't only from embarrassment. I wanted to kiss him again and again.

zachary

My blood pounded in my veins. Amber's lips were swollen and red from our kiss, and I wanted to press my mouth against hers again, wanted to kiss her until she lost all sense of herself. But it was late and my cock was already getting hard in my pants. I shifted, dropping my hands in my lap to hide the bulge. Amber didn't need to see it. We were making progress, and I didn't want to ruin it because I wasn't able to control my dick.

I wanted to take Amber to my room, wanted to lower her to my bed and find out if every part of her body tasted as good as her mouth. Fuck, she would be my undoing. I rubbed a hand over my face. "I'm tired."

Disappointment flickered across Amber's face. "Oh, right. It's late." She stepped back from between my legs, suddenly looking self-conscious.

"I can't wait to kiss you again and again," I said, and she lit up. She leaned forward and brushed a quick kiss across my lips. This was sweet torture.

"Sleep tight," she whispered before sneaking out of the kitchen.

I wouldn't sleep for a long time. When I was sure that Amber was in her room, I got up. My pants were too fucking tight for my hard-on.

In my room, I sank down on my desk chair and pulled out my cock, dropping my head on the backrest. I gripped my dick and started rubbing.

Images of Amber filled my head as I came all over my hand. I cleaned myself up, pulled on boxer shorts, and fell back on my bed with a groan. Jerking off alone in my room wasn't nearly as satisfying as I'd hoped it would be, but I'd just have to get used to it for now until Amber was ready for more. I really hoped that would be the case soon, but I knew I couldn't pressure her. *I wouldn't*.

Screams tore through my sleep. I sat up, blinking into the darkness of my room. What was going on? I tried to shake off the remnants of my tiredness. Another scream sounded. I tensed. It was Amber. I threw off the blankets and leaped out of bed then bolted out of my room and toward hers. Brian opened his door, his hair a mess. I stepped into Amber's room, not caring if Brian disapproved. She was thrashing in her bed, the blankets tangled around her feet. She was only wearing a nightgown, and her bare legs were slick with sweat. I tore my eyes away and walked up to the bed. She was crying, tears trailing over red cheeks. I wasn't sure what to do.

I needed to free her from the horrors of her nightmare, but I didn't want to scare her. Brian was watching me from the doorway. I bet he hoped I'd turn on my heel and tell him I couldn't deal with this. I bet he'd love to see me fail now, when the relationship between Amber and me was still new and would be easy to end. Amber whimpered, her arms flailing against an invisible assailant. Bile rose in my throat at the thought of what she'd been through. I wanted to kill the bastards that had hurt her, wanted to rip them to tiny shreds. I sank down on the edge of the bed and reached for her shoulder. The second my palm brushed her naked skin, she jolted awake, her eyes wide and fearful. She lashed out with a cry, catching my face with her hand. My lip burned, but I fought my instinct to grab her arm to protect myself. I wouldn't restrain her. I'd been hit far worse in fighting matches. Her eyes froze when they found my face. It took a moment for her to recognize me. Then the panic and fight drained out of her. She sat up, breathing heavily. She scanned my face and her eyes grew wide. She touched a fingertip to my lower lip and looked at it. There was blood.

"Did I do that?" she asked in horror.

"It's nothing."

"I'm sorry." She covered her face with her palms.

"It's okay. Everything is okay." I was about to get up when she lowered her hands and looked at me pleadingly. "Can you stay? Just for a little while."

I was shocked by her request. I would have thought that she wouldn't want anyone near her after a nightmare. "Of course," I said.

Brian gave me a warning look. Did he think I'd actually try something after what I witnessed just now? I wasn't that much of an asshole. He slipped out and quietly closed the door. Amber had never even noticed he was there. She moved to the side, so I had more room on the bed. I sat back against the headboard with my legs stretched out in front of me. Amber put her head back on the pillow. Then she linked her hand with mine and closed her eyes.

"I feel safe with you," she murmured.

"You are. I won't let anyone hurt you again." I stroked her head. "I'll protect you."

Slowly, her breathing became even and her face relaxed. She was still clutching my hand, and I was worried I'd wake her if I tried to let go. Pumpkin glowered at me from his spot on the desk chair. I shifted until I was half lying down, extinguished the lights, and closed my eyes. Amber snuggled closer until her head was resting on my arm, and her breath fluttered over my naked chest. Fuck. I should have thought of putting on a shirt before I came into the room. At least I was on top of the covers. I moved the hand Amber was holding, but she only tightened her grip. It felt good to have her at my side, even though I hated the reason for why I was there in the first place.

chapter fourteen

Amber

When I woke the next morning, I was alone in my bed, except for Pumpkin who was sleeping on his usual spot by my feet. I remembered how I'd been saved from my nightmares by Zach, how I'd asked him to stay with me, and how good it had felt to fall asleep with my hand in his. I felt safe. I slept without nightmares after that. When did he leave? I didn't even hear him move. The spot beside me was cold, so it must have happened a while ago. Why did he leave? Maybe being torn from sleep by my pathetic cries finally made him realize just how broken I was. What kind of guy would want a girlfriend that was haunted by nightmares from her past?

I walked into the kitchen, wearing a fluffy bathrobe over my nightgown, to feed Pumpkin and to grab a bite for myself. Zach was sitting at the kitchen table.

"Don't you have classes?" I asked, hovering near the door. Pumpkin tiptoed over to the spot where he was always fed.

Zach glanced up from his cereal bowl and smiled. "Not until later." His lower lip was slightly swollen, and there was a tiny cut that was already scabbing. Embarrassment washed over me as I realized that I had done this to him. No wonder he'd fled my room the moment I'd fallen asleep. Who would want to be close to someone who acted like a lunatic?

"Hey, are you okay?" Zach asked gently, getting up from his chair.

I nodded then gazed up at Zach as he stopped in front of me, not touching my body. Was that because he'd changed his mind about me, about us, or because he still wasn't sure if it would scare me? Everything was still new and tentative. "You weren't there when I woke this morning."

Surprise crossed Zach's face. He reached for my hand and slowly pulled me closer. "You wanted me to stay with you? I didn't want to startle you when you woke."

He was worried about me. "I *asked* you to stay. It's not like you snuck into my bed while I slept." He grinned. I stood on my tiptoes and he leaned down, touching his lips to mine. He winced and pulled back a few inches, licking his lower lip.

"Does it still hurt?"

Zach shook his head. "It's nothing, really. I've had far worse."

I wanted to ask him if he could spend every night in my room. Last night with him by my side I felt safe. I knew he couldn't protect me from my nightmares, nobody could, but somehow his closeness had at least kept the horrors of my past at bay. But the words wouldn't leave my mouth. I couldn't ask him for something like that. It couldn't have been comfortable for him sitting on top of the covers. Was I ready to really share a bed with somebody? I wasn't so sure.

Zach's eyes darted toward the clock on the wall. "I should probably get my ass moving or I'll be late again."

I took a step back. "Again?"

Zach shrugged. "So are you going to meet that girl Olivia again tonight?"

"Yeah."

"I'll drive you." He gave me a quick kiss and rushed off toward his room to get ready for his day.

Ten minutes later, I was sitting alone in the apartment. The silence pressed down on me. I had to find something to do during the day. If I wanted to start college next spring, I'd have to apply in the next few weeks. I wasn't convinced I was ready for a room full of people yet, but applying couldn't hurt. And in the meantime, I needed to find a job. There had to be something I could do. I couldn't hide in the apartment forever. If I really wanted to move on from the past and break free of its hold on me, I had to take control of every part of my life. Having a boyfriend was only a small part of it.

Olivia watched me over her cup of tea. "You seem happy." Her cheeks looked even more hollow than last week, but according to our rules, I wasn't allowed to talk about weight or food. So I didn't.

"I am happy. Being with Zach is something I never thought possible."

She smiled but her eyes were distant. "I'm happy for you."

"Are you okay?"

She set down her cup of tea. "Yeah, sorry. I just remembered how it felt to be in love. Well, at least I was in love. He on the other hand…" She trailed off.

I knew her old boyfriend was another off-limits topic, but she had kind of mentioned it first. "Your ex-boyfriend. What happened?"

"He cheated on me," she said slowly. "We'd been dating for a little over a year when I found out he'd been sleeping around." She gave a helpless shrug. "Maybe it was my fault. Maybe he got sick of my problems. He never got why it was so hard for me to take control over my eating disorder. I guess he wanted a normal girl. Or maybe he couldn't stand to look at my body anymore. Who knows?"

"Sorry, Olivia. You'll find someone better." Worry started to gnaw at me. Olivia's boyfriend had cheated on her because of her issues. What if Zach did the same? I quickly banned the thought from my mind. Zach had promised. We both wanted to give this relationship a chance. He wouldn't do what Olivia's boyfriend had done.

"Now I ruined your evening," Olivia said with a frown. "Are you worried about Zach?"

"Is it that obvious?"

"Well, you mentioned that he's been with many girls before you, and my story wasn't really happy. Just because my boyfriend was an asshole doesn't mean you shouldn't trust yours. From what you told me, Zach seems to adore you, so other girls are probably very far from his mind."

"Maybe, but Zach can't even really touch me."

"Most cheaters cheat even though their girlfriends sleep with them. Men always like to blame their infidelity on their frigid women, but in truth, they are just horny assholes. A cheater cheats no matter what his girlfriend does."

I couldn't help but laugh. "That's a pessimistic way of seeing things."

"Yeah, I'm bitter. You shouldn't listen to me. Let's change the topic. There's a reason why I banned my ex from our conversation. Nothing good ever comes from being reminded of him."

I nodded. "So, the latest episode of *Game of Thrones*. I can't believe—" My ringing phone interrupted me. "Sorry," I said as I pulled it out of my purse. It was Brian. I picked up. "Hi, Brian, what's up?"

"I'm going to pick you up from therapy."

Olivia raised her eyebrows.

"It's not therapy," I reminded him. *My brother*, I mouthed at Olivia. She rolled her eyes, and I grinned. Then Brian's words finally registered. "Zach was supposed to pick me up."

"Yeah, I know. He called me. His dad is in town and wants to meet him, so he asked me to jump in."

"Oh, sure. See you then."

"I'll be there in ten minutes."

Brian hung up.

"Let's go. We need to get there before my brother arrives. He'll freak out if I'm not waiting for him. He constantly worries."

We packed our things and strolled back to the hospital building. Brian's car, an old Corolla, pulled up a couple of minutes later. He got out and jogged toward us, his eyes darting between Olivia and me. It was the first time he met her. Zach had picked me up the last two times. I introduced them. Olivia brushed a strand behind her ear and smiled shyly at my brother. Oh no. I needed to tell her next time I saw her that Brian had a girlfriend.

"How was your talk session?" Brian asked, looking at Olivia.

I rolled my eyes. I knew he wasn't happy that I wasn't in an actual support group, but for now this was better for my goal of pretending to be normal.

"That's my lift," Olivia said with a nod toward her mother's car. "Nice to meet you." She gave Brian another smile then gave me a meaningful look before heading toward her mother.

"She seems nice," Brian said the moment Olivia was out of earshot. "Does her mother know that she's not in therapy and that she's spending her time drinking coffee with you instead?"

"I don't think so. It's Olivia's business. She and I are old enough to make our own decisions," I said. "It helps me to talk with her."

"I don't get it. She didn't even experience the same thing as you did."

"Few people have," I muttered.

Brian grimaced. "I mean, she's not a victim of abuse. She has an eating disorder; that's something entirely different."

"I know. But I feel comfortable with her because she struggles with other demons," I said as I sat down in the passenger seat. "I hope Zach's father doesn't give him trouble." And I hoped Brian would get the hint and stop talking about my meetings with Olivia. I would join a real support group when I felt ready for it.

Brian grimaced. "He usually does. Zach really hates him. Have you talked to him about his parents yet?"

"Once, but he didn't say much."

"He doesn't like to talk about them."

"Maybe I'll try to talk to him when he gets back from meeting his father."

"I doubt he'll be sober enough for that."

"What do you mean?"

"Usually, after a conversation with his father, Zach goes out, gets drunk and picks up a random girl—" Brian snapped his mouth shut. "I shouldn't have said that."

I wrung my hands as I tried to keep my face neutral. "It's okay. I can deal with Zach's past."

"He probably won't go out tonight. He's got you now, after all, so don't worry." Brian sounded doubtful and that didn't help. Was he doing it on purpose, trying to put a wedge between Zach and me?

We didn't speak for the rest of the drive, and when we arrived at our apartment, I disappeared into my room. Zach wasn't home yet.

I kept glancing at the clock the rest of the evening while searching the internet for possible jobs I could apply for. Brian called for me once, asking if I wanted to order Chinese, but I had eaten a slice of carrot cake earlier and was too anxious for Zach to get home so I wasn't hungry.

Close to midnight, when I was already dressed in my nightgown, the front door slammed shut, and I heard Zach's cursing. I put on my bathrobe and peered out of my room. Heavy steps sounded in the living room. I held my breath and listened for the sound of a second pair of shoes, but I could only hear Zach. Immediately, I berated myself for thinking Zach would bring someone home. Brittany had happened before Zach and I started dating. I shouldn't have let Brian's comment get to me.

Zach appeared in the corridor, a tall silhouette in the darkness. His movements were unsteady, and he bumped into the wall. I flicked the switch and the lights came on. Zach shielded his eyes with his hand.

"Fuck. That's too bright." His words were slightly slurred.

He staggered in my direction, and a hint of unease settled in my gut. One of the men who'd broken me had been drunk. I still remembered the smell of alcohol on his breath and coming out of his pores. Shuddering, I shoved the memory out of my head. Zach stopped in front of me, his hand still hiding his eyes from me. I considered turning on my heel and locking myself in my room, but I wasn't afraid of Zach, drunk or sober.

"You're drunk."

Zach dropped his hand, and his gaze focused on me. He stumbled a step forward, and I stiffened, but didn't back away. His eyes grew wide and he shook himself. "Fuck. Sorry, Amber. You shouldn't have to see me like this … fucking wasted. I'm probably scaring the shit out of you."

He walked backward and almost lost his balance. "You don't scare me," I said firmly.

Brian's light came on and spilled out from under his closed door. If he found Zach like this, he'd start another fight. Not that Zach didn't deserve it, but I really didn't want to have another discussion with my brother about my relationship with Zach. I took Zach's arm and quickly ushered him into his room then closed the door.

"Amber?" Brian called.

"I'm fine. I'm with Zach. Go back to bed."

"Zach's home?"

Brian's door creaked and groaned. He was opening it further. Since Zach had pushed Brian into it, the door couldn't be moved without making a sound. "Is he drunk?"

"No, he's fine. Go back to sleep. I just need to talk to Zach."

Eventually I heard the click of Brian's door shutting and turned around. Zach had passed out. He lay sprawled out on his bed, his limbs spread wide, legs dangling over the edge. We definitely wouldn't talk tonight. I crept closer. He was still fully dressed. I bent over his feet and slid off his shoes then straightened and considered my options. I could leave him as he was. It would serve him right. I knelt on the bed beside Zach's upper body and tried to free him from his jacket. It couldn't be comfortable for him to wear it during the night, but he was heavy to move. When I finally managed to pull one arm out of the jacket sleeve, Zach mumbled something in his sleep. I leaned closer but couldn't hear what it was. He shifted suddenly and wrapped one arm around my waist, pulling me closer to him, then he rested his head in my lap. I swallowed a gasp, my body frozen in shock. My heart pounded in my chest as panic tried to take hold of me. This was only Zach and he was doing nothing, just sleeping. He didn't even know what he was doing. There was no danger. Slowly, I relaxed. Zach was fast asleep, his head warm in my lap. What now? I tried to wriggle away, but his grip on my waist kept me in place. I drew in a deep breath. *I was in control of the situation*, I reminded myself. I could wake Zach, and he'd immediately release me and probably be embarrassed. Everything was okay. I lowered my back onto the mattress. Zach let out a sleepy sigh. I stroked his head and watched his relaxed expression. Apparently my lap was very comfortable. The lights were still on, my position was uncomfortable, and Zach smelled like an ashtray, but I closed my eyes and tried to relax. Tomorrow I'd have to ask Zach what happened. He'd been in a club or at a bar, that much was certain. But what else had he done?

zachary

I had the mother of all headaches. This must be what it was like when Dexter used a drill on his victim's head. I groaned as I shifted in bed then froze. That wasn't a pillow under my head. My hand rested on a hip and my head on a stomach. Soft skin pressed against my cheek. Dread shot through me worse than any headache could. Holy fuck. I was with a woman. I'd been dating Amber for what … two days? And already I'd cheated on her. Brian was right. I was a fuckup. I couldn't remember much from last night, except that after meeting my father I'd gone off to a bar with Jason and Bill and got shitfaced. At some point, I must have met someone and taken her home. Amber would be heartbroken. She'd hate me forever, as she should.

Maybe it was for the best that I messed up so soon. That way at least we never got the chance to get emotionally invested. Oh fuck, as if I wasn't already emotionally invested.

But I had to own up to my mistakes and just take the hint the universe was sending me: I wasn't cut out to be in a relationship. Every woman I dated would only end up like my mother: heartbroken, bitter, and an alcoholic.

I had to get away from whomever it was I screwed last night. There really was no easy or polite way to do it. Over the years I'd honed my craft of slipping out undetected, but I'd never woken up snuggling someone before. Fucking great. I took a deep breath and opened my eyes, immediately stunned to find myself in my own room. I raised my head off the soft stomach and stared down at the woman I'd spent the night with. Amber. She was sprawled on my bed, one arm draped over her head, the other beside her body, her hair fanned out around her head like a dark halo. She looked peaceful. How had she gotten here? My eyes traveled the length of her body. Her nightgown had ridden up almost all the way to her ribcage, revealing her long legs, creamy stomach, and her thin white hipster panties. I stifled a groan. The outline of her folds and the curls on her mound were visible through the fabric. All I wanted to do was lean down and kiss her there. I wanted to press my palm against her core and feel its warmth. I wanted to bury myself in her. My cock was already rock hard and straining against my jeans. *Get a fucking grip on yourself, asshole.*

"Zach?" Amber's sleepy voice almost gave me a heart attack, and I ripped my gaze away from her panties and found Amber watching me with obvious embarrassment, her cheeks flushed. Fuck, she'd caught me ogling her in her sleep. I sat up further to give her more space and shifted one of my legs to hide the fucking bulge in my pants. She lowered her arm, wincing. It probably had fallen asleep. She hadn't slept in the most comfortable position. Instead of sitting up, she lay there, searching my face. I wished I could read her mind.

"What happened?" I asked instead.

She finally sat up, pulling her nightgown down and curling her legs under her body. She couldn't meet my eyes. I really wished I could remember what I did last night. I hoped I hadn't dragged her into my room. Since she was still mostly dressed and not crying, I couldn't have forced my touch … or something worse on her.

"I was hoping you could tell me that," she said, peeking up at me through her lashes.

I ran a hand through my hair. "I don't remember much except for getting shitfaced and taking a cab. After that it's pretty much a blur."

"You were very drunk," she said quietly.

"Did I do something? I didn't drag you into my room, did I?"

She smiled. "No. I dragged you inside to hide you from Brian. I didn't want him to see you so drunk. And then you passed out."

"Thanks for staying with me," I said. Silence settled between us, and

I could tell that Amber wanted to ask me something. "I bet the girls in the club wear sexy lace underwear."

I frowned. "I didn't do anything with other girls."

She played with the hem of her nightgown. "I mean the girls you used to … go out with. I bet they didn't have boring *white panties*."

Did she think I'd been staring at her panties because I didn't like them?

She met my gaze, questions swimming in her eyes. "Why do you even want to be with me? Pity?"

I snorted. "Amber, I want to be with you because I like spending time with you and because you turn me on. I was staring at you because you're sexy. I'm fucking hard for you. I don't think I could be any harder if you wore lace or nothing at all."

Her eyes widened then darted toward my crotch, finding proof that I wasn't lying.

Zach, you fucking moron, now she'll flee the room. But she didn't. She slowly raised her head, biting her lower lip. "Oh."

I raised my eyebrows. "Oh?"

She shrugged then made a vague motion toward my erection. "I'm sorry. This must be frustrating for you."

"Don't worry. I'll take a shower and take care of business." I grinned at the sight of her blush deepening. I gave her a quick kiss then swung my legs out of bed and hurried out of the room before I could pounce on Amber and lick every inch of her body.

In the bathroom I realized how much my clothes reeked of cigarette smoke. Amber was a saint for putting up with me. When would she realize I was the lucky one, not her? I almost sighed in relief when I was out my clothes and stepped under the hot shower. My cock twitched when I grabbed it, calling up the image of Amber's white panties, the outline of her folds, and I started jerking off. After I'd come, I leaned against the shower stall and released a harsh breath. I'd never had to go without sex for a long period of time. This was the sweetest form of torture I could imagine. It hadn't even been that long, but it probably felt that way because of the wait that lay ahead. I wondered how long it would take for the skin of my palm to become hard and calloused from jerking off so often. I laughed, then shook myself. Maybe I'd be better at controlling my dick if Amber didn't sleep in my bed, half naked.

amber

My skin flushed when I recalled the bulge in Zach's pants. It was hard to believe that my simple white panties did that to him. Maybe I should have felt scared, but there was only a hint of nervousness mixed with excitement. Even with a drunk Zach at my side, I slept better than I ever could alone. I was bursting with energy and couldn't sit still, so I was glad when Reagan came over after Zach had gone off to class. She was wearing her jogging clothes.

"Why don't you join me?" she asked as she stepped into the apartment.

"Running?" I hadn't exercised in years. I didn't think I would last for more than a few minutes. Back in junior high, I was on the track team. I loved it. I never felt freer than when I was flying over the track, my pulse pounding in my veins, and the sound of my shoes slapping the pavement in my ears.

"Brian mentioned that you used to be on the track team."

I stared off toward the window. "Yeah. The day I was attacked, I was out running a trail in the forest. Usually my best friend went with me, but that morning she didn't feel well and instead of cancelling my run, I went off alone."

Reagan's face twisted with regret. "I'm sorry. I didn't know. I didn't want to bring bad memories back."

My love for running was another thing those men had taken from me. Hatred ignited in me. Sometimes I wished I had a way of hurting them just as they had hurt me. Sometimes I wondered how it would be to kill them. How it would be to hear them begging me, only for me to laugh in their faces. I didn't like that vicious, hateful part of me. Before the attack I wouldn't have been capable of murder. Now I wasn't so sure.

"Let me get changed."

Surprise flashed across Reagan's face as she followed me toward my room, where I put on sweatpants and a T-shirt. I preferred to run in shorts like the ones Reagan was wearing, but I didn't own any and I wasn't sure I was comfortable with showing that much skin yet.

When we stepped outside into the fresh fall air and started stretching, I said, "Go easy on me. I need to learn running again." Just like I needed to learn how live again or how to let people get close to me. As we pounded the pavement at a leisurely pace, I could feel the familiar euphoria of running flowing through my body.

"So how's it going with Zach?" Reagan asked, not even sweating yet while I was already panting. I was so out of shape.

"Good, I think?" I said between gasps of breath. "We shared a bed last night."

Reagan lost her footing and almost stumbled, but then she fell back into a trot beside me. "What?"

"He came home drunk last night and passed out, so I spent the night with him."

"And?"

"It was nice. I love falling asleep beside Zach, and I love waking up next to him even more."

"You've got it bad," Reagan said with a grin.

There was no use denying it. I was falling for Zach scarily fast. I'd been depraved of emotion and physical contact for three years, and now I felt like I needed to make up for it.

"Promise me to be careful."

I threw her a confused look.

"Just don't think that Zach's the only one who can make you feel that way. If things between you two don't work out, there are many other guys out there who'd be lucky to be with you." She stopped and I was glad for it because my heart felt like it was going to jump through my ribcage. We started stretching again. "Kevin is my second boyfriend. When my first love broke up with me, I thought I was going to die. I thought I could never love someone again. But then I met Kevin and we're so much better together than I was with my first boyfriend."

I nodded, but I didn't want to think about Zach and I splitting up. I knew it was a possibility at some point, but right now I needed to believe that the feelings he gave me would last forever.

The next morning Brian told me that he would bring Lauren for dinner. I was glad that he finally decided to introduce her to me. He probably realized that I wasn't bothered by relationships all that much if I could date Zach.

I decided to cook something special and bought everything for my favorite fish curry as well as a mango chutney, cucumber raita, and naan bread. I was chopping and humming when Zach stepped in, holding up the new season of *Game of Thrones* that had released on DVD today. Pumpkin hopped off the chair he'd been napping on and began rubbing his body against Zach's legs. Zach bent down and patted my cat's back.

"That smells delicious," he said, taking a whiff as he walked up to me and pressed a gentle kiss against the crook of my neck. I leaned back against him and tilted my head all the way back until our lips could meet. "I thought we could have a DVD marathon tonight?" He dipped a finger into the mango chutney, and I swatted him away. "Stop. Lauren is coming for dinner. I don't think she'll be happy if she finds out you had your finger in her food."

Zach grimaced. "That girl is never happy unless everyone around her is miserable. I bet my father would love her."

Deciding this was the best chance I had, I asked, "What did your father say yesterday that made you go out and get drunk?"

"He thinks I'm not taking law school and life in general seriously enough. He wants me to get my ass in gear so I can finally join him in the family business. But I'm used to that by now." He shrugged. "What made me want to go out and drink was that his fucking affair arrived at the end of our dinner so he could take her to a hotel and fuck her."

My eyes widened. "Your father openly cheats on your mother?"

"For years. He doesn't even try to hide it. My mother tries to pretend it's not happening and drowns her sorrows in alcohol."

"Like you do." It slipped out before I could stop it. "Sorry."

He shook his head. "No, you're right. Whenever I'm pissed at my father, I end up at a club getting shit-faced." He nodded toward the array of ingredients. "Is there something I can do?"

"Do you know how to debone a fish?"

"Yep. My grandfather used to take me fishing before he died." He unwrapped the fish and set out to work.

"I can't imagine you in fishing gear," I said.

"I look sexy as hell as always."

I laughed then continued chopping the red pepper.

After he was done helping me in the kitchen, Zach went into his room to study. It was the first time I'd actually seen him do it. His talk with his father must have had some type of an effect on him. I used the time to choose a casual dress and put my hair up in a neat ponytail. I wanted to make a good impression on Brian's girlfriend, even if Zach didn't like her and said things between Lauren and my brother wouldn't last. Brian probably thought the same thing about Zach and me.

When I heard the sound of the front door being opened, I was already back in the kitchen and setting the table. I wiped my hands and walked into the living room where my brother stood with a tall girl with straight blond hair and black-rimmed glasses. She was impeccably dressed in black dress pants and a white blouse. She looked like she belonged in law school. Brian was gnawing on his lower lip. He was nervous. He had a hand on her lower back but kept almost an arm's length between them as if he worried seeing them standing so close would upset me.

"This is my sister Amber," he said. "And this is Lauren."

I smiled. "It's nice to finally meet you."

She walked up to me and held out her hand. Brian was about to protest, but I quickly shook her hand, trying not to show that I still wasn't used to physical contact with other people. "Brian has told me a lot about you," she said in an even voice. She let go of me with a polite smile. She seemed like a reserved person. From Zach's description, I was expecting a raging bitch.

"I see the guest of honor has arrived," Zach said from the doorway to the corridor, a smirk on his face. I could hear Pumpkin meowing in protest. I'd locked him in my room, so he wouldn't bother Lauren; Brian had mentioned that she wasn't an animal person.

"Zachary," Lauren said with contempt. "Shouldn't you be studying for M&A? You don't want to fail, do you?"

Zach's lips curled. "Don't worry. I won't." He strode toward me and wrapped an arm around my waist. Lauren turned to Brian and gave him a look I couldn't quite read.

"I made dinner," I said, trying to dissolve the tension. "Fish curry and Indian starters."

"I don't have time to cook, but it's nice that you do."

I wasn't sure if she meant it as an insult or if she was just being insensitive. Zach's hand on my hip tightened.

"Then let's eat," Brian said.

We walked into the kitchen and took our seats around the table. I was still wondering which topic to choose when Lauren began talking about law school. She seemed really enthusiastic, but the more she talked, the more Zach's face darkened.

"I'm working my ass off every day. Not all of us are as lucky as Zach to have a multi-billion dollar business waiting for us to manage. He doesn't have to get good grades."

"Not everyone has the same ambitions," I said diplomatically.

"Some of us don't have any at all."

Zach narrowed his eyes. "Better than having too much ambition. You'd do anything to get ahead."

Two red blotches appeared high on Lauren's cheeks, and her lips thinned. She put her fork down. She'd hardly eaten any of the fish curry. "This was very tasty, Amber. Thank you." She turned to Brian. "I'm tired. Let's go to your room."

Brian glanced at me. "Lauren is going to spend the night."

"You don't need to ask my permission," I said with an embarrassed laugh.

Lauren nodded. "See, that's what I've been telling you for *weeks!*"

Brian and Lauren got up and left the kitchen. I was actually glad and released a sigh. Zach was still glaring at her chair.

"What did you mean when you said she'd do anything to get ahead?" I asked quietly.

Zach grimaced. "You don't want to know."

"Now I really want to know."

Zach lowered his fork and leaned back in his chair. "Before Lauren and Brian started dating, I knew her. We shared several classes, and she knew about my father and the business. She started coming on to me really hard. I quickly figured out it was to score an internship or maybe even a job."

"So you blew her off? Is that why she dislikes you so much?"

Zach avoided my eyes.

"You slept with her," I whispered.

Zach didn't deny it. "It was a long time ago, and I'm not exactly proud of it."

"Does Brian know?"

"No. And I don't want him to. It was before they started dating anyway."

"I won't tell him," I said. "But why don't you tell him? Maybe he'd break up with her. That's what you want, right?"

"Yeah, but it would hurt Brian. He needs to figure out just how much of a bitch Lauren is by himself."

"How many girls have you been with?" I asked as I started clearing the table.

Zach got up to help me. "Many."

"More than you can count?"

"No, but more than I'm willing to admit to you."

I snorted. "That's an answer in itself, you know?"

"I know," he said quietly, pulling me into his arms. I was still amazed that I didn't dissolve into a puddle of panic whenever he did that. I lifted my head and brushed my lips against his. "Past is past," I murmured. Nobody wanted that more than I.

When we were done with the dishes, Zach and I headed for the living room. Then I hesitated.

Zach turned. "Is something wrong?"

"I don't know if this is what you want, but I'd really like to sleep in your bed tonight." The moment the words left my mouth, I was stunned.

Zach froze.

"I mean," I rambled. "I feel safe with you close. But if you don't like to share your bed …"

"No. I want you in my bed." For a moment, we stared at each other.

"Just sleep," I said.

Zach smiled. "Just sleep."

"Go ahead, I'll change and then I'll join you." I flushed but Zach kissed my lips and headed for his room.

As I stood in my bedroom, I suddenly wasn't so sure anymore if it was a clever idea. Sleeping in the same bed with someone was a big deal, but it wasn't as if it would be the first time. Zach and I had spent two nights together in the same bed already, albeit under different circumstances. Instead of a nightgown, I chose my satin pajamas. I didn't want to flash my panties at Zach again, even though he hadn't minded.

On my way to Zach's room, I passed Brian's door and froze when I heard a moan behind it. I quickly moved on, not wanting to hear any more. I really didn't need an image of Brian and Lauren in my head. Zach had left his room open, and I cautiously stepped in. He was kneeling in front of his flat-screen TV attached to the wall across from his bed. He glanced over his shoulder and smiled. "I thought we could watch one or two episodes of *Game of Thrones* before we sleep?"

"Sure." I closed the door, feeling self-conscious. Had Zach heard Lauren's moan? He must be disappointed. While Brian and Lauren had sex with each other, Zach could only look forward to a night sleeping beside me. He straightened, and for the first time I noticed that he was wearing a shirt over his boxer shorts. He'd always slept bare-chested in the time that I'd known him. It was for me. He didn't want to intimidate me.

Before I could lose my nerve, I slipped under the covers, and Zach joined me a moment later. He turned on the TV, and I leaned against his chest, linking my fingers with his. How could something as simple as this feel so right? Zach extinguished the light so that the glow of the screen was the only illumination. As we watched the first episode, I felt myself relax more and more. Zach's warmth and his scent enveloped me in a cocoon of safety. But there was more. The feeling of his muscled chest against my cheek, the feeling of his abs against my arm, made me want to touch him, to slip a hand under his shirt and find out how soft his skin was.

I didn't even pay attention to the second episode. I untangled my fingers from Zach's and ran my hand over his chest until it came to rest on his firm stomach. He tensed under my touch and held his breath. Biting my lip, I inched my hand to the edge of his shirt. Zach might have been carved from stone he'd become so still. I hesitated then gathered my courage. *Take control, Amber.* I eased my hand under Zach's shirt and rested my palm on his abs. He sucked in his breath. His skin was hot against mine, and his muscles quivered against my hand. I peered up into his face. His eyes were focused on me, the TV forgotten.

"Is this okay?" I whispered.

Zach laughed hoarsely. "Yeah. More than okay." He repeated the words I'd said after our first real kiss. "I can't even begin to tell you how much I want to kiss you right now."

"Then do it."

He brought his face down, and I propped myself up on his chest as our lips met. We kissed slowly, and I could feel a sweet pressure building between my legs. I shifted, half embarrassed and half excited, and completely glad that Zach didn't know what kind of an effect a simple kiss had on me. Eventually, I pulled away. Zach kissed my forehead, his grip around me tightening for an instant before he sat up. "I just need to go to the bathroom real quick." I nodded, suddenly tired. Who knew kissing could make you sleepy?

With a half smile, I watched Zach creep out of the room, probably worried about disturbing Brian. I let my head fall down on the pillow and closed my eyes. I wasn't sure how much time had passed before the mattress sank under Zach's weight, and he snuggled up to me from behind, one of his arms slung over my waist.

"Is this okay?" His voice was a deep rumble against my ear.

"Hmm," was all I got out in response before sleep claimed me.

The next morning, I woke with my head on Zach's chest, his arms still wrapped around my body. I could get used to that.

zachary

Over the past few weeks, Amber and I found a routine. We always watched a bit of TV, then we kissed until I had to pretend I had to go to the bathroom to take a leak while really I needed to jerk off because I was close to bursting, and then after I'd come in my own fucking hands, I would return to Amber and hold her in my arms until we fell asleep. I loved hearing her rhythmic breathing beside me and seeing how her face lit up with a smile every morning when she saw me. But fuck, having Amber's body pressed against mine was torture. Even jerking off didn't stop my balls from feeling like they were under constant pressure. Sometimes I caught myself wondering if it would be better for our relationship if I picked up a random girl to fuck to release some of the tension. Amber would never have to find out, and I could keep being patient for her. But as soon as I thought, it I felt like the biggest asshole in the world. I couldn't do that to Amber. I'd be no better than my father if I did. But it was getting increasingly difficult to hide my boner from Amber every morning. One day I'd actually come in my fucking pants with her lying beside me.

"You look as if you're tasting something foul," Kevin said as he slid into the chair across from mine. We sometimes met for coffee between classes. I could only imagine what he'd say to my thoughts of cheating on Amber.

"Is this all because you're not getting any?" he asked as he settled in with his pumpkin spice latte. I wasn't sure how he could drink the sweet stuff.

I made a noncommittal sound.

"Stop acting like a pussy."

"Says the man who drinks skinny milk like an anorexic girl."

"That's not very PC of you."

I rolled my eyes. "Once I'm joining my father in the company, political correctness is all people will ever get from me on the outside. Might as well enjoy my numbered days of having a foul mouth for as long as they last and before I become a backstabbing corporate lawyer and manager."

"Then don't join the company and do what you want."

"That would go over well with my father."

"So what?"

"I like my life. I like not having to worry about money. If I became a human rights lawyer, my father would disown me."

"Zach, you told me yourself that you've invested a lot of the money your grandfather gave you when he was alive and that it's going well. You could live on that money easily."

I probably could. But I'd been living by the rules of my father all my life. Money had never been an issue because of that. And my father would probably make my mother even more miserable just to punish me, though I wasn't sure how that was even possible. Maybe he'd divorce her out of spite. She'd actually despair if the asshole left her. Love always meant trouble. "I don't want to talk about it."

"Then let's talk about you and Amber." I wasn't sure I wanted to talk to him about that either. "Have you tried talking to her?"

"I can hardly tell her that I'm an asshole who spends every waking moment fantasizing about getting her naked."

"Maybe she'll surprise you."

Or maybe she'd run away screaming. I couldn't risk that. Sometimes I wondered if I was on the verge of breaking my rule about never loving a woman.

Amber was lying on my arm, her firm butt pressed against my erection. The friction was almost enough to blow my load right there. I tried to remove my arm from under her head, but it didn't work. She made a small sound and shifted her butt. I groaned. I wanted nothing more than to slide up her nightgown and move her panties aside and bury myself in her. She felt so hot against my cock. I could only imagine how much hotter her core would feel wrapped around me. I closed my eyes and nuzzled her neck, drawing in a deep calming breath. Her hair smelled like the vanilla shampoo she always used. I started to relax when Amber began to wake. The way I was spooning her, there was no way I could hide my erection, especially if I didn't shove her off me.

amber

The sun's rays tickled my face. I blinked away the sleepiness. Zach's chest was pressed against my back, one of his long legs between mine. I was wrapped in his arms. As I shifted, I noticed an insistent pressure against my butt, and my eyes opened wide. I waited for the panic to set in, but it never came. Instead there was only curiosity and embarrassment. I tried to wriggle away to spare Zach the mortification once he woke, but when he groaned, I realized it was too late. I gasped and couldn't help it. Zach stiffened and quickly rolled away, leaving me cold.

"Fuck," he mumbled. The mattress shifted as he sat up. "Sorry." He sounded angry. "I didn't want you to wake like that."

Did he think he had scared me? I turned around, grasping his arm to stop him from getting out of bed. His expression was pained. "Don't go."

"I really need to deal with this," he said, gesturing to his lower region.

Heat surged into my face. How often had he been taking care of things himself in the last few weeks? He swung his legs out of bed and stood. My eyes were drawn to the bulge in his pants. A mix of anxiety and curiosity filled me. It was stupid to be anxious at all. I had no reason to be afraid of Zach, much less of what was in his pants. Zach would never hurt me. I was in control of my fear, my wants, my life. That had become my mantra. I had to claim my life back.

"I'll be back soon," Zach promised before he left the room.

I turned onto my back and stared up at the ceiling. Zach and I had been dating for four weeks. All we'd done was kiss. After my brief moment of courage, when I touched Zach's stomach that first night we watched TV in his bed, I hadn't even seen his stomach since. He always wore a shirt in bed. Sometimes he caressed my cheek or put a hand on my hip, but he never attempted anything else. He was waiting for a sign from me. I wished I knew how far was too far for me at this point.

The door swung open, and Zach came back in. I couldn't help but blush at the thought of what he'd done in the bathroom. He perched on the edge of the bed and reached out to brush my hair away from my forehead. "Do you want to get up?"

I shook my head. It was Saturday, so we could stay in bed. Zach slipped back under the covers, but I sat up. Zach's brows drew together in confusion. My pulse was pounding in my veins as I reached for my long sleeved pajama top and pulled it over my head. I was still wearing a very thin spaghetti top underneath, and I knew Zach had seen me like that before when he woke me from my nightmare weeks ago, but this was more. I lay back, feeling Zach's intent gaze on me.

"Can you remove your shirt?" I asked in a whisper.

Zach sat up at once and slid his shirt over his head. I touched the tattoo on his shoulder blade. It was bigger than my hand, an intricate design of intertwined lines.

"It's a tribal tattoo," Zach said before I could ask. "It was a spur of the moment kind of thing. I loved the design."

"It's beautiful." I traced the edges. "Maybe one day I'll get a tattoo too."

Zach lay down beside me, a curious look on his face. "Really?"

"Yeah. I once saw one I really liked. It was a quote 'Sometimes you've gotta fall before you fly' with birds fluttering away from the words."

Zach cupped my cheek and kissed me. "Where?" he whispered against my lips. Drawing up my courage, I lifted my shirt up to my ribcage and motioned along my side. "The birds are supposed to fly over my scar." I couldn't meet Zach's gaze.

The scar below my ribs on the upper left side of my stomach was ugly. It was almost as long as my hand. Over the years it had paled, but it was impossible to miss. I knew Zach was looking at it. How could he not?

He reached out and put his hand over my scar. "Is this okay?"

I nodded, not able to speak. "It's ugly. I know."

"No, Amber," Zach said fiercely. "No part of you could ever be ugly." He leaned down very slowly, eyes on me as he placed a kiss on the scar. Goose bumps erupted all over my skin. I shivered at the feel of his mouth.

"Does it still hurt?"

"No. It'll always be a reminder of that day. Whenever I see or feel it, I'm forced to remember." My voice broke. Zach's eyes flashed with emotion. I could see that he wanted to ask what had happened. "They beat and kicked me when they were done with me. And when I passed out from the pain, they tried to strangle me. They thought I was dead, so they left me. My spleen was ruptured and several ribs were broken as well bones in almost every part of my body. They had to remove my spleen. That's why I have the scar."

It was strange hearing myself say the words. They sounded detached, as if I was talking about something that had happened to someone else. Zach's jaw twitched, and he closed his eyes for a moment before he opened them again. He touched his forehead to mine.

"I wish I could turn back time and kill those men before they got you. I would make them suffer. I wished there was a way to take away the memories."

Tears filled my eyes as I stared at Zach. "Every day with you makes it better, Zach. I never thought I could have what you've given me. Those men said nobody would ever want me after what they did so they were being merciful by killing me. For a long time I believed them."

He swallowed hard. "Everything they said was a lie. I want you, Amber, scars and all." He grasped my left arm and turned it over revealing the long scar from my second suicide attempt. He rubbed his thumb over it with a strange expression on his face. "I'm so glad your father found you in time."

"He almost didn't. I put a lot of research into my second try. When I woke in the hospital, I was so angry at my father because he'd saved me. I hated him because he couldn't let me go, because he loved me too much." I choked out a laugh.

"Have you ever thought about trying again since then?" Zach was still running his fingers over the soft skin of my forearm. I considered lying, but his eyes compelled me to say the truth. "Almost every day." Zach's grip tightened. "But I won't. It's more like a light at the end of a tunnel for me when the darkness of living gets too much."

Zach pressed his face into the crook of my neck. "God, Amber. Promise me you won't ever try it again."

"I won't try again." I knew it was something I couldn't promise. Could anybody ever promise something like that? I'd learned to live with the horrors of my past, but I couldn't tell what the future would bring.

I curled my fingers around Zach's neck and brought his face up to mine for a kiss. My tongue traced over his lips, and slowly our kiss morphed into something that sent tingles through my body. I pressed my palms against Zach's chest as we kissed before taking one of Zach's hands and putting it over my ribcage. I pulled away to speak.

"It's okay if you touch me," I said quietly.

"Do you *want* me to touch you? That's what really matters."

"Yes, I want you to touch me." My cheeks flamed, but I returned Zach's heated gaze. "Where?" I bit my lip and lowered my eyes. "Everywhere above my waistband."

For a moment, nothing happened, and I risked a peek up at him. Zach scanned my face as if he was trying to see if I was serious. "You tell me if you don't like something I do, okay? And if something scares you, you say stop at once. No trying to bear anything on your own just for me. I want you to enjoy this. Promise me."

"I promise." Zach kissed me again, his tongue making every nerve in my body snap to attention. His hand on my ribcage inched upward until his fingertips grazed the underside of my breast. He traced his fingers along the crease toward my side then up to my armpit and up to my shoulder. His touch was feather-soft and made my body buzz with a pleasant ache. It felt so good, and he wasn't even doing all that much. His eyes bored into me as he stroked his thumb over my collarbone then slowly he moved lower, over the swell of my breast. Although his finger was so close, he didn't touch my nipple. Instead he drew slow circles around it. I gasped against his mouth at the sensation his teasing sent through my body. Something warm pooled between my legs, and I squirmed in surprise. Zach's eyes darted toward my thighs as if he knew exactly what his touch did to me. A grin curled his lips when his gaze returned to me. My nipples were hard and straining against the soft material of my top. I wanted Zach to finally touch me there. I made an impatient sound.

"What do you want?" Zach murmured against the skin below my ear, softly kissing the spot.

"More," was really all I could articulate.

zachary

"More."

Fuck, how I wanted to give her more. I wanted to dip my fingers into the wet heat between her legs. The way she pressed her legs together, I knew she was aroused. But seeing Amber's scars, hearing a bit more of what happened, made me realize that I had to push my wants to the backburner. Amber had been through too much for me to be a selfish dick and pressure her into something she wasn't ready for. I wouldn't mess things up between us.

I licked her throat slowly, feeling her pulse against my tongue. She moaned and it was the most beautiful sound in the world. I wasn't even sure she realized she'd made it. I propped myself up and brought my hands up, cupping her breasts. I massaged them gently watching Amber's face. Her eyes were half closed, her lips parted. I captured her nipples between my thumb and forefinger, eliciting a whimper from her, then I slowly rubbed them back and forth. She arched her back slightly and squeezed her legs even tighter together.

"Do you like that?" I definitely did. My cock was already rock hard in my pants.

Amber gave a small nod, her lips pressed together. I kissed her softly, my fingers keeping up their teasing. It felt so good to kiss her, to give her pleasure. I trailed kisses down her chin and collarbone. When my lips brushed the swell of her breasts, I paused. Amber's body was taut with anticipation.

"Yes," she whispered before I could even ask. I smiled against her skin as I nudged the edge of her top down with my nose. Then I licked the skin I'd exposed. Amber shifted her hips, and I gently pressed my palm against her stomach, rubbing it with my thumb. As aroused as Amber was, I knew she'd feel it all the way in her core. I wanted to give her body what it wanted. Fuck. Amber was so fucking responsive. I pushed her top down until one nipple sprang free. What a sight.

I closed my lips around it and began sucking gently. She tasted so sweet, and I closed my eyes, relishing in the feel of her hard little nub in my mouth. Amber gasped and moaned and lifted her hips off the mattress in small, desperate thrusts.

Releasing Amber's nipple, I kissed her parted lips. Her eyes were hooded with pleasure, but I couldn't give her what she longed for if I didn't touch her pussy.

"Do you want me to touch you between your legs?" Hesitation filled Amber's face, and I shook my head. "I won't. How about you touch yourself…" I kissed her earlobe "…while I tell you what to do?"

Amber's eyes widened.

"I know you ache. Let me help you."

Amber nodded. I wrapped an arm around her shoulders and pulled her against me, my lips grazing her ear. I slipped my other hand under her shirt and started twisting her nipple softly.

"Put your hand into your pajamas," I said in a hoarse voice. I was so turned on, if I wasn't careful I'd come in my pants. Amber slid her hand below her waistband, and I had to bite back a groan. Fuck. Fuck. Fuck. "Are you touching yourself?" She gave a small nod, her eyes squeezing shut. It was so fucking sexy when she was embarrassed by her own arousal. "Are you wet?" Another nod, her cheeks flushing red. "Good. Run two fingers up and down between your folds, slowly." She made a small sound of pleasure, and I gave her nipple a firmer tug. Her hips buckled. "Coat your clit with your wetness, and now rub your fingers over it."

She shuddered in my arms, and I bowed my head over her breast and sucked her nipple into my mouth while my fingers teased the other. I kept watching her. I could see her hand moving in her pajamas, and I imagined how it would be if my fingers were there. Amber's movements became faster, her shudders more violent, and her hips bucked over and over again. I sucked harder on her nipple and grazed the other with my fingernail. Amber jerked and let out a long moan, her entire body seizing. I glanced up at her face. It was fucking beautiful. I wanted to make her come every day. I wanted to give her so much pleasure that there was no more room for darkness in her thoughts. She pulled her hand out of her pants, and before I even thought about it, I brought it up to my lips. I licked her fingers clean. Amber gasped, eyes wide as she watched me. I circled her finger with my tongue, tasting her. My cock twitched so hard a simple touch would have been enough to make me come.

"I can't wait to really taste you," I said in a rough voice. I knew some guys didn't like to go down on a girl, but I loved it. There was no better way to give a woman pleasure. Amber buried her face against my chest. "I can't believe what just happened. It felt so good."

I kissed the top of her head. "It'll get only better from here."

Amber became still.

"Is—" The rest of my question was lost in a groan.

Amber's hand rested lightly over my cock. There was still the fabric of my boxers between us, but fuck I was so horny it didn't even matter. I put my hand over hers and gave myself a few hard squeezes with her hand, and then I fucking came in my boxers like a horny teenage boy. I jerked my hand back, releasing Amber's, feeling horrible.

"Fuck, sorry. I didn't want to force you to do that."

She shook her head and kissed me. "I touched you. I wanted to give back."

I closed my eyes. "Please don't think I always come that quickly. I'm usually more controlled." She laughed and put her head down on my chest. My boxers stuck to my skin. I really needed to clean myself, but I couldn't bring myself to leave Amber yet.

amber

The next morning I woke with Zach's arm around my waist, and again I could feel his erection digging into my lower back. I couldn't believe what had happened yesterday morning. I'd never felt anything like it before.

"I'm going to take a shower," Zach said in a strained voice, sitting up. He probably didn't want to come in his boxers again. I flushed with the memory. He pressed a quick kiss against my forehead then left the room and closed the door behind him. Before I could change my mind, I hopped out of bed and followed him. I hesitated in the corridor. The bathroom door was closed and the shower was running. I sucked in a deep breath and slipped in before quietly closing the door. Zach stood under the streaming water, head tilted back and eyes closed. I was glad he didn't watch me because my face slipped into an expression of shock when I saw him completely naked. Images from long ago nibbled at my mind, but I pushed them back. This was nothing like the past. I walked closer, my eyes never leaving Zach. He was gorgeous. Rivulets of water traveled over the ridges of his hard body, his muscled chest, his abs, his narrow hips. It didn't surprise me that girls wanted him. He curled his hand around himself and slowly began stroking up and down. He was big, bigger than … No. That was the past.

I took another hesitant step closer, and Zach's eyes opened, his gaze meeting mine. "Shit, Amber!" He jerked upright, hitting his head against the shower, and released his erection. I drew my eyes back up to his face. Shock was plainly written all over Zach's face. He didn't try to cover himself up. "What are you doing here?"

My cheeks were flushed, and I fumbled for an answer. "I was curious."

Zach relaxed slightly and his expression shifted. "Curious?"

"I wanted to watch you."

Zach's cock twitched in response. He groaned then shook his head. "I think I hit my head too hard, because I could swear you just said you want to watch me jerk off."

I walked closer until I was directly in front of the glass stall. Nerves twisted my stomach so tightly I was worried I'd throw up. *Calm down, Amber. This was your idea. Now go through with it.* It was stupid that a completely naked Zach made me anxious. Zach was watching me intently.

"Amber? I need you to be very clear about what you want," his voice was a hoarse plea.

What did I want? My eyes traveled the length of his body. I wanted to run my hands over his skin. "Can I watch you touch yourself?"

Zach stared. Then he snapped out of it. He wrapped his palm around his length. "You mean like that?"

I nodded then opened the shower door. Water sprayed my face. I didn't care. I stepped inside still wearing my pajama pants and top. I needed that barrier, even though it wasn't really a protection from anything.

"Amber?" Zach asked.

He leaned back against the tiled wall. The water was soaking my clothes, plastering the fabric to my skin. The pajama pants and the top were both white, so they probably didn't leave much to the imagination. I should take them off. It would be so easy, but I couldn't bring myself to do it. Cold air flooded the stall, and I closed the door. Zach stood across from me, only an arm's length away, his hand curled around his shaft.

He slid his hand up and down then stopped. "Do you want me to move?"

I nodded, biting my lip. He began stroking himself again, eyes burning into me with a hunger that made heat gather in the pit of my stomach. I pressed my legs together and tried to tense the muscles of my core to alleviate some of the tension. It was almost painful. I needed some relief, but I didn't know what to do. I couldn't touch myself, not like this. Why not? In bed with Zach's arm around me, it hadn't felt strange. And he was touching himself too. Zach was panting, his strokes becoming faster, his knuckles turning white from the iron grip on his length. I wondered how it would be if I was the one doing that to him. I could feel myself getting wet between my legs. He let out a long groan, hand curling around the tip of his length as he came. I sucked in a deep breath, waiting for a flicker of fear, but there was none. Only fascination and desire. I wanted to touch Zach. I wanted him to touch me. He would make me feel good. I knew it. Zach stared at me, still clutching himself as the water washed away the signs of his orgasm. He looked as if he was expecting me to freak out any moment. It was almost comical. I burst out laughing. It felt as if I'd ripped down another one of my walls, and it felt incredible.

Relief washed over Zach's face and he chuckled. "That was..."

"Weird?"

He shook his head. "Hot. At least for me."

Suddenly, I felt daring. Maybe it was because Zach's penis was softening, and he wasn't posing an immediate threat, which was a stupid thing to think but my brain was messed up so its logic wasn't exactly reasonable.

"I want to get out of my clothes," I whispered.

Zach stopped washing himself. "Okay?"

I couldn't look him in the eyes when I said, "No touching." God, could I sound any more pathetic? Why was Zach putting up with me?

"No touching," Zach said quietly. He put his hands behind his back, trapping them between the wall and his butt.

I gripped the hem of my top then paused.

"Amber, you don't have to do anything you're not comfortable with. But I swear to you I won't ever touch you if you don't ask me to."

"I know," I said. "But what if you don't like what you see?"

"Your clothes aren't hiding all that much, and I saw almost all of you yesterday. And believe me, you are fucking beautiful."

My fingers on the hem tightened, and I quickly pulled it over my head, my arms dropping to my side. The top landed in a wet heap on the ground and was quickly joined by my pajama pants as I slid them down my legs. Then I hooked my fingers under my panties and pulled them down as well. I had to force myself to stand still and not cover myself. Zach's eyes roamed my body. Then they settled on my face. I tried not to notice that he was getting hard again. He was turned on by me, by my body. The knowledge excited and frightened me at the same time. The warm water rained down over us as our eyes locked. *I was in control*, I reminded myself again. I took a step closer to Zach, who still leaned motionless against the wall. His eyes followed my movements as I reached out and lay my palms flat against his naked chest. He was almost completely hard again, and if I moved any closer his erection would brush against my stomach. For a moment I was overwhelmed by the situation, by the realization that I was naked in a shower with a man. Not any man ... this was Zach. I trusted him more than I thought I could ever trust a man again. I inched my hands lower, coming to rest on his lower abdomen. For a moment, I considered wrapping my hand around his length, but then I lost the courage. The pressure between my legs hadn't lessened, and I shifted again.

Realization flashed across Zach's face. "What do you want, honey?"

It was the first time he'd used that term, and it made me feel warm in an entirely different way. "I don't know," I admitted. I almost wished Zach would take lead and touch me. He didn't.

"Did it turn you on to watch me come?"

"Yes." The word was a breathless whisper.

Zach brought his face closer without moving his body. He gently kissed my lips. "Do you want to come too?" he asked in a husky voice, and my face exploded with embarrassment. Zach could be direct about these matters without ever blushing. It must have come with experience. I gave the tiniest nod.

Zach shook his head. "That's not enough," he said quietly. "I need you to tell me or I won't move."

I searched his eyes, but his gaze was unrelenting. He wouldn't touch me without my verbal agreement. "Yes, I want to come," I finally got out. "I want you to touch me this time."

Zach's chest heaved. "Let's go back to my room, okay?"

"Okay." Zach turned off the shower and stepped out, handing me a towel before he took one for himself and began drying himself. I had to bite back a smile when I watched him rub his length. How would he hide it on our way to his room? He wrapped a towel around his hips but that didn't really hide anything. When I'd covered myself with my towel, I followed Zach back to our room.

I felt nervous, but the tension between my legs spoke louder than my worry. Filled with uncertainty, I stood in the room, waiting.

Zach put his hand on my shoulders. "Tell me if you changed your mind."

I shook my head. I walked over to the bed and sank down on it, a towel still around me. Zach crouched in front of me. He cupped my face in his hands. "I want to make you feel good." He leaned forward then whispered against my mouth, "Let me lick you. I want to kiss every inch of your body."

My lips parted in surprise. The thought of Zach's mouth between my legs sent a thrill through me. That wasn't something that could remind me of what happened. I loved when Zach kissed me. How much better would it feel if he kissed me down there? "Okay," I said.

"Scoot up," Zach rasped. I did and watched him wide-eyed as he settled on the bed beside me. He hooked one finger under my towel then looked at me. "Can I take it off?"

I nodded then remembered Zach's rule and said, "Yes."

Zach opened my towel, and I lifted my butt and back from the bed so he could slide it out from underneath me. "I'm going to tell you before I kiss or touch you somewhere, and you say 'yes.' If you don't, I'll stop, okay?"

"Okay."

"Okay," Zach breathed, eyes intense as they roamed over my naked body.

zachary

My eyes took in every inch of Amber's beautiful body. I couldn't believe she'd watched me jerking off. The memory of the look on her face when I stroked myself was enough to make me hard again.

But my boner didn't matter right now. As Amber lay before me, naked, with trust in her eyes, all I cared about was showing her what pleasure meant. I wanted to prove to her that yesterday had been nothing. I leaned over her breasts then looked up into her eyes. She closed them quickly, her cheeks turning red. "I'm going to kiss and lick your breasts now," I murmured, my lips an inch from her nipple. I had done it yesterday, but I could tell that Amber was more nervous today because she was naked and vulnerable. And with only a towel around my hips, I wasn't exactly dressed either.

"Okay," she said in the barest of whispers, her muscles taut. I darted my tongue over her nipple, and her body jerked. I cupped my lips around her hardened nub, circled it with my tongue, first slow then faster. Her lips parted, eyes squeezed shut, but she didn't make a sound. I'd lick her and kiss her and suck her until I got another moan from her. I loved her taste, the feel of her warm skin against my lips, the pressure of her hard nipple against my tongue. I pulled back a few inches and blew on her wet skin. Her skin rippled with goose bumps, and I allowed myself a few seconds to admire her breasts and pink nipples. Then I took one nub back into my mouth and sucked very lightly then a bit harder. Amber squirmed, her lips pressed together. I wanted to get her slick with arousal before I tasted her. I darted my eyes down to her pussy. She was clamping her thighs together. I knew I'd find her already wet if I slipped my hand between her legs. My cock twitched in response. Fuck. I wanted to touch every inch of her. I let her nipple glide out of my mouth slowly and trailed my tongue around her breast then sucked at the skin over her ribs. Amber let out a small laugh. "That tickles."

I grinned and dusted my fingertips over her ribs teasingly. She buckled, giggling. "Zach!" I moved my mouth a few inches lower and kissed her waist, her hipbone, the soft skin of her belly. She became still under my ministrations, and I risked a glance up at her. She was biting her lip as she watched me. Then she looked away.

"I want to kiss you between your legs." *I want to eat your pussy* would probably have been a bit too direct for Amber.

"Okay," she murmured. "But no fingers," she added in obvious embarrassment. I paused my kissing and licking of her hipbone and searched her face. "You mean no touching, or you don't want me to put a finger in you?"

Her blush had spread over her breasts by now, but I needed for her to say what she wanted. With other women I'd always known what to do, and they'd mostly been quite vocal about their needs anyway, but with Amber I wouldn't take the risk of pushing past her comfort zone.

She buried her face in her palms. "God, this is so embarrassing." She took a deep breath. "The second." The thought of why she was so scared of having anything pushed into her turned my stomach, and I could feel my dick softening.

"I won't put my finger in you, I promise, but I really want to touch you, okay?" I also really wanted to slip a finger into her core to show her that it could feel really good, but I wouldn't do it, not before she asked me to.

She lowered her hands and met my eyes briefly before settling back against the pillow. "Okay."

I brought one hand up to her hipbone then slid it over her stomach down to the edge of her soft brown hairs. She tensed and I paused with my fingers, just brushing her mound. When she relaxed, I cupped her with my palm. She was so fucking hot and wet. My middle finger rested against her clit, and I pressed lightly. A small noise escaped Amber. I slowly pushed her legs apart, revealing her glistening pink folds. I groaned and pressed another kiss against her hipbone. God, I wanted to lick her, but this wasn't about me. I caressed her outer folds with my fingers then slid one finger up to her clit and drew small circles around it. She was so slick my finger glided easily over her small nub. She moaned then tensed.

"I love your moans. Don't hold them back. Just relax and let me make you come."

She did, and as my finger circled her clit faster, her moans and gasps came faster as well. She was close. I quickly sucked one nipple into my mouth and gave her clit a flick with my thumb, and she arched her back, her muscles trembling as she came under my hand. I lavished her breast, and my finger on her clit slowed its ministrations to a soft caress. She would be over sensitive right now, so I had to start my licking very slowly to bring her toward her second orgasm. "Now I'm going to lick you," I warned her.

She watched me through hooded eyes as I lay down between her legs, spreading her wider. Her pussy was dripping, and I pressed a kiss to her folds just as gentle as I would to her pink mouth. Soft and slow, my tongue slid out and along her slick folds. Then I trapped one between my lips to suckle lightly and was rewarded with a soft moan from Amber. Nothing was more satisfying for me than knowing I was giving Amber pleasure with my mouth. I wasn't cocky but I knew I was good at eating pussy. That was the one good thing about being a man-whore. I kissed her folds then her clit. She gasped. I parted my lips and nudged her with the tip of my tongue.

"Zach." Her voice was breathless.

I reached down and grasped my cock under the towel and started stroking myself as I circled her nub with my tongue very slowly.

"Mmm," I hummed and Amber got wetter.

I took her clit into my mouth and gently sucked on it while flicking my tongue over it then slowly around it. She put her hand on my head, raking her fingers through my hair. I didn't think she realized it, and that was the best thing. I couldn't help a satisfied grin as she nudged her pelvis up again in encouragement. She was so wet. I knew my finger would have slid in easily, and maybe even my cock. God, how I wanted to feel her juices around my cock right now. Instead, I circled her opening with the tip of my tongue before dipping it inside. Amber gasped, and I waited to see if she felt uncomfortable, but her legs opened a bit wider to give me better access. Satisfaction swelled in my chest. I slowly slid my tongue in and out of her opening and stroked her clit with my thumb as I rubbed myself in rhythm with my tongue's thrusts. Amber was close. She squirmed and gasped and whimpered. I quickly cupped my mouth over her folds and clit and sucked. She cried out and shook under me. Closing my eyes, I relished in the feel of her pussy on my face. I squeezed my cock hard, pressing my lips together as I came on my leg. I rested my cheek on her inner thigh for a few more moments, enjoying the feel of her heated skin. Eventually I sat up and cleaned myself with the towel before lying down beside Amber. She snuggled up to me.

"I think we'll need another shower," I said teasingly. She laughed.

Her laughs, her moans, her smiles … There were so many things I couldn't get enough of.

chapter fifteen
Amber

When Zach and I stepped into the kitchen, Brian was seated at the table with his laptop in front of him. Pumpkin perched on the windowsill, giving me the cold shoulder. He was probably annoyed that he always had to sleep alone in my room because I spent my nights with Zach.

"I fed Pumpkin. I wasn't sure if you'd ever emerge from Zach's room." Brian scanned my face, and I couldn't meet his gaze after what Zach had done to me this morning. My skin still tingled. Had Brian heard something? Did he know? This was too embarrassing. I hid my face behind the fridge door, but when I emerged with a yogurt, Brian was still glancing between Zach and me.

"Are you going home for Thanksgiving?"

Was that why he'd been staring? I hadn't even thought about

Thanksgiving, but it was only two weeks away.

"Of course," I said. I couldn't believe that I hadn't seen Dad in so long. Brian's eyes darted to Zach, who was busy spreading Nutella on a slice of bread. "I'll call Dad."

Brian nodded. "I need to leave or I'll be late for my lunch date with Lauren."

Zach made a face behind Brian's back. I managed to keep my face neutral, but when Brian had left the kitchen, I jabbed a finger against Zach's chest. "You're impossible."

Zach took a bite of his Nutella bread and shrugged. I wrapped my arms around his waist, and he lightly stroked my back. "Do you celebrate Thanksgiving with your parents?"

He snorted. "They celebrate Thanksgiving at their country club. They don't expect me to come home."

"So what do you usually do?"

"The last few years I went out partying with the guys."

"Oh, of course," I said. "Do you want to go partying this year too?"

"I'd rather spend the day in bed with you." He kissed my throat, lighting off small fireworks down my spine.

"Why don't you come home with me and Brian and celebrate with my family? I'd love to officially introduce you to my father as my boyfriend." Or was that too fast for Zach? When did people usually introduce their boyfriend to their parents? I really wished Mom was still here to meet Zach as well.

"I've met your father before," Zach joked. Then he sobered. He actually looked hesitant. "Are you sure?"

"I am. I really want you to come."

"Okay," he said slowly. "But won't your dad mind?"

"I think he'll be happy for me."

"I wouldn't be so sure about that. Look at Brian. I don't see happy when I look at his face."

"Brian is happy for me … for us."

Zach looked doubtful, but he nodded. "Family Thanksgiving it is, then."

I grinned. "I'll call my dad and tell him." I pressed a quick kiss against Zach's lips before I hurried into my room to grab my phone.

As always when I called Dad, he answered on the second ring. "Amber?" And as usual worry filled his voice. I hated that his first reaction to a call from me was concern that something might have happened to me.

"Hi, Dad," I said.

"Are you alright?"

"Yes, I'm fine." I could hear him release a breath. "I wanted to talk to you about Thanksgiving."

"You're coming home?"

"Yes, and I want to bring Zach."

There was a pause on the other end. "Are you still dating?"

"Don't tell me Brian isn't giving you daily updates."

Dad coughed. "Well, it occasionally comes up in our conversation."

"It's probably the only thing you talk about."

"Not the only thing," Dad said. "We're both just worried about you. And to be honest, it's difficult for me to imagine. You've changed so much since I last saw you, I can already tell from just talking to you on the phone."

"Zach helps me. Living here helps me. So is it okay if I bring him?"

"Sure. I want a word with him anyway."

"Oh no, Dad. Brian's made Zach's life hell for dating me. Promise you won't do the same."

"I can't promise that. But I'll do my best not to embarrass you." I could hear a smile in his voice. God, I couldn't remember the last time Dad sounded so much like the old-Dad from *before*. I wasn't the only one who'd been changed by the incident. Brian's and Dad's lives had been turned upside down as well. "Will Aunt Lynn and Uncle Barry come as well?"

"Actually, we'll celebrate at their house because you won't be here to cook. Lynn is going to make dinner for us this year."

"Oh, right. I didn't even think about it." The past few years I'd prepared our Thanksgiving meals. Cooking had been pretty much the only thing that had given me some sliver of joy, but of course I wouldn't be able to do it this year unless I arrived a few days early prepare. I couldn't expect Zach to stay with my dad for that long. What if they didn't get along?

"I miss you, sweetheart. I'm counting the days until Thanksgiving."

"I miss you too, Dad."

After we hung up, I smiled. I wanted Dad to see how far I'd come. He always wanted a normal life for me, and I was getting closer to that goal every day.

"You look happy," Zach said, leaning in the doorway to the kitchen.

"I am happy." He advanced on me then leaned close. "Maybe we can schedule a repeat performance of this morning?"

I blushed, but my body responded with a flood of tingling between my legs. I peered at the clock. "I'm meeting Reagan for a run in thirty minutes."

Zach pouted playfully. I laughed. "Maybe later then?" he said in a low voice that made my legs go weak.

"Later," I promised.

I couldn't stop thinking about this morning even as Reagan and I jogged through the neighborhood. I would have never thought something could feel this good. Zach's mouth and tongue had made me forget everything. There had been no room for horrible memories. I couldn't believe I was even capable of being this aroused. The word alone seemed wrong before. Now I couldn't wait to let Zach do it again. I knew this didn't mean the past wouldn't come crashing back down on me again. It always did and always would. After what I had gone through, it couldn't be any other way, but it was slowly pushed to the back of my mind.

"I don't know what's going on, but you're positively glowing," Reagan said as we paused to catch our breath. "I guess it has something to do with Zach."

A blush crept up to my cheeks. "Yeah." I avoided her gaze. I wanted to talk to her about these things, but I didn't even know where to begin. And did people even talk about that stuff? The friends I'd had before the incident talked to me about everything, but back then *everything* had meant only kissing and the occasional boob grab. This was something else entirely.

"Oh, oh. That expression. I need details. What did lover boy do?"

I nodded toward the general direction of my vagina. Reagan smirked. "He touched you there?"

I shook my head and Reagan grinned. "Oh boy. He went down on you, right?"

I pressed my lips together to stop myself from letting out a ridiculous giggle.

"That good, hm?" she whispered. My skin burned with embarrassment as I nodded. Reagan leaned against a tree. "There's nothing better than a guy who knows how to do it right. And I assume Zach's one of them."

"He is." That's what I assumed at least. It wasn't as if I had anything or anyone to compare his skills to. Nobody had ever gone down on me. A flicker of the past shoved itself into my mind. A hand ripping my panties, gripping me cruelly, but I forced the memory out of my head and focused on my most recent experiences. Zach. His tenderness. "I can't believe how good it felt."

Reagan bit her lips impishly. "And did you return the favor?"

My face fell. "No. I haven't even really touched him yet."

"Oh, that's okay." She tilted her head in consideration. "Are you scared?"

I thought about it. I wasn't really scared about touching Zach's erection. "I don't think so. It's just intimidating. But I think I want to touch him."

"Have you seen him yet?"

"Yeah."

"And?"

I frowned. "Everything about Zach is gorgeous." God, had I just said that?

Reagan burst out laughing, but not in a mean way. "And big I bet." She grimaced. "Is that what you're worried about?"

"You mean am I worried that it's going to hurt when Zach and I ever sleep together?" I shook my head. "I'm not worried about pain. Not anymore." It wasn't as if I was a virgin, and nothing could possibly hurt as much as what those men had done to me. I didn't fear pain. What terrified me was the idea that sleeping with Zach, or even just touching his erection, would always evoke memories of that day. What if there was an end to how much I could change? What if there would eventually be a wall I couldn't break down? "I want to touch Zach. I really do. But I'll probably disappoint him."

"Nonsense. Zach will be thrilled, believe me. And I'm sure he can tell you what he likes. I don't think he's shy about these things."

"No, he definitely isn't." I paused then gathered my courage. "Do you go down on Kevin?"

Reagan nodded without hesitation. "Yeah, I love giving him head."

"Really? Don't you think it's degrading?"

"Why? I feel powerful when I do it. Kevin is totally in my hands when I do it. I think I could ask anything of him in that moment." She giggled. "And he goes down on me too, so why shouldn't I do the same?"

I pondered that. "What about ... you know?"

"You mean swallowing?"

I looked away. "Yeah."

"Some women do, others don't. That's your decision. I personally don't. I just don't like the taste. That's all. But Kevin doesn't care. He enjoys the rest too much." Reagan smiled.

I wanted to give Zach what he'd given me. I wished there was a way of knowing I was ready.

I shuddered as the last waves of pleasure rolled through my body. Zach kissed my stomach, the skin between my breasts, and at last my lips before he settled beside me. I could taste myself on him and it was strange. My eyes flitted down to the bulge in his boxers.

"Can you remove them?" I asked, my voice utterly relaxed. Zach looked surprised, but he pulled down his boxer shorts and tossed them on the ground. He lay back. I propped myself up on my arm and allowed myself to stare at his erection. My eyes darted back to Zach's face. I could see how much he wanted me to touch him, but he wasn't moving. Love for him surged through me. Lowering my gaze to his erection once more, I reached out and brushed the tip with my fingers. Zach sucked in a deep breath, and his erection jerked, a drop of liquid coming out. I rubbed my forefinger over it, spreading it over his tip.

Zach moaned. "You don't have to do this," he managed to drag out, but I could tell how much he wanted it, and I wanted to give him pleasure. I actually caught myself enjoying the power I had over him. I wrapped my fingers around him and began stroking him. I worried that my grip was too tight, but Zach seemed to enjoy it. I moved my hand faster.

Zach's eyes were closed, and his jaw clenched tightly. I shifted until I was leaning over his erection. I waited for a moment of unease, but there was only need and curiosity. This was okay for me. I pressed my lips to Zach's tip. "Fuck!" He sat up so fast he almost knocked me out with his arm. His eyes were wide with shock. I flushed. For a moment, we stared at each other. "You startled me," he said, out of breath.

"I see that," I said with a smile. He looked so adorably shaken. My hand was still wrapped around the base of his erection, but I'd stopped moving.

"Don't you want me to *you know?*"

"What? Fuck, yes, of course I want you to do that." He looked torn, his chest heaving. "But I don't want you to be uncomfortable. I…" he shook his head "…fuck. I'm not good at this being noble thing. Fuck. I really want you to, but—"

"Shh," I said. "It's okay. I know you don't want to pressure me."

He rubbed a hand over his head.

"Lie back," I said firmly. Zach dropped his hand and slowly did as I'd asked. I bowed my head over his erection again and licked over the soft head. Zach's lips parted as he watched me. I wasn't sure if I was any good. I did what felt right and what I wanted to do, taking Zach's moans as encouragement. He tensed in my mouth. Before I could react, he grabbed my arm, wrenched me back and squeezed the tip of his erection, his head falling back as he came on his hand and leg. "Sorry," he said quietly, his eyes opening slowly. "I didn't want to come in your mouth."

I let out a nervous giggle, suddenly overwhelmed by my own courage.

Zach pulled me into his arms, eyes searching mine. "Are you okay?" The worry in his tone banished my nerves, and I nodded. Zach seemed unconvinced. "Tell me if I'm a selfish bastard for letting you do that."

"I wanted to do it. You didn't coerce me into doing it."

"But still. Maybe I should have stopped you. A decent guy would have done that."

"A decent guy lets the woman decide what she wants to do and doesn't make the decision for her," I said.

"You are too fucking perfect."

"Now I get why people say love makes you blind." I cringed as soon as the words left my mouth. Zach ignored my comment altogether and kept stroking my arm.

It was definitely too soon for the L-word. Except I was pretty sure I was already in love with Zach. But I understood that he didn't want to talk about love. We all had things that scared us, and maybe voicing his emotions was one of Zach's.

chapter sixteen

Amber

When Zach parked his Hummer in the driveway of my old home, my stomach coiled with nerves. The last time I'd been here, I was a completely different person. So much had changed in these last couple of months, and yet I was terrified that I would somehow revert back to my old self once I set foot into the house where I'd hidden myself away for three years. Zach squeezed my hand. Brian didn't wait for us. He slipped out of the backseat and opened the trunk to unload our luggage and Pumpkin's carrier. "You look nervous," Zach said. "Shouldn't I be the one who's nervous? After all, your father's going to roast me for dating you."

"He promised to go easy on you."

"Well, that's a consolation." Zach kissed my cheek. "Now come. We don't want to make your dad wait. He's already watching us."

My head whirled around. And indeed Dad was standing on the porch, his eyes focused on us. I opened the car door and got out. Zach grabbed our bag before he came to my side and took my hand. Together we walked toward Dad, who was staring at me like I was an apparition. His eyes kept darting to my hand, which was linked with Zach's. We stopped in front of him, and Zach let go of me to shake hands with my father—who didn't say anything. I didn't think he was doing it to intimidate Zach; he looked too stunned for words. When Zach stepped back, I moved toward Dad and wrapped my arms around him. He froze, but then he hugged me back lightly. His hands barely touched my back as if he was scared of breaking me. I still didn't exactly feel comfortable with physical contact most of the time, but this brought back only good memories. Memories of a time when everything was still as it was supposed to be. I drew back after a moment, and Dad's eyes were filled with tears. He still didn't say anything. I could see how hard he was fighting for composure. Heat pressed against my eyeballs, but I didn't want to cry today.

Dad squeezed the bridge of his nose, drew in a deep breath. Then he nodded toward the front door. "Let's go in. It's too cold to stand on the porch all day."

The moment I stepped inside, my throat tightened. I wasn't sure why. It was ridiculous to be scared of a place. This wasn't even where I'd been attacked. But it was the place where I'd tried to kill myself twice, where I'd learned to hate life and myself, where I'd spent hours resenting my father for saving me and my brother for leaving my father alone with me. Three years of darkness and despair, of fear and frustration ... that was what the house meant for me. The memories of those three years covered up every good memory I'd made in the sixteen years before the incident. What if the darkness and despair harbored in these walls were strong enough to destroy every good memory I'd made since I'd moved out? I still remembered the day I tried to kill myself for the second time. I'd taken one of the razorblades Dad kept hidden in his sock drawer, and I sat down on the bathroom floor because I didn't want to ruin the carpet in the other rooms. And then I drew the blade across my skin. It had hurt like hell, but I didn't get a deep cut on the first try so I had to do it again with more pressure. My palms were slick with blood and sweat, but I wasn't crying. I was calm, my hands steady. I watched the blood trickling out of my wound for a long time until eventually I had to lie back and lost consciousness. Today, I couldn't imagine doing something like that again, not only because I didn't want to hurt those around me, but also because I wanted to live. And yet I could remember the despair of that day as if I was actually living it right this second.

Dad was talking but I didn't hear him. Oh God, not a panic attack. Please. I didn't want to lose it in front of my dad, who actually looked happy for once, or Brian, who had been looking forward to Thanksgiving, or Zach whom I'd almost convinced that I could be a normal girl. I wanted to be normal. I wanted to go through life without fear and anxiety and panic attacks.

Zach cupped my cheeks, and his face filled my vision, his eyes intent on mine. I focused on their blue color until there was no room for anything else. I breathed in and out, tried to calm the pounding of my pulse, tried to forget the past. Zach didn't say anything, but even without words he anchored me in the present, built an invisible barrier between me and my hurtful past. I swallowed then released a long breath. "Okay?" Zach whispered.

I nodded. He dropped his hands. Brian and Dad were watching us, and I couldn't help but feel ashamed for freaking out like that.

zachary

Amber disappeared in the bathroom so she could splash her face with water. The moment the door closed behind her, her dad turned toward me. "Let's go into the living room and talk."

Brian, the traitor, didn't join us. He went up to his room. I was surprised he didn't want to be present when his dad roasted me. I sank down on the brown sofa, and Amber's dad took a seat in an armchair across from me.

"Call me Joseph," he said. Then he eyed me closely. "You've been dating Amber for a while now."

"Six weeks," I said. I decided not to mention that I'd never been in a serious relationship before. Fathers usually didn't like hearing that.

"Brian told me a lot about you."

Of course he had. "Okay," I said slowly.

"I don't care about that. Well, I did before I saw you and Amber together, but now …" He trailed off. "Today I saw glimpses of the daughter I lost years ago. I thought she was gone completely." I could tell that he was struggling for his composure. He clenched his hands at his side, and his gaze flitted to a frame at the wall. In it was a photo of his entire family: Amber, Brian, Joseph, and his wife. It was the first photo I'd seen of Amber's mother. She had Amber's nose and eyes. Amber didn't have family photos in her room. She didn't have any photos of herself or her life before the rape anywhere. "But Amber has gone through a lot. First her mother's death. She and Brian had to see their mother waste away slowly … and then the attack. That leaves scars. I'm not sure what would happen if things between you and her ended badly. A little over two years ago, I came home early from work because of a migraine, and Amber didn't answer when I called her name. I ran upstairs and found her on the bathroom floor in a pool of her own blood, barely breathing. If I had returned home later, she would have been dead. I don't ever want to experience that again. Don't break her heart. I've lost my wife. I won't lose my daughter too."

I didn't even know what to say to that. I nodded, feeling as if a heavy weight had been dumped on my chest.

amber

I froze in front of the living room, shocked. I couldn't believe Dad had made it sound as if Zach could be responsible for another suicide attempt if he left me. It would hurt horribly if things between Zach and me didn't work out, but I'd come too far to kill myself over something like that. I wanted to live with or without Zach.

I made sure to let them hear my footsteps as I entered the living room. Dad got up at once, smiling. He still looked at me in wonder. "I need to call your aunt."

I waited until he was gone before I sat down beside Zach. "You look like you saw a ghost."

He smiled, but it wasn't as bright as usually. "Your dad is an intimidating guy," he joked.

I snorted. "No, he isn't." Zach didn't say anything else about the conversation, and I didn't want to bring it up. I wanted to enjoy Thanksgiving.

My aunt and uncle were as surprised about the changes in me just as my dad had been. It was wonderful to sit around a table with everyone without having worried glances thrown my way. In the last few years everyone had always waited for me to have a nervous breakdown, but today Zach was the center of attention. Everyone loved him, especially my little cousins. Zach carried them around on his shoulders and told them about his fights when he studied martial arts. Even Brian laughed like he hadn't laughed in years. Life was good.

chapter seventeen
Amber

It was only one week till Christmas. I'd bought a calendar with gorgeous photos of Patagonia for Zach, but I still needed something else. I was bad at buying gifts for others. Maybe I needed to take Reagan up on her offer to help me with my Christmas shopping this year. One pre-Christmas gift I'd planned for tonight wasn't exactly a gift, though I had a feeling that Zach would be more excited about what I had planned than about the calendar.

Zach and I were snuggled against each other on the sofa, and he was trailing his fingers up and down my arm. It was distracting. The credits played on the TV screen, but I was barely paying attention. Zach's hand moved lower and began drawing gentle circles on my hip. All through the movie, I'd been thinking about my decision. I wanted to be absolutely sure that I was ready before I told Zach. I didn't want to have to push him away. He'd been so patient with me.

Zach leaned back and stretched, revealing a sliver of his muscled stomach. I loved running my hand over it, over Zach's entire body. I loved how velvety his penis felt in my palm, how I could make him tremble under my touch. I felt powerful when we were in bed together. Since the incident, I had always equated sex with being powerless and losing control, but with Zach I'd discovered that it didn't have to be that way. I wanted Zach. I really wanted to be with him, wanted to finally rid myself of that last barrier from the past. Butterflies swarmed in my stomach. My body yearned for Zach's touch, for the feel of his skin against mine.

Zach noticed me staring and cocked one eyebrow. I wished I could do that. For me it's either both eyebrows or none. "Do I have something on my face?"

For a few moments I didn't say anything. Then I shook my head. I wrapped my hand around Zach's and stood, tugging at his arm. Without hesitation he got to his feet, confusion clear on his face. "Amber? What's the matter?"

I bit my lip, embarrassed to voice my request. I curled a hand around his neck, pulled him down to me, and kissed him. Then I murmured against his mouth. "I want to sleep with you."

Zach pulled back to search my eyes. "Are you sure?"

I nodded and began leading him toward his bedroom. He followed silently. I closed the door. Brian was at Lauren's, but I didn't want to risk him walking in on us. It was still difficult enough for him to watch Zach and me kiss. I turned. Zach stood in the middle of the room. There was a bulge in his pants. I smiled at him, walked toward the bed, and sat down. Zach watched me with so much intensity that it sent a thrill through me.

"Won't you join me?" I asked in amusement. I scooted up on the mattress and patted the spot beside me.

Zach shook off his stupor and came toward the bed. He lay down beside me and leaned over me until our faces were only inches apart. "You can say no any time. You know that, right?"

"I know." I caught his lips in another kiss, my tongue darting out to meet his. Our kiss became more urgent, kindling a fire of desire in my belly. I pushed my hands under Zach's shirt, feeling his hot skin, the firm muscles, the trail of fine hairs that disappeared in his waistband. Zach groaned as my palm grazed his bulge. He sat up and I pulled the shirt over his head, revealing his perfect chest. He pressed against me and slid a hand under my shirt, tracing the edge of my bra then flicking a finger over my nipple through the material. I twitched at the sensation. He cupped my breast through my bra, running his thumb back and force over my hard nub, sending small shivers of pleasure down my spine. I hummed in agreement when he helped me out of my shirt and unhooked my bra, revealing my breasts.

He bent over me and placed a soft kiss against the hollow of my throat then slowly worked his way toward my left breast. Oh God. He licked the underside then circled around until his tongue reached the edge of my nipple. I arched my back, wanting him to lick it, but he only kissed it very softly. I bit my lip as he kissed my nub over and over again, the touch feather soft. Wetness pooled between my legs. "Zach," I half moaned. He was playing around. And while I loved this side of him, right now I wanted something else.

He peered at me over my breast and pressed another gentle kiss against my nipple. I was burning up with need, and his teasing drove me almost insane. "Hm?" he said, bringing one hand up to circle my other breast. His thumb lightly grazed one nipple as he kissed the other.

"I need more," I coaxed.

"More?" Zach raised his eyebrows as if he didn't know what I meant. I pressed my knee against his crotch and found him rock hard. He pulled back with a growl. "I want to take this slow, Amber."

"This is too slow," I protested and caught a glimpse of his smirk before he lowered his head and his hot lips closed around my nipple. He suckled it, first slowly then faster, and his thumb on my other nipple flicked back and forth at the same pace. I could feel every jolt of pleasure all the way between my legs. Zach watched me as he teased my breasts with his tongue and lips. I closed my eyes, still not able to meet his gaze when we were intimate. He sucked my nipple harder, and a moan slipped past my lips. I was so wet. How was that even possible?

Zach's hand moved away from my nipple, but his mouth kept up its sucking. He unbuttoned my jeans then sat up to slide them off. His eyes trailed up my legs as his hands glided over them, then over my hips and stomach until they cupped my breasts. He kneaded them gently, lowering his mouth and licking my left nipple. His hand brushed my stomach, one finger slipping beneath the edge of my panties teasingly. *Yes.* I made a sound deep in my throat, and I could feel Zach smiling against my breast. *Tease.* He moved his hand down until his finger slid between my folds, my soaked panties clinging to my core.

"Fuck," he ground out. "So fucking wet."

He rubbed his finger back and forth, causing more wetness to pool out. I lifted my hip, hoping he'd get the hint. He chuckled, sat up, and spread my legs. Then he propped himself between them. He looked at me and grinned like the cat that ate the canary. *Do it.*

He kissed my opening through my panties, spreading me even wider. His mouth was so hot against my center as he dusted soft pecks against my clothed folds. Tingles spread from my center through my entire body. My toes curled. He moved the crotch of my panties aside and kissed the skin there, drawing in a deep breath. He drove me insane. I pressed my lips together, almost not able to bear the tension building in my body. He trailed his tongue along the ridge between my thighs and my core, back and forth, slowly, teasingly.

"You smell so good," he moaned. "But I know you taste even better." He hooked his fingers under my panties then looked up. His eyes were hooded with desire. At one time a look like that would have sent me into a panic, but now my body responded with a sweet tingling between my legs. I raised my hips so Zach could easily slide my panties down. He dropped them on the ground then slid his hands below my butt, squeezing the cheeks. He gripped my waist, pushed me further up the bed, and knelt before me on the mattress before he spread my legs and lay down between them. His breath fanned over my wet folds, making me shiver. "I can't wait to taste you," he whispered as he kissed my opening, then my folds and my clit.

I jerked and gasped at the feel of his lips against me. He was so good at this. His fingers parted my folds and his tongue darted out, nudging my clit for the briefest moment before his mouth closed over it. I threw my head back and shut my eyes.

"Oh God," I groaned. He gently sucked on me, slow and unhurried, sending spikes of pleasure through me with every tug of his lips. I squirmed under his ministrations. Every time I got close to shattering in pleasure, Zach released my clit and kissed my inner thigh, driving me so insane with need I wasn't sure I could stand it much longer.

"Please," I whispered.

He brushed another kiss over my folds, then my clit, before closing his lips over it and continuing his sucking. Slowly, he increased the speed of his lips, and I could feel my pleasure building again. This time Zach didn't pull back. He sucked harder and faster, his hands moving up my body to knead my breasts. He clamped my nipples between two fingers and twisted and at the same time sucked my clit hard. I squeezed my eyes shut, my legs shuddering as my orgasm crashed over me, riding through wave after wave of pleasure. My fingers clawed the sheets, my butt lifting as I gasped and moaned. Slowly I came down. Zach was still between my legs, kissing me and occasionally trailing his tongue over my core and clit.

"I love licking you."

And I love being licked by you, I thought but was too shy to say aloud. He brought one of his hands between my legs and gently rubbed a finger between my folds, then over my opening but he didn't enter me. Zach glanced up at me.

"We don't have to do this," he said quietly, and I realized I'd tensed up at the light pressure against my opening.

"I want to," I said, trying to relax.

Zach didn't take his eyes off me as he slid his fingertip into me. I was wet and it felt nice, especially when Zach started rubbing my clit again. I relaxed even further. He eased his finger into my core, pumping it in and out at a leisurely pace. As my pleasure started building again, he pulled out, then nudged my opening with two fingers. Kissing my thigh, he slid them in very slowly. My muscles contracted, but I was so wet it wasn't uncomfortable. Zach hummed in satisfaction as he began pumping in and out.

"You are so wet, honey. I love that I did that to you. I could spend my whole life with my head between your legs." I was too turned on to be embarrassed about his words.

"Zach," I said. "I want you now."

Zach pulled his fingers out and shoved down his pants, his penis standing at attention. I'd touched his hardness more than once, but now that he knelt between my legs, a tiny hint of nervousness overcame me. He pushed a condom down his length and lowered himself to his forearms, his erection pressing against my thigh. He kissed my throat then my cheek and temple before meeting my eyes.

"You can say 'no,' Amber. Any time. Always." He kissed my lips. I shook my head. I wanted this. I'd wanted this for a while. He captured my mouth in another kiss, and I met his tongue with mine, but Zach made no move to push into me. He drew back a couple of inches. "Then tell me you want this. I need to hear you say it." My heart swelled with love for him.

"I want this." After a kiss, I added, "I want you."

Zach shifted and brought a hand between us, guiding his erection until the head was pressed against my opening. Then he slid his arm back up and cupped my cheek in his palm, his eyes fixed on mine. I lay my palms flat against his back, feeling his muscles flex as he moved his hips and slid into me inch by inch. My eyes fluttered shut at the feeling of him inside me.

"Is this okay? I'm almost all the way in," Zach ground out in a strained murmur. "Tell me if I'm hurting you. If you need me to stop."

"It's okay." It didn't hurt. There was only the sensation of being full. I was worried sleeping with Zach would bring back haunting memories, but this had nothing to with what had been done to me years ago. This was loving and gentle and perfect. The feeling of Zach's body on top of me, the feeling of him in me, made me feel safe and cherished. Tears prickled my eyes and slid out. Zach tensed and started to pull out, but I held onto him. "No. Don't."

"You're crying," he said quietly.

I opened my eyes and smiled before kissing him. "I'm fine."

Zach looked relieved. "So you don't want me to stop?"

I shook my head. "I want you to move."

Zach pulled almost all the way out then pushed back in, slowly picking up the pace. Every stroke of his erection sent a shiver of pleasure through my body. I moaned against Zach's lips, and his own pants were coming faster. He reached under me and lifted my butt, changing the angle. I gasped at the sensation, but I didn't look away from Zach. I wanted to be with him physically and mentally. Our eyes were locked, and with every thrust I could feel a tiny piece of my past breaking away. *They didn't win.* They wanted to break me, wanted to destroy me and my future, but as I looked into Zach's loving face I knew this was only the beginning of my life. The past no longer had a choke hold on me.

"Come for me, Amber," he whispered. I was barreling closer and closer toward my peak with every thrust, and then I tumbled over. I cried out, my entire body tensing, my core muscles clenching. Zach moved even faster, low growls slipping from his lips. His muscles tensed under my fingers, and with a shudder he let out a low moan as his own release gripped him. His movements slowed as he rained down kisses all over my face. Then he stopped, his eyes searching mine. He wiped a tear from my face and kissed the tip of my nose before he pulled out and threw the condom into the trash. He lay down beside me and wrapped his arms around me, pressing my head against his sweaty chest.

"Are you okay?" Zach whispered when our breathing had slowed.

I nodded then raised my head to kiss him. "Better than okay." I put my cheek back down on his chest. "I love you, Zach."

His fingers paused their stroking of my hair. Then he brushed his lips against the top of my head. He didn't say anything, and eventually I was too spent to wait any longer and drifted off to sleep.

We were awoken the next morning by the ringing of Zach's phone. He reached for it and answered the call with me still snuggled against his chest. From the way his voice hardened, I knew he was talking to his father.

"Tomorrow?" He paused. "Yeah, sure. I'll see what I can do. Yeah. I'll let you know ASAP." He hung up and flung his phone back on his nightstand.

"Your father?"

"Yeah, he and my mother want to meet you. They invited us over for lunch tomorrow."

"Oh," I said, not able to hide my surprise. Zach had never mentioned that he'd talked to his parents about us, and I guess I never asked. "Your parents know about me?"

Zach pulled back to give me a strange look. "Of course. It's been more than two months. I told my parents about you."

"And what do they think?"

Zach's lips tightened. "My mother is happy, I guess. My father doesn't believe in relationships."

"He's married."

"Yeah, and that's working out perfectly," he said, his voice dripping with sarcasm. "Sometimes I think marriage was invented to make people miserable."

I stared. "My parents loved each other. They were happy. My dad still isn't over my mom. Since she died seven years ago he's never seen anyone else."

"Must be lonely."

"I suppose it is."

"Would you be angry if he found someone else?"

I pondered that thought for a minute. "No, I want to see him happy. He's gone through so much. First losing my mom to cancer and then what happened to me. Nobody deserves happiness more than he does."

After that we steered clear of topics like marriage and love, even though I felt like it was something that we should discuss at some point. Not that I was even considering marriage right now, far from it, but it was something I might want later in my life. Zach propped himself up and hovered over me, his fingers untangling my hair. "How do you feel?"

I smiled. "Good."

"Not sore?"

I shook my head. Zach kissed my throat. "How about a repeat performance?" His fingers slipped under the covers and began their work.

Later, our skin covered with sweat, I was back in Zach's arms. "So will you meet my parents tomorrow?"

"Of course," I said, trying to catch my breath.

"Expect the worst."

"I'm sure it'll be fine."

"It won't. My father loves to drive me up the wall. He'll probably go on about law school and why I'm such a failure and all that."

"Why don't you do something else, then, if you hate law so much?"

"I don't hate law in general. I like human rights law. I'd love to do something that helps people and not multi-billion-dollar companies."

"Then do it."

Zach shook his head. I didn't press the matter and rested my cheek against his chest. "I got the job in the café around the corner."

"Why didn't you tell me sooner?"

"I kind of forgot to mention it because of my plan to seduce you."

Zach laughed. "So when do you have to start?"

"The day after tomorrow."

"Before Christmas? That's going to be tough."

"I'm actually excited. I know it's nothing special, but at least I'm doing something until I decide what to do about college."

"That's good. Take your time with your decision."

The words I love you hovered on the tip of my tongue again, but this time I swallowed them. I didn't want Zach to feel pressured into saying it back if he wasn't ready. He'd been patient with me, and I could be patient with him.

chapter eighteen
Amber

Zach's parents' house was just outside of New York, but his father had an apartment in Manhattan where he spent most of the time away from his wife. As we pulled up in front of the villa, because you couldn't really call it house, I was stunned. It had a vague resemblance to the white house and lay in a gated community. Everything about the lawn, flowers, and house itself was immaculate. Zach's parents probably had people who took care of everything for them.

The moment I met Zach's father, I knew he didn't like me. He was polite, charming even, but there was a trace of condescension in every twist of his mouth and look he sent me. He was almost as tall as Zach but not as broad, though it was obvious that he took care of his body and probably went to the gym whenever time allowed. His hair was still mostly dark-brown, except for a few streaks of grey. He was a good-looking man, and I didn't doubt that his appearance and his money made it easy for him to find women for his affairs.

His grip on my hand was firm, and it took everything I had not to squirm away. Apart from Zach, I still had trouble with physical closeness, especially with strangers. He didn't let go of my hand when he said, "So you are Zach's girlfriend." The word sounded like an insult coming from his lips, but I kept a polite smile plastered on my face. "You can call me Robert."

Zach cleared his throat, and his father finally released me. I exhaled quietly, but tension lingered in my muscles. "Where's Mother?" Zach asked, a hint of worry in his voice.

"She's getting ready."

"Ready?"

"For the luncheon at our country club. Didn't I mention it? We'll eat there so you can meet a few of our business partners, and they can meet you and your *girlfriend*."

I tensed and peered up at Zach. I wasn't wearing something that was fancy enough for a country club luncheon. I probably didn't even own anything that was remotely close to being acceptable for such a club. Robert's deprecating expression as he took in my skirt and blouse made that more than clear.

Zach narrowed his eyes at his father. "We aren't dressed for a fancy luncheon."

"We still have a few of your business suits and dress shirts upstairs. They should still fit."

"And what about Amber?"

"She can borrow something from your mother."

Zach dragged me away from his father and led me upstairs. "I'm sorry. He's doing this on purpose. He loves to put me on the spot." He turned to me. "We can cancel. We don't have to go to the fucking luncheon."

I smiled. I knew Zach needed to go there. Once he started working in his father's company, he would have to deal with these people all the time. "Maybe it won't be too bad? It's good practice, right?"

He kissed me. "You're too good for this world." Then he shook his head. "My mother is a bit taller than you. I hope we find something that can work. I hate this."

We stopped in front of a door and knocked. "Mother?"

"Come in," came a soft voice.

Zach pushed open the door, revealing a huge bright bedroom. His mother stood in front of a long mirror with a glass of red wine in her hand. She was wearing a tight blue dress with a pencil skirt and high heels. She looked sophisticated, almost regal, but an air of sadness clung to her. She took another gulp from her wine then set the glass down on the vanity next to a half-empty wine bottle. Zach's grip on my hand tightened before he let go and wrapped his arm around his mother in an awkward hug. She patted his back, her eyes on me. Her expression wasn't hostile nor friendly. It was, if anything, resigned and hollow.

She pulled back then strode toward me. "Nice to meet you."

Close up, it was obvious that she had done something to her face, maybe Botox, to get rid of the wrinkles and hide her age. Her breasts didn't look natural either. Had she done it because she hoped Zach's dad would stop cheating on her if she changed?

"Father said you would give Amber something to wear for the luncheon."

"Of course," she said, her eyes drifting toward the wine glass. "Get ready. We don't have much time. I will take care of your girl."

Zach looked at me, and I nodded. He pulled the door closed. I twisted my hands, suddenly nervous about being alone with Zach's mother. She snatched up her wine glass and emptied it in one long gulp. Then she smiled wistfully. "I was once as wide-eyed and hopeful and happy and young as you are now." She filled her wine glass again. I wondered if she'd drunk what was missing in the bottle before we arrived and if she intended to finish it. I wouldn't be able to walk on high heels after that much alcohol. I probably wouldn't be able to walk at all. "That was such a long time ago." She looked down into her glass as if she hoped to find something there that she'd lost. I could feel for her.

What happened? I wanted to ask but didn't. Wine glass clutched in her hand, she led me through a door into a walk-in closet. It was bigger than my room in the apartment.

She turned toward me as if remembering something. "You can call me, Abi." Then she began rifling through her dresses until she pulled out three pieces. None of them were something I'd normally wear. I pointed toward a black dress with a high collar and a beige flower at the waist. "Try it on. I'll be outside," Abi said and left with her wine glass.

I quickly got out of my thick winter tights, skirt, and blouse then slipped the dress over my head. It reached my knees and was a bit too wide around the chest. It wasn't very obvious since it wasn't meant to accentuate that area, but the waist could definitely have been a bit smaller for me.

Abi knocked before she came in, her eyes scanning me from head to toe. "Not perfect, but it should do." She took an unopened package of nylons from a drawer and handed them to me then moved over to the shoe shelf and grabbed a pair of very high beige high heels. They matched the color of the flower belt on the dress. "Can you walk in these?"

"I don't know," I admitted.

"Put on the nylons. Then we'll try."

I put the nylons on and took the shoes from her. When I stepped into them, I swayed for a moment. I was really tall. I took a few hesitant steps. It didn't help that the shoes were one size too big for me.

Abi shook her head. "No. That's not going to work." She went back to her shoe shelf and searched for a long time then picked up black pointy sling back heels. I tried them on and while they were also too big, the heel was moderate, and I could actually walk like a normal human being in them. I didn't want to embarrass myself at the luncheon by falling on my face.

Abi nodded. "Good. Let's go. Robert doesn't like to be late."

I followed her into the hallway, where Zach was already waiting. He was dressed in a light gray pinstriped business suit, a light blue dress shirt, and a tie in a darker blue color.

He straightened when we came out, his eyes roaming over me. He'd never seen me in an elegant dress before.

"I'll give you a moment," Abi said with a wistful expression. Then she was gone.

I shrugged, embarrassed. "It's not perfect."

Zach put his hands on my waist and pulled me toward him for a kiss. "I prefer you in your own clothes anyway, but you look gorgeous."

"Zach?" Robert called in an impatient tone.

Zach and I stopped kissing and walked downstairs. His father scanned me from head to toe as we arrived in the entrance hall. He didn't look impressed, even though he gave a tight-lipped smile. I hoped the other guests of the luncheon would be more like Zach and not like his father.

Unfortunately, most of the guests were exactly like that … or worse. Every smile seemed fake, every word loaded with innuendos I didn't get. I smiled and laughed, but I wanted to be anywhere but there. It wasn't as much a real lunch as an occasion to drink expensive champagne—that didn't even taste all that good—and nibble at small appetizers that did nothing to satiate my hunger. Zach kept his hand on my waist, and I was grateful for it. Mostly, I watched the people around me and occasionally answered a question directed at me, but the other guests were more interested in small talk with Zach anyway. Despite the amount of wine Zach's mother had drunk, her appearance was immaculate as she talked to other women of the country club. But every once in a while, her gaze would seek out her husband, who never once returned it, and a ripple went through the perfect mask she wore like a second skin. Was that what longing and loneliness looked like?

I excused myself to go to the bathroom and released a long breath when I was hidden in the bathroom stall. This wasn't my crowd. When I stepped out, I froze. Brittany stood in front of a washbasin and was reapplying lip gloss. Her eyes met mine in the mirror. This wasn't an accidental run-in.

"You're here?" I said in surprise.

She straightened, a thin smile on her face. "Of course, my father and Zach's father are best friends and have been members in the club forever." She shook her head. "You look like a fish out of water out there. You hate those people. But it's what you'll have to get used to if you stay with Zach. Those people will become your people, and their ways will become your ways, and eventually you'll be a hopeless alcoholic like Abi."

I frowned. "If it is so bad, then why do I get the feeling that you wouldn't mind being at Zach's side for all that."

"Because," she said, taking a step closer to me, "those are already my people. I'm one of them. I've always been one of them. Their games and backstabbing are what I do best. And I'm too strong to become alcoholic. I won't have a breakdown because my husband cheats on me. That's what pool boys and masseurs are for. I'll find someone to distract me." She turned to leave. "Don't look so shocked. That's how it works. That's the world Zach has grown up in. He might try to be an average law student right now, but eventually he'll become what he was meant to be."

After she left, I needed a couple of minutes to compose myself before I joined Zach again, but I couldn't stop thinking about Brittany's words.

It was late afternoon when we returned to the house, and I was exhausted. Keeping up a front *was* exhausting. Even Zach's mother, who'd been charming and almost exuberant at the country club, seemed to retreat into herself the moment we were inside.

"Could I have a word with my son?" Robert asked with an all too polite smile.

Zach narrowed his eyes at his father, but I let go of his hand and followed his mother into the kitchen. She opened the fridge in search for something. I assumed some kind of alcohol. When she didn't find it, her shoulders slumped, and she turned to me.

"Zach's trying to be a good boy," she said quietly. "But he's his father's son. Maybe he won't leave you because he's worried what you'll do if he does, but he won't love you. I know because I'm living that reality." My lips parted in shock. She smiled. "I really like you, Amber. I want you and Zach to be happy ... Please excuse me. I have to leave you for a moment." With that, she walked out of the kitchen, leaving me alone.

After a moment, I also left the kitchen and headed for the guest bathroom, but froze when I heard Robert's voice coming from the living room.

"You brought her here because you knew how I'd react. You knew I'd say what you are thinking but are too polite to say aloud or too cowardly to admit to yourself. That girl is not for you."

"Why? Because she makes me happy and you prefer me miserable?"

"Don't be ridiculous. The girl is not for you because once you join me in the company, you need someone at your side who can charm the pants off of clients. Someone who has no trouble lying through her teeth. Someone who can be every bit the trophy wife men in our position need. Someone like Brittany."

I stifled a gasp. I peered through the gap in the door and saw Zach and his father facing each other.

Zach scoffed. "Brittany? You think she's a good match because she's the daughter of one of your best clients. She means better business."

"So what? It's not like she's hard on the eyes. And she's like you."

"Like me?"

His father smiled coldly. "You're both not exactly faithful."

Zach's face hardened. "I have Amber now."

"Amber is shy and polite and barely able to hold my gaze. She won't impress anyone, believe me. She's your flavor of the month, but that won't last. Whether you're able to admit it or not, Zach, you are like me. You can't be monogamous. You will always look for the next hot piece of ass, and what happens to Amber then? That girl wouldn't survive a marriage to you. Look at what marrying me meant for your mother, and she was never as weak as that girl. Do you really want that for Amber? Let her go. Let her find some boring accountant who will make her happy."

Weak. I wasn't weak.

Was I?

"I can't," Zach said. I can't? What kind of answer was that? Shouldn't he have said I won't? 'I can't' sounded as if I was stopping him.

"Why? Your mother told me a bit about the girl. Are you worried she's going to kill herself if you dump her? Believe me, I know how it feels to be shackled to a woman because she threatens you with suicide. They won't go through with it, don't worry."

Zach didn't say anything. I felt like I was falling. Was he staying with me because of what my dad had said? Was he scared I'd kill myself if he left me?

Robert put a hand on Zach's shoulder. "Think of your future, of Amber's future, and then do the right thing and cut her loose as long as this isn't serious. If you wait longer, it'll only get worse." Zach's father shrugged. "If you're too selfish to let her go, then keep her on the side. If she's good in bed, then keep her for that for all I care, though I can't see the appeal unless you like them meek and submissive."

I stumbled back, not able to bear another moment. My heart pounded in my chest as I hurried back toward the kitchen. I'd always thought that Zach could do better than me. Apparently, I wasn't the only one who thought like that. What about Zach? He didn't exactly disagree with his father. Maybe deep down he knew that we wouldn't make it. Maybe he'd realized that I wasn't enough. Maybe he was tired of vanilla sex. Maybe he wanted to escape but couldn't because his conscience wouldn't let him. Brian and my dad made sure he knew how fragile I was, and seeing my suicide scars probably hadn't helped matters. I wasn't sure what to think anymore. Zach's father was right with one thing: I couldn't live like

Zach's mother did, knowing that my husband was cheating on me and drowning my sorrows in alcohol. I'd gone through too much, had come too far to let that happen to me. I had a past I hated being reminded of; I at least wanted at a future to look forward to. And there was another thing I was absolutely sure about: I wouldn't force anyone to stay with me by threatening him with suicide. I'd been pitied by everyone around me for years. I didn't want Zach to be with me out of pity or duty.

zachary

I ground my teeth together to keep back the things I wanted to call my father. He was a cheating, misogynistic, money-grubbing asshole, but he was still my father. When I was sure I wouldn't curse him, I said, "Don't talk about Amber like that. You don't know anything about Amber or about our relationship. I can't leave Amber because I love her." Shock shot through my body at the realization. I did love her. I should have realized it sooner.

"Love, please don't be ridiculous, Zach."

I glared. "Just because you aren't capable of loving anyone except for yourself that doesn't mean I'm the same way. I'm nothing like you."

"You are. Tell me now that you've never once considered cheating on Amber, and then maybe I'll believe that you are less like me than I think."

I tensed and my father let out a sharp laugh. "Maybe you aren't ready to accept it yet. Keep your Amber for now, string her along, but mark my words: that girl won't be at your side once you take over my company."

"Coming here was a mistake," I said firmly. "Amber and I are leaving now." I turned around to pick up Amber in the kitchen.

"Yes, run away. But you can't run from the truth of who you are, Zach." I pushed through the door and almost ran toward the kitchen. Amber was inside, staring out of the window. Alone.

"Where's my mother?" I asked.

Amber glanced over her shoulder. She looked shaken. "She said she needed to go upstairs."

God, was my mother getting wasted with Amber in the house? "I need to check on her," I said and went upstairs. Mother was in the bedroom, bent over her vanity. I approached her cautiously and put a hand on her shoulder. "Mom?" She raised her head a few inches. The remains of cocaine dusted the vanity and her chin. "I thought you stopped with this shit?" I whispered harshly. I helped her to her feet and led her toward the bed, where she lay down with a hazy smile. "I did. For a little while. A little while. But I need it to feel something, to feel numb and forget."

Did she realize that she contradicted herself? There was only one thing cocaine did. It ruined your life. "Does Father know?" The answer was obvious. Cocaine was expensive.

"He tells me to be careful." I closed my eyes for a moment then pressed a kiss to my mother's forehead and left.

I couldn't remember how old I was the first time I'd found my mother like that. I was young, maybe six or seven, and Father had lost it completely. I didn't think he cared that much now. When I came back downstairs, Father was putting on his coat.

"Where are you going? Mother just sniffed coke, you can't leave her alone."

"Nina is on her way."

"You're going to let the maid take care of Mother?"

He glared. "It's worked for the last few years. Now leave and get your affairs sorted. I'll be back in a couple of hours. Don't worry, I'll spend the night with your mother."

I wanted to hit him so much in that moment. Instead, I walked into the kitchen and took Amber's hand before leading her outside. Father was already getting into his Porsche when we stepped onto the porch. "Is your mother alright?"

Nina waved at me from a ways down the street. "She's ... as she's always been." That was the only way to describe it. I couldn't remember a time when my mother hadn't been addicted to something. Pills, anti-depressants, alcohol, pot, cocaine. She was getting worse at hiding it and that was what really worried me.

Amber was awfully silent during our drive back to Boston. She was probably shocked by the state of my family. Some people equated money with happiness, but that wasn't true. I didn't think my mother had been truly happy in many years.

"Are you okay?" I asked eventually.

She looked almost surprised that I'd spoken, as if she'd forgotten that she wasn't alone in the car. "Yeah. Tired. The country club was exhausting."

"I know. It'll get better. Eventually your facial muscles learn to keep a constant smile and the right words will come naturally."

Amber scrunched her brows together as if she doubted that. And maybe she was right. Some people just weren't meant to be part of this kind of backstabbing, two-faced group.

When we returned to the apartment, Amber led me into my room at once and began undressing me almost desperately. I was startled by her initiative. She slipped my shirt over my head, her lips hot against my chest as she kissed me. Her fingers fumbled with my belt then the buttons of my dress pants. Finally she pushed them down. I was already rock hard. Her expression was so intense, so focused. I sank down on the bed, and Amber removed my last pieces of clothing, freeing my cock.

"Amber, are you okay?" She didn't reply. She knelt beside me on the bed, bent her head over me, and closed her mouth around my cock. I closed my eyes and put a hand on her head, stroking her hair as she worked her mouth up and down, licking and sucking. It was only the second time that she'd given me a blowjob, and I missed it. I loved the feel of her warm, wet mouth around my cock. I shifted my hips up and down. "Yeah, that feels so good, Amber. Yes, honey."

Sometimes her teeth grazed me by accident, but I was so horny by Amber's boldness that I didn't even mind. I could feel myself getting closer and closer, and when Amber cupped my balls and began massaging them, I almost came at once.

"Amber, I'm going to come," I warned.

I tried to move her away because I didn't want to come in her mouth, but she didn't budge. Instead she sucked even harder, and I couldn't hold it in anymore, I threw my head back and exploded in her mouth. I groaned, as my cock twitched and my balls tensed. Amber kept sucking and it felt so fucking good. I opened my eyes and watched her sucking my softening cock slower and slower. That was a fucking fantastic sight. I ran my hand gently over her head and kept my eyes on her as her lips remained on me until the aftershocks of my orgasm were over. She sat back on her haunches and wiped her mouth. I sat up and helped her out of her dress and bra, suckled and licked and kissed her breasts as I peeled off her panties. Then I slowly moved down her body and started licking her. She was already wet, but I took my time nibbling and teasing her clit. I pushed one finger into her and began pumping slowly as my mouth worked her clit. I wasn't sure what had gotten into Amber to make her so horny, and I didn't care. Seeing her like that was fucking hot.

amber

This was the last time. The thought kept whirring in my head as Zach licked me. I needed him. Just one more time. I pushed his head back. Zach looked surprised. I couldn't say anything. Instead I made him sit back against the headboard and straddled him. Zach released a low breath as I curled my fingers around him and slowly guided him into me. He wrapped his arms around my back, our chests pressed against each other as I started to move. We kissed, slowly, unhurriedly. I wanted to taste him one more time, wanted to feel him one more time. Zach suckled my throat as he guided my hips in a slow rhythm. I could feel pressure building in my core. I moved faster and wrapped my arms tightly around Zach's neck, burying my face in his hair. Tears started to trickle down my cheeks as I relished in the feel of our skin sliding against each other. I choked back a sob. Zach sneaked a hand between us and rubbed my clit, driving me higher and higher. My orgasm gripped me, and I cried out as pleasure shot through my body. I moved my hips faster and faster until Zach's hand grabbed my hips and he groaned when his own orgasm overwhelmed him. I clung to him as the tingling ebbed and he softened in me. I didn't move, couldn't move. I wiped the tears off my face so Zach wouldn't see and stared at the wooden headboard. This was it.

Zach lay down, taking me with him. I rested my cheek against his chest, breathing in his scent, listening to his quick heartbeat, running my fingertips up his muscled arms. He stroked my back, his touch soft and gentle as he always was with me. I wanted this moment to last forever.

One more night, I told myself, and tomorrow I'd break it off before he could break my heart ... or worse: stayed with me for the wrong reasons until he learned to regret it and maybe even resent me. I'd never feel comfortable around the society women who smiled at you while hating everything about you and the business men with their overconfident smiles. That wasn't my world. But it would be Zach's soon. It was already Brittany's. My heart tightened. Reagan had told me to take control, to always be in control. I wouldn't lose control ever again. Control was what had helped me leave my past behind. I wouldn't let anyone have control over my life again.

I breathed in his scent again, letting it engulf me entirely, wrapping me into a cocoon of blissful safety. He was the only one who made me feel like that. Only him. But whatever we had, it would ... it could never be more than an interlude. Zach didn't disagree with his father, and that was as much a confirmation as there could ever be one. Maybe Zach was really too kind to admit it. Maybe he was worried he'd lose Brian if he left me. Maybe he was worried I'd shatter if he was the one to end things between us, so I had to make it easy for him. I loved Zach, loved him more than I thought possible after what had happened, but he would never say it back. I thought maybe it was a guy thing, but now I realized it was a Zach thing. He couldn't say it because he didn't love me. When we started dating, he always said he would try to be a good boyfriend but he couldn't make me any promises. Trying hadn't been enough; I realized that now.

One more night. I closed my eyes and buried my face in Zach's chest. I was suddenly very calm. One more night.

chapter nineteen

Zachary

When I woke, Amber wasn't snuggled up to me. I sat up and rubbed my face. She'd probably gone to the bathroom, but when I touched the side where she usually lay, it was completely cold as if she'd left a while ago. I got out of bed, put boxer shorts on, and went in search of her. I knocked at her door but got no response. Eventually I found her in the kitchen, leaning against the counter and staring intently at a cup of coffee cradled in her hands. She looked like she hadn't slept at all last night. I walked up to her for a kiss, but she shook her head and took a few steps back. Confused, I stopped.

"We need to talk," she said quietly.

Something was wrong. Very fucking wrong. "What's going on?"

"This isn't going to work. I want to break up."

Shock shot through me as I stared at her. She was looking right back at me, completely serious. Her eyes were guarded. I'd never seen that look on her face.

"What do you mean?"

"What I said. I think we should break up. When we started dating we always knew it might not work out, and I just realized it isn't going to work out." She said it like she'd rehearsed those lines all night. When had she decided to break up with me?

"It's because of yesterday, because of my mother, right?"

She shook her head, but I could tell from her expression I'd hit a nerve. She thought she'd end up like my mother if she stayed with me. She'd finally realized what my father had known all along: that I was just like my old man, that I was a destructive force bound to fuck up her life. My father had said the best thing I could do for Amber was letting her go so she could find someone else, someone nicer, someone better.

I nodded once. "Okay. If that's what you want. It's probably for the best."

She looked surprised for a moment. Then she put down the coffee and walked past me. "Yes, it is." She slipped out of the kitchen and a moment later I heard the front door shut.

What the fuck just happened? I sank down on the chair and didn't move for a long time. I'd never felt so fucking empty. I buried my face in my palms. Why was I feeling so bad? I was doing the right thing. Amber needed someone, a decent guy who loved her, so then why was the mere idea of her being with another man feeling like I'd been stabbed in the heart?

"What's up with you?" Brian asked as he entered the kitchen.

"Amber and I broke up."

There was silence. "I knew it. I fucking knew it! I warned you not to get involved with her. I knew you'd break her heart. Did you cheat on her? Did you get tired of being with only one girl? What the hell is wrong with you, Zach?"

Everything, apparently. I looked up. "She broke up with me, and I didn't cheat on her."

"Then what did you do?"

"Does it have to be me who did something?"

He gave me a look.

"She think it's not working out. She's probably right."

Brian shook his head with a frown. "Great, now I have to pick up the pieces. Where is she?"

"I don't know. She didn't tell me. She left."

"You're an asshole, Zach." Brian left the kitchen.

"Don't I know it," I muttered to myself.

amber

I couldn't breathe. I rushed out of the building and into the nearby park where I collapsed on a bench. I pressed my chest against my legs, staring down at the gravel, trying to calm my breathing, trying to stop my heart from feeling like it was shattering. Tears burned my eyes.

I really broke up with Zach. God, why? Why? Now I realized that deep down I'd only wanted to get something from him, some kind of sign that he loved me or at least cared about me as much as I cared for him, but he'd given up on us without a fight, without as much as a protest even. He let me go like it meant nothing. Everything his father had said yesterday was right. That was why Zach hadn't argued with him. Zach probably hadn't broken up with me because he didn't want to leave the poor broken

Amber. Was it pity that had made him stay with me for this long?

But I'd survived worse. I would survive this. I'd move on. I wasn't that broken girl anymore. I was stronger than her. With shaky fingers, I pulled out my cell from my jeans pocket and dialed Reagan's number. She answered after the third ring. "Hey, Amber!"

"I broke up with Zach."

"Whoa, okay. What?"

"I broke up with Zach."

"How did that even happen? Do you want me to come over? I could be there in thirty minutes."

"Yeah, that would be great. I think I need a shoulder to cry on." I let out a choked laugh.

"I'll be there soon."

Then I remembered that I couldn't go back into the apartment, not yet. If I met Zach now, I'd lose it. "I can't go back into the apartment. What do I do now?"

"Let's meet in the Starbucks around the corner."

"Okay." We hung up and I stared at nothing for a long time. Then I got up and walked slowly toward the Starbucks.

Reagan arrived twenty minutes later with wet hair and a panicked look on her face. When she found me sitting at table in the corner, she rushed over and hugged me. "Amber, what the hell is going on? Tell me everything."

And so I did, and when I was done, Reagan frowned. "Maybe Zach was just stunned and that's what he didn't fight for your relationship. Maybe it's not really over."

"It is. He never told me he loved me. He never spoke about the future."

"Did you sleep with him?"

I nodded. Then I blinked quickly to keep tears at bay. "And I don't regret it. I've never felt so loved." I snorted. "I didn't think I could ever feel so safe with someone."

Reagan squeezed my hand. "I could talk to Zach."

"No," I said quickly. My phone vibrated for the tenth time. It was Brian, and I finally picked up.

"Amber, where are you? I talked to Zach. I'm worried about you. Are you okay?" He sounded close to his own meltdown.

"I'm with Reagan, and I'm okay. You don't need to worry. I broke up with Zach, not the other way around."

"Did he hurt you? If he did, I'll kill him."

"He didn't hurt me," I said quietly. "It's nobody's fault. It just wasn't meant to be. Can we talk later?"

"Okay, but don't stay out too long. I'm really worried."

"I know." I hung up then sighed. "This is such a mess. I thought if I was the one breaking up with Zach before he could, I'd feel better about it. That being in control would make it hurt less."

"It doesn't," Reagan whispered.

"No, it doesn't. It hurts so much." I closed my eyes and pressed my face into my palms. Reagan wrapped an arm around me. "Shhh. It'll get better. And you can still talk to Zach. Nothing's lost yet. Talk to him about your feelings and worries and why you really broke up with him. It'll be fine."

I didn't think it would be. If Zach didn't feel the need to fight for us, then why should I? But Reagan eventually managed to convince me, and we walked back to the apartment together. Brian was already waiting for me in the living room.

Before he could question me further, I asked, "Where's Zach?"

"He went over to Jason's to go out. He's doing what he's good at. Getting wasted. They want to hit a club."

Reagan cursed. "What is wrong with him?"

I put on a brave face. "It's for the best. A clean cut." I wished I could really believe that.

I lay awake almost all night in my bed, but Zach didn't come home. He'd probably found someone new to spend the night with. After having been shackled to me for months, he must have been desperate for a one-night stand.

I could barely keep my eyes open the next morning, but I got dressed and headed out for work in a trance. I managed to smile and take orders without messing it up. Life went on as if nothing had happened. That was a small consolation. In a few years I'd look back to this moment and see it as another step toward becoming who I was supposed to be. God, I sounded like a Hallmark card.

Reagan waited for me when my shift was over, and together we walked over to the apartment. "I think I need to find a new place. I can't keep living in Zach's apartment now that we've broken up." It still felt surreal, as if any moment I might wake up from a nightmare. But things like that never happened. I learned that in the past.

"You could crash at my place for a while. My roommates wouldn't mind. They practically have their boyfriends over all the time, so what's one person more?"

"Thanks. Maybe I'll take you up on that offer."

"Have you seen Zach again since the breakup?"

"He didn't come home all night, and I didn't see him this morning." Reagan shook her head. "I can't believe he's acting like this."

"He seems to be coping well with the breakup," I said miserably. "Better than me."

zachary

I couldn't remember the last time I'd been so wasted. I couldn't even remember how much I had to drink. Kevin was giving me the dirty eye. What the fuck did I care? I emptied my glass. Day three after Amber broke up with me, but no matter how much I drank even thinking her name still felt like a canyon ripped open in my chest.

Fuck it. Fuck it all. Fuck my father most of all for making me turn out like him.

"Don't blame your father," Kevin said in exasperation. I hadn't even realized I'd said anything aloud. I glared. "There's a small voice called choice, Zach. You could try it. Try to act like a grown up and don't get shitfaced. Go to Amber and make up. Tell her you can't live without her. Tell her you love her and stop throwing yourself a pity party."

"I'm not fucking capable of loving anybody. Just like my father said. I ruined it."

"Then why, if you didn't love Amber, are you acting like this? I've never seen you so miserable."

"I'm not miserable. I've having a fucking perfect time."

"I can see that."

"Hey, Zach, I'm surprised to find you here," Brittany said, suddenly appearing at my side. "Where's your girlfriend?"

"Gone. We broke up."

"Oh, that's a pity." She leaned close to me. "Need some company?"

Kevin shook his head and left. Good. He was driving we crazy with his talking.

"We always have a good time, don't you think? We're meant for each other."

Had she talked to my father? She ran her hand up and down my chest. "Let's have some fun. You must be hungry after all the vanilla sex with Amber."

"Don't talk about her," I growled.

"Okay, okay. Still a touchy subject." Her hand grazed over my groin. "We can go to my place, or we can do it in the alley like old times. What do you say?"

"Alley," I said simply, and she took my hand and led me across the dance floor, through the backdoor into the alley. It was fucking cold. But I didn't care. I couldn't believe Christmas was in two days. My present for Amber would rot in my desk drawer for all of eternity. Brittany started kissing my lips. I pulled away and gripped her shoulders, pushing her down. She grinned and opened my zipper. I closed my eyes as she curled her hands around my cock. All I could think about was Amber, her smile, her soft lips, the way her hair smelled, her laughter when I tickled her sides. What the fuck was I doing? I pushed Brittany's hands away, took a few steps back, and zipped my pants. "I can't." I actually felt like I was going to throw up.

"What do you mean?" She stood up. "Don't tell me this is because of Amber."

I closed my eyes but quickly opened them again when I almost lost my balance. Too much alcohol. I was like the worst possible combo of my father and mother. A drunk cheat.

"You said it's over between you and her, so what's the fucking problem?"

"The fucking problem is that I still love her." I froze. Love. I still loved her. Loved her so much it fucking hurt. I should have told her a long time ago. And it took a breakup and this to figure it out. Too late as always. "I'm sorry. But I can't do this."

I stumbled back into the club, bumping into several people and almost falling flat on my face a few times. Kevin stepped in my way and slung one of my arms over his shoulders.

"Already over?" His voice was harsh, angry.

He could be angry with me all he wanted. He couldn't possibly hate me more than I hated myself right in this moment. I'd lost the first woman I ever loved because I was a stupid asshole.

"I couldn't go through with it," I muttered. "I still love Amber. I fucking love her so much it hurts. And I fucked it up. I let her go."

"Let's get you home," Kevin said. "Maybe when you aren't wasted anymore, we can figure out a way to get you back together with Amber."

Why could I possibly do or say to make Amber give us another chance?

chapter twenty

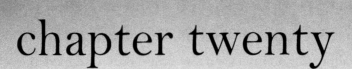

Loud knocking woke me. I glanced at my alarm clock. It was after midnight. I slipped out of bed and walked out of my room. "Brian?" I called out, but he wasn't home. Maybe he was with Lauren. I headed for the entrance door but didn't open it, even when the knocking got more insistent. I peered through the peephole but it was empty. "Who's there?" I asked.

"It's me, Kevin." He sounded strained. "Could you let me in? Zach can't find his keys."

After a moment of hesitation, I unlocked the door and found Kevin holding Zach up against the wall in the corridor. Zach was totally drunk. I sighed. "Do you need help carrying him?"

Kevin grunted when Zach stumbled against him. "Yeah. Maybe we can get him onto the couch. His room is definitely too far away."

Kevin and I half-dragged, half-carried Zach over to the couch where he fell back and passed out.

"What happened?" I shook my head. "I probably don't want to know."

"He's never been like this. I mean he's always drowned his sorrows in alcohol after a talk with his father, but he's been drunk every day since your breakup. He's miserable because of you."

"Because of me?"

"He misses you," Kevin said softly. "He loves you, Amber."

"Did he tell you that? Because he never once said he loved me. And it doesn't matter anymore. We would have never made it. Zach's going to run a company, and I'm not the right person to be at his side for that."

"The last thing Zach wants is to join his father's company."

"But he's going to anyway. What does it matter what he … what *we* want, if we don't act upon it?" That made me pause. I acted against what I really wanted when I'd broken up with Zach.

"Do you want me to stay? Someone needs to keep an eye on him in case he throws up."

"No, it's okay. I'll stay with him," I said quietly. When Kevin left, I perched on the armrest above Zach's head. I couldn't resist. I reached out and ran my fingers through his hair. He stirred and turned his head toward the ministrations. I closed my eyes against the emotions rising up in me. I wanted nothing more than to stretch out beside Zach, to feel his heartbeat against my cheek, to snuggle up to him and fall asleep with his comforting scent in my nose—even if he smelled of smoke and beer right now. I rested my head against the backrest and kept stroking Zach's hair until I fell asleep.

My body was stiff from my awkward position draped over the backrest. I opened my eyes to find Zach staring at me. He was stretched out on the sofa, and my hand was still in his hair. I pulled it away and sat up.

"You kept watch over me?" he said in a gravelly voice. I loved his morning voice.

Looking at his face, I realized I still loved him just as much as before I broke up with him. Maybe it took longer to forget someone who helped you find yourself again. "Someone had to. You were really drunk."

I slid off the armrest to create some distance between Zach and me. Zach's eyes followed me. I couldn't read the emotion on his face, but I couldn't stand it a moment longer.

"I need to pack," I said.

Zach stood. "You're leaving?"

"For Christmas. I'm spending a few days at home. Brian's going as well, remember?"

"Oh, sure."

Before our breakup, Zach and I had planned to celebrate with my family because his parents always spent Christmas and New Year's in the Bahamas. "You could still come with Brian and me, you know?" I wasn't sure if that was a good idea, but I didn't want Zach to spend the holidays alone.

"No," Zach said quickly. "I still need to do some stuff for school. And I could watch Pumpkin for you. Then he doesn't have to do the long drive again."

It cost me everything I had not to storm toward Zach and kiss him. "Are you sure? You don't have to do that."

"I want to. Pumpkin isn't any trouble."

"Okay," I said slowly. Then I quickly walked toward my room before I lost it.

Brian and I were on our way out of the apartment when Zach walked out of the kitchen carrying a package in his hands. "Amber, wait."

Brian glanced between Zach and me. "I'll wait in the car." He closed the door after him.

"I wanted to give you this," Zach said. He stopped in front of me and held out a medium-sized parcel covered in reindeer wrapping paper. "I bought it for you for Christmas. I still want you to have it." An envelope was attached to the top.

I took the parcel, my throat tightening. "Thanks." I opened my mouth to say something else, but then I left instead. Brian didn't say anything when I got into the car with tears on my cheeks.

zachary

I moved away from the door as Amber closed it. My legs bumped against the back of the sofa, and I sank down on the backrest. I should have told Amber that I loved her. I wanted to, but something in her expression made it clear that it wasn't the right moment to voice my emotions. Maybe the right moment would never come again, but I'd given her my present and the card anyway.

Pumpkin leaped onto the headrest beside me and bumped my arm with his head. I began stroking him and was rewarded with a deep purr. I picked him up before I headed toward my room but froze in front of my door. On the ground was a gift. It was longer than my arm. I set Pumpkin down, who sniffed the gift, before I picked it up. There was a small card at the top right corner with 'For Zach' written in Amber's neat handwriting.

She probably intended for me to wait until Christmas morning, but I walked into my room where I immediately ripped away the wrapping paper, revealing a calendar with nature photography from Patagonia. Another note fell to my feet. 'I hope you get to live your dreams one day.'

I swallowed and sat on my bed. One dream had left the apartment less than fifteen minutes ago.

amber

Dad and Brian hovered near me almost every moment of the day. I knew they were expecting for me to have a nervous breakdown after what had happened with Zach, but I didn't let them see how much I missed him. Brian could probably guess, but he never mentioned anything. I probably wouldn't have been able to keep my composure in front of my brother and father if I opened Zach's present in the living room with them. Instead, I was hidden away in my own room.

Inside the bigger present, I found three smaller presents, each accompanied by a note. I opened the first. There was a pair of soft black leather gloves inside. 'For our next visit to the ice rink,' the note said, and my throat started closing up. With shaky fingers, I opened the second present. It was a gift certificate for a tattoo parlor. 'If you ever decide to get your tattoo.'

As I opened the last present, I sank down on my bed. Inside the small box was a beautiful gold necklace with bird silhouettes. 'You can fly,' was written on the accompanying card.

Tears prickled my eyes. Zach could have gotten anything for me and I would have loved it, but this was so much better. Every present had a meaning. He really thought about it, had listened to what I said. I took out the necklace and put it on then rested my hand over it, closing my eyes. Would he have given me such a thoughtful gift if he didn't care for me? But caring for someone wasn't loving someone. I took a few deep breaths before I dared to read the letter Zach had attached to my present.

Amber,

I've always been good at screwing up and eventually I learned to expect it. That's why I didn't fight for you when you left me. That's one of the things I regret the most. Sometimes you have to lose something to realize that you don't want to live without it. I should have said it a long time ago: I love you. There are many questions in my life right now, but you are the one thing I'm sure about.

Please give me another chance.

Zach

I couldn't see through my tears, and yet I couldn't avert my eyes from the note in my hand. Zach had said he loved me. He wanted another chance. My first impulse was to grab my phone and call him, but I couldn't rush into this. I was too emotional to make a decision like that.

zachary

Amber had been gone for three days. She must have opened my present by now, must have read the letter I wrote her, but she never called. The first night of not hearing from her I wanted to go out with Jason and get shit-faced. That was my solution to any problem, after all, but I stayed at the apartment instead. If I didn't want to become like my parents, I had to act differently.

Brian and Amber were supposed to return to Boston today, but I half expected Amber to stay with her father. Maybe she decided that she couldn't face me anymore. I'd have to accept it, even if I wasn't sure if I could let her go that easily now that I'd realized I loved her. I never believed in love, and even now I was wary of it, but there was no denying I loved Amber.

I heard a key turning in the lock, and the door swung open, revealing Brian with two bags. One of them was Amber's and relief flooded me. She was a couple of steps behind him, but she didn't look at me as she entered and closed the door.

"Hey, Zach," Brian said then glanced at Amber. "I'll be in my room." With a pointed look in my direction, he headed for his room, leaving me alone with Amber. She stood near the door. Pumpkin, who'd been sleeping beside me on the sofa, strode toward her and pressed his head against her shins. She scratched behind his ears with a small smile. I couldn't stand it anymore. I rose from the sofa, drawing her eyes toward me. The smile disappeared from her face. Instead we stared at each other. She was wearing the necklace I'd given her, so she had at least opened my presents. "Did you—" I said at the same time as she blurted, "Yes."

We both fell silent. "Yes?" I asked. I wasn't sure if she'd anticipated my question and her answer meant 'yes I read your letter' or if it meant something else entirely.

She walked up to me. "I read your letter." She paused. "And yes, I want to give us another chance." I could hear the silent 'but' in her answer. "But I won't ever be the trophy wife you need at your side."

I frowned then it dawned on me. "You heard what my father said."

"I didn't mean to eavesdrop, but …" She trailed off.

My father was really fucking me over in every way possible. "I don't want Brittany or anyone else at my side. If my father and his business partners can't deal with it, then they can go fuck themselves. And I don't even know if I want to work in my father's company. Payne Enterprise can do without me for now. My father will work until he drops dead anyway."

"Then what *do* you want to do?"

"I want to become a human rights lawyer. But first I want to travel through South America."

"Oh," Amber said. Then she smiled. "Living your dream."

I bridged the remaining distance between us and took her hands. "I want you to come with me. Let's figure out together what we want and who we really are meant to be. There's no better way to do that than travel the world, right?"

Amber's eyes widened. "Are you serious?"

"Yes. I actually bought this already." I pulled out two tickets for a one-way flight to Buenos Aires. "One for you and one for me. I know it's presumptuous of me to think you'll come with me when I don't even know if you still want to be with me, but I can't imagine doing this without you. I can't imagine life without you."

Amber stared down at the tickets. Then she slowly met my gaze. "You're really serious."

"I've never been more serious about anything in my life. The flights leave January 25, less than a month from now. So will you give me another chance?"

Amber wrapped her arms around my middle, and I embraced her tightly, pressing my nose into her hair. "Of course. The first 'yes' when you interrupted me was already a yes to the question in your letter. I love you, Zach, and I want to be with you. Even if you decide to start working in your father's company at some point, I'll stand by your side. Together we can do it."

I lifted her head and kissed her. Fuck. I'd missed the feel of her lips against mine. Her taste, her smile. Everything. "So you'll travel through South America with me?"

amber

I was still stunned. I couldn't believe Zach had bought a plane ticket for me. "Yes, but—" His face fell. "I can't let you pay everything by yourself."

"Amber, I have more than enough money to take every resident in this apartment building to South America with me."

"I know," I said with a smile. "But I'd feel bad if I didn't contribute to this trip. I have some money in my savings account that will pay for food and for accommodations for a couple of weeks."

Zach looked like he might protest, but then he kissed me. "That's why I love you. Brittany and most of the other girls I met would have let me pay for everything without batting an eye. You don't even care about my money."

"I care about you. Money is a nice cushion to fall on, but it can't buy you happiness or love or anything that really matters."

Zach tightened his hold and pressed his lips against me. He deepened the kiss almost immediately and I clung to him as if I was drowning and he was my lifeboat.

"So how long do you want to spend traveling?" I asked, feeling more and more excited by the minute. And what was even better: I was back in Zach's arms and we wanted to try again.

"I don't know. As long as it takes to see what we want to see or until we feel like returning home. It's summer in Argentina and Chile right now, so we don't have to be worried about the weather in Patagonia."

"That could take a while," I teased.

"I don't care. I want to make love to you in every country of South America, and on every continent in this world."

I laughed. I linked our fingers. "How about you make love to me now?" Zach didn't say anything, only led me toward his room. We fell on his bed and kissed and touched every inch of each other. When we made love, it was slow and sweet and gentle and loving, almost reverent. Afterward, when we lay wrapped in each other's arms and listened to our ragged breathing, I knew this was the start of something new, something even better.

I'd come a long way, had torn down walls that seemed impenetrable, had discovered that sometimes you have to let go of the things you lost to discover that there's more to each of us than we thought possible. I'd become someone new; my broken self was still part of me, would always be a part of me, but I'd learned to live with it and learned to see beyond what wasn't meant to be to find new happiness.

"I love you," Zach murmured against my neck.

"And I love you."

Please consider leaving a review.
Readers like you help other readers discover new books!

If you want to be among the first to get updates on books, please join my Facebook group **Cora's Flamingo Squad** for bonus content and news, subscribe to my newsletter!

more books by
cora reilly

THE CAMORRA CHRONICLES:
Twisted Loyalties
Twisted Emotions
Twisted Pride
Twisted Bonds
Twisted Hearts

BORN IN BLOOD MAFIA CHRONICLES:
Luca Vitiello
Bound by Honor
Bound by Duty
Bound by Hatred
Bound By Temptation
Bound By Vengeance
Bound By Love

about the author

Cora is the author of the Born in Blood Mafia Series, the Camorra Chronicles and many other books, most of them featuring dangerously sexy bad boys. She likes her men like her martinis—dirty and strong.

Cora lives in Germany with a cute but crazy Bearded Collie, as well as the cute but crazy man at her side. When she doesn't spend her days dreaming up sexy books, she plans her next travel adventure or cooks too spicy dishes from all over the world.

www.ingramcontent.com/pod-product-compliance
Lightning Source LLC
LaVergne TN
LVHW012345150625
813932LV00011B/576